CW00521660

I'm Coming to Take You Home

Pauline North

Copyright © 2023 I'm Coming to Take You Home

All rights reserved

The characters and events portrayed in this book are fictitious. Any similarity to real persons, living or dead, is coincidental and not intended by the author.

No part of this book may be reproduced, or stored in a retrieval system, or transmitted in any form or by any means, electronic, mechanical, photocopying, recording, or otherwise, without express written permission of the publisher.

ISBN-13: 9798858388340
ISBN-10: 1477123456

Cover design by: Art Painter
Library of Congress Control Number: 2018675309
Printed in the United States of America

For Brian. My rock

Contents

Title Page

Copyright

Dedication

Chapter 1   1

Chapter 2   15

Chapter 3   28

Chapter Four   36

Chapter 5   50

Chapter 6   62

Chapter 7   82

Chapter 8   95

Chapter 9   108

Chapter 10   122

Chapter 11   135

Chapter 12   147

Chapter 13   157

Chapter 14	169
Chapter 15	180
Chapter 16	189
Chapter 17	203
Chapter 18	216
Chapter 19	230
Chapter 20	240
Chapter 21	252
Chapter 22	265
Chapter 23	280
Chapter 24	291
Chapter 25	306
Chapter 26	320
Books By This Author	327
Books By This Author	329

Chapter 1

The narrow gap in the curtains allowed a sliver of moonlight to fall along the carpet and over the dressing table. I lay in the shadowed bed, in the house that was my prison, waiting.

The body lying beside me grunted and turned over. Shit. Don't let him wake up. Please. No – it would be alright – the snoring soon started again. I breathed out. I would give it another five minutes, then I would make my escape. I watched the minutes click by on the bedside clock.

At last, with daybreak only an hour away, I slipped out of bed and walked out through the bedroom door. As though I was only going to the bathroom, not sneaking away in the still of the night. Then, instead of turning left, I made my way one slow step at a time across the landing and down the stairs. When I reached the kitchen, I took a moment to listen. To reassure myself that he wasn't creeping down the stairs and about to catch me, because that was the critical moment. Until then I could give a reason for my actions – 'I felt like a glass of water, just coming back.' – But no longer, from that moment on everything changed.

At the connecting door to the garage, I took a deep breath to calm my pounding heart, turned the key in the lock, took hold of the handle and slowly pushed it down. The door opened without a sound. I stepped through and closed the door. The familiar garage smells of oil, petrol and metal wrapped around me. I switched on the light and lifted my car keys off the hook by the door. I opened the boot of my car and removed the backpack and the bundle of clothing I had put there that afternoon.

With fingers that were stiff and clumsy with fear I removed my dressing gown and shoved it into the boot. Then I dressed in the clothes from the bundle, dark leggings and sweatshirt, jacket, and trainers, then finally a cycle helmet. I put on the backpack containing everything I would take with me. Then I lowered the boot lid and gently clicked it shut.

I couldn't use my car. I had tried that once, been traced too easily and brought back. The beating he had given me that night had been the worst. This time I had to get away.

I had learned to plan and scheme. It had taken a long time. I diverted housekeeping money into a new, secret account and waited until I had enough put by to last me a while. I bought a bike and rented a garage to store it in, a safe distance from the house. I used the hours he was out of the house to practice riding it, at first in the safety of the local park, then the streets. Increasing the distance, building endurance and confidence. All that time, at home, I was careful to behave as he expected. To smile and make small talk when we had guests. To stay in the background, and never speak out of turn.

I was ready. The external garage door was too noisy for me to leave that way, so I stepped back into the kitchen. I was listening so hard for movement upstairs that my footsteps seemed to echo round the house. The walk through the kitchen, along the hall and out of the front door, was a nightmare. I took it steady, fighting the urge to rush at the door and slam through. Once outside, with the door closed behind me, I paused for a moment on the top step to breathe in the cold night air. Then, after a last look back at the house, I walked away.

I kept to the shadows until I turned out of the drive, then the possibility of success caught my breath and my nerve cracked. Instead of a sedate walk to my garage, I panicked and ran, thankful that the thick soles of my trainers muffled my footsteps. I dreaded someone seeing me. I didn't see anyone, no lights flicked on in the houses, no dogs barked at me.

I arrived at the garage gasping for breath. I leaned against the wall until I had regained a degree of calm. Then I unlocked the garage and wheeled out my bike. I didn't bother to lock it behind me. Whether I succeeded or failed, I wouldn't be back. I climbed onto the saddle and set off through the quiet streets.

As the night slowly eased into dawn the streetlights clicked off. By the time the roads started getting busy, bringing the smell of exhaust fumes, I had taken to the quieter side streets, nervous of the heavy traffic and looking for a café where I could get breakfast. I found one among a row of shabby shops, tucked between a newsagent and a betting shop. Looking through the window. I saw a handful of small tables with yellow laminate tops and an assortment of mismatched chairs. The floor and tabletops looked clean. The window gleamed in the early sunlight.

There was a woman behind a counter at the back and at one of the tables an old man crouched over a cup of tea. It would do. I left my bike propped against the window, where I could keep an eye on it, walked in and sat at a table. The woman behind the counter looked over and called out, 'Yes, love, what can I get you?'

'Full English and a tea, please.'

When my breakfast was ready, she called me over to the counter. I paid, took cutlery from a tray, and carried it all back to my table. The egg was perfectly cooked, I poked it with the fork and the rich gold yolk flowed over the toast. I sighed with satisfaction and tucked in.

As I worked my way through the meal, I took time to reflect on the progress of my escape, satisfied that the café was worlds away from my usual haunts.

When Phillip sent his men after me, they would look in the smart coffee shops and restaurants, or in the kind of hotels that he would expect me to use. They would check the closed-circuit recordings from the train stations and airports.

Well, they wouldn't find me like that. With this low-speed escape, in fact the complete change of everything in my life, I wanted to confuse anyone searching for me. I had in my pack a list of holiday parks scattered over the south of England. I planned to find one where I could rent a cabin on a semi-permanent basis.

Phillip had delighted in reminding me, as one of his control mechanisms, that he found me when I was struggling to support myself – working as a waitress – living in a single room and drinking away too much of my meagre wage.

'Wasn't I indeed a lucky woman to have been rescued from that life?' he would demand. 'Shouldn't I be more grateful for being taken into a life of luxury?' And at the start, I had been. Thrilled, excited, and yes, grateful. I had fallen for the charming, attentive man who lifted me from my poverty. I promised I would love him and cherish him. I would be the best damn wife I could be.

My little cloud of fluffy happiness imploded almost as soon as my wedding dress hit the floor. Once I was his, he dropped the tender attentions. He made it abundantly clear exactly how he expected me to behave. Then, when I failed, he showed me the error of my ways.

When I had absorbed the shock of finding that my charming man had turned into a monster, I learned the hard way to show a compliant face. But inside I nurtured the flame of pride and hope. All of that had, at last, led me to my freedom.

I wiped the last of the toast around the plate to collect the last drop of flavour, finished the tea and carried the empties back to the counter. The woman smiled and took them from me. 'Alright, was it love?'

'Yes, really good, thank you. Would you re-fill my water bottle for me, please?'

As she passed my bottle back over the counter she said, 'Off on a bike ride then, are you?'

'Yes, with my sister, we're trying to get fit. I'd better get going, she will be wondering where I am.' We exchanged the understanding half-smiles of reluctant exercisers as I left.

My plan was to travel south by the minor roads between the A3 and the A24. At last, with London behind me, I was happier than I could ever remember. The day was bright and clear. The choking smell of concentrated exhaust fumes replaced by fresh, clean air. At that moment, I could have gone on like that forever.

Much later, pedalling along a quiet country road, the euphoria had faded. I had been in the saddle too long, I ached, I was tired and sore. I needed to rest. I would give it a few more minutes and then I would check my map for a possible overnight stop.

I was freewheeling down a winding lane when I noticed, half hidden by the new spring growth, a sign for a Bed and Breakfast. Hanging crookedly from the board was a smaller one proclaiming: 'Vacancies.'

With a feeling of relief, I took the track off to the left and bumped along over the stones and ruts until it turned right through a gateway. The B and B turned out to be an old stone farmhouse, mellow in the afternoon sunlight. In front, there was a cobbled courtyard. By the far wall were the guest parking spaces. Further on, I could see sheds and a barn. I leaned my bike against the mossy wall at the back of the yard, walked to the door and knocked. A woman's voice called, 'Just a minute.'

While I waited, I took off my helmet and speculated on the owner of the voice. I imagined she might be the traditional farmer's wife – comfortably plump, middle-aged, wearing an apron. The door opened to a tall, long-haired, blond, somewhere in her late twenties, holding a grumpy baby on her hip.

'So sorry, Lacey is having one of her stroppy

days. Can I help you?'

'I'm hoping you have a single room available for tonight.'

'Yes, we do, please, come in.

She stepped back into a hallway and over to a small counter, bounced the baby to a more comfortable position, opened a book and picked up a pen. 'You will be the only guest tonight, so you can choose between the room with the best view or the one furthest away from Lacey's room. Which do you fancy?'

I smiled at her, 'No offence, but I'll go for the room without a view.'

She grinned back. 'It's fifty pounds for the room and breakfast, an extra ten if you would like dinner, no choice on that I'm afraid it will be what we are having. Tonight, it's cottage pie with fresh vegetables and blackberry cheesecake, is that alright?'

'That sounds lovely, so yes, I would like to order the dinner please.' She scribbled into the book. 'Can I please take your name for the register?'

I had already decided on my new name. Now I could try it out, to see how comfortable it felt. 'Jess Hampshire.

'I'm Fleur. Sign here for me. Then I'll show you to your room. Do you have luggage to get from outside?'

I held up my backpack, 'Only this, I'm on a cycling holiday. I left my bike against the wall, is that alright?'

'I'll get my husband to put it in the shed where we keep ours; it will be safe and dry there.'

Fleur, along with baby Lacey, took me up a narrow staircase and along to a bright, clean room. 'Your en suite is through that door. Feel free to use the lounge. That's the first door on the right downstairs. Dinner will be at seven. See you later, Jess.'

After she had closed the door behind her, I stripped off, took a long shower, and changed into my spare set of clothes: jeans and a tee-shirt with a sweater over the top. Then I took my map and list of sites from my backpack and sat on the bed to study them. I decided to head to The Green Valley Holiday Village, a bit northwest of Brighton. I thought maybe two more days of easy riding if luck was with me.

With time to kill before dinner I wandered down to the lounge. I chose an armchair and carefully eased my exhausted body into the comfort of it.

Fleur came in to check if I needed anything. I asked for a coffee. When she brought it in, she said, 'Feel free to watch the TV. I'll give you a call when dinner is ready.' Instead, I sat in the still peace of the room. The whole house felt welcoming. Now and then I heard Fleur's voice chatting to her daughter and happy sounds from the child. A door opened somewhere. There was a brief conversation between Fleur and her husband, his voice warm and deep, then the sound of an outside door closing again.

I got to my feet and crossed to the window. A tall chunky man with a shock of sandy hair was collecting my bike from its position against the wall. He walked it to the left, out of my sight. I went to sit again, feeling touched by that simple act of kindness.

I was almost dozing when Fleur popped her head around the door. 'I'm just about to bring out your starter. Let me show you to the dining room.'

In the small, cosy dining room my place was set on a table by the window. There was a white linen cloth and a small posy of fresh flowers. Through the window I saw a large kitchen garden and beyond that there were fields, patched by stands of trees in their new seasons green.

The starter, when Fleur brought it in, was a goat's cheese salad. The cottage pie was richly flavoured and the homemade cheesecake delicious. All through the meal, I could hear snatches of sound from the kitchen, a raised voice, a laugh. Happy sounds.

The husband brought my coffee and cleared the table. After he left, I sat with the coffee and thought about the day. I could hardly believe I had got away. I could still taste the fear – feel the pounding of my heart. And yet, here I was, with almost an entire day of freedom. I had to keep alert, watch for his men in every place I went, but I could do that. There was no way I would go back there.

Back in my room after dinner, I spent a short while with my tablet searching for a place to stay the next night. If all went well, it would be the last of the journey. I needed to have a destination. It had been a random stroke of luck happening upon the B and B, it would have been a much longer ride to the ones on my list. I was reluctant to trust to chance again. I found a hotel close enough to the Green Valley site to leave me what should be a leisurely ride.

I turned on my mobile and booked a room at The Hurst Hotel, turning the phone off as soon as I finished. Then I climbed into bed and, despite the early hour, dropped into an exhausted sleep.

The patch of sky visible through the window when I woke was the threatening dirty grey, that sometimes comes before rain. I climbed out of bed and walked over to the window. I watched the husband walk across the yard with a bucket in each hand. He disappeared around a corner. I opened the window to get a feel of the temperature. The air on my face felt chilly. Even with my eyes closed, I would have known I was on a farm from the faint smell of animals on the breeze. Somewhere close by, chickens were making their soothing clucking noises.

I dressed in my cycling outfit then I took the waterproof jacket out of my pack and laid it ready on the bed. I packed everything away safely, then I went downstairs for breakfast. Fleur came to take my order. I opted for bacon and scrambled eggs. A great, fluffy pile arrived, along with three slices of perfect bacon and a stack of crispy toast. I had three cups of coffee to finish.

After breakfast I went back to my room to collect my pack. Picking it up from where it hung on the back of the chair, I caught sight of myself in the mirror. I stood a moment and considered the woman who looked back at me. Did I look different? Apart from the cycling gear instead of a designer dress and with my hair tied back, the solemn face was much the same. I had always known how to hide my feelings. Perhaps the brown eyes were more open. I thought I saw a new boldness in the depths. I gave that person a nod of approval then I went down to pay and check out.

'I hope everything was alright for you, Jess.'

I was a little startled to hear my new name spoken. It felt strange.

'It was all perfect, thank you Fleur. I wish I could have stayed longer.'

'You will find your bike outside ready for you, have a safe journey.'

Outside, I slipped on my waterproof. The rain would be along soon. I buckled the helmet and rode out of the gate. I took the lane very carefully, avoiding the worst of the bumps and holes. At the end of the lane, I turned left. I had the route in my mind. I knew where I was going.

There was no need to rush. I roughly calculated my journey time as around four hours, so I peddled along enjoying the fresh air and the country views. My contentment lasted until the rain came. I could smell it, even before the first drops fell, the extra richness of damp earth on the freshening wind. Then occasional fat drops that soon became a steady drizzle. The sky grew dark with thick piles of purple clouds. Not so bad, I could deal with that, but soon the skies really opened and dumped a whole ocean of water on me, lashing my eyes and blowing me off course.

I lowered my face and ploughed on, desperately hoping for somewhere to shelter, preferably somewhere with a toilet. I said a silent prayer of thanks when I passed a signpost, I was only a mile from a place named Storrington. This turned out to be a small town, where I easily found a pub: The Anchor. I took the time to chain my bike to a nearby signpost and dashed gratefully into the bar.

Inside it was warm and welcoming. I waited for the barman to finish serving an elderly couple and then asked for a coffee. As an afterthought, I ordered a whiskey to go with it. I took the drinks to a table and retreated to the toilet.

When I had finished in the cubicle, I washed

my hands and dried them under the hot air dryer, then bent down and gave my hair a blast. Finally, I took off my, gave it a good shake and kept the drier going a few minutes more to dry off the worst of the wet.

From my table back in the bar, I could see the rain on the windowpanes. I took my time with the drinks, but it was still raining when I finished, so I ordered a sausage sandwich and another coffee. By the time I had finished the sandwich and my drink I was beginning to worry about the time. I was relieved to see the rain had finally eased. It was time for me to go.

I stepped through the pub door and stood dazzled by the sudden sunlight reflected from the slick pavements and the puddles. With soaring spirits, I collected my bike. I had started riding on when I spotted a drinks cabinet in the window of a shop. I left my bike leaning against a wall and went in to get a bottle to stick in my pack.

As I closed the shop door, with my hand still gripping the handle, I caught sight of a familiar black car. For a moment I froze. Cruising through the town, his eyes searching both sides of the road was one of Phillip's hard men. What the hell was he doing here?

Chapter 2

He was looking for me, of course. I didn't think he knew where I was. He was simply covering the ground. Doing a blanket search, but less than a minute earlier I would have been standing, in full view, outside The Anchor.

I moved further into the shop. My mind was racing. Pretending to study the tins on the shelf in front of me, I tried to think logically. I had always lived in the southeast of England, so I blended in. Of course, I expected this area to be searched first and most thoroughly. It was only a coincidence that he chose this road. Not yet though, surely, they can't have already checked the more obvious escape routes. Why were they on the road so soon? Had Phillip brought in extra men?

I moved closer to the door, where I could see in both directions. There was no sign of the car and, although I waited for a while, no familiar figure walked along the pavement searching for me.

I collected a bottle of lemon drink from the cabinet and took it to the till. Outside I checked my reflection in the shop window. Wearing my cycle helmet, with my hair covered and the shape of my head obscured worked quite well as camouflage. So, I did the only thing I could do. I climbed on my bike and got back on the road. I didn't see the car again.

The spell of bright, sunny weather didn't last long. Ominous clouds drained the light from the sky, darkening the afternoon and threatening more rain. I consoled myself with the thought that the hotel couldn't be much further.

The dark clothes I was wearing were a deliberate choice. What happened later was partly my fault, because of that decision and partly because of the broken edge of the road. Also, the driver of the large SUV should have noticed me and given me space instead of blasting past me so frighteningly close. I wobbled, caught a wheel in a hole and went flying down a bank and into the roadside bushes.

I landed hard. My hands hit first, scraping over twigs and gravel. Something cracked as my legs arrived. I curled up and waited for the worst of the pain to pass, cursing the car, the driver and myself for being so careless.

Very carefully, I got up onto my knees, which seemed alright, so I made it up to my feet. Where one of my shins had landed, I had broken a dried out brittle branch an inch or so thick. I was fairly sure I hadn't broken any bones, but I would have some colourful bruises. I was covered in mud and saturated leaves. I scraped off as much as I could, then heaved my bike up the bank onto the roadside verge and looked it over. It surprised me that apart from a few scratches it seemed undamaged.

I didn't know how far it was to the hotel. When I arrived, I would have to approach carefully, in case whichever of Phillips men was in that car had stopped there, asking questions, maybe demanding to be informed if I showed up, I ached like hell, but there was nothing for it but to keep moving. I wheeled the bike back onto the road and was about to mount it and ride on when something caught my eye.

On the opposite side of the road was a narrow track, leading into the dense woodland. Perhaps it led to a house. If I explained to the householders what had happened, would they let me leave my bike there overnight? I could find out where I was and call a taxi to take me to the hotel.

Figuring that the worst that could happen was they could tell me to clear off; I stepped into the deeper gloom of the woods. It was late afternoon now and the light was fading fast. It was too dark to ride. I found the rough surface treacherous, stones and deep ruts caught at the wheels, trying to trip me.

Soon, with my spirits starting to lift a little, I thought I glimpsed lights between the trees. Then, under the scent of the woods, carried on a faint breeze, I caught a whiff of food. There must be a house up ahead.

I had focused my attention on where I had seen the lights. The voice that snapped out from only a few feet away stopped me instantly.

'What the fuck are you doing here?'

A figure stepped out from the trees to my left, I couldn't see the expression on his face, but there was no mistaking the aggression in the way he moved towards me.

I stepped backwards, shocked, and more than a little afraid. 'Sorry, I'm only looking for help. Look, I'll go, ok?'

'No, not ok. Didn't you see the private property sign at the entrance?'

Bloody stupid question in this light, I thought. 'No, only the entrance of this track leading off the road, that's all.'

He took a step closer. A beam of torchlight dazzled me for a moment; I stood in a pool of light while he looked me up and down. I raised my head and glared at the dark figure holding the torch.

The voice was no softer, but a little curious, 'What happened to you?'

'I came off my bike, I fell into the bushes, I'm cold and wet, I hurt, and I don't think I can ride any more today.'

There was a long pause before a resigned sigh. 'You had better come along with me then.'

He turned and walked away, not even

checking if I followed. Still struggling to control the bike, I fell behind, so by the time I reached the end of the track and stood rooted to the spot by the sight of what was all around me, he had called over two other men. They all turned to stare at me.

There was a quick explanation in a language I didn't understand. While the three men stood there, muttering, I looked around and tried to make sense of the scene in front of me.

It could only be a Gypsy camp. We were standing at the edge of a large clearing. Arranged around a central space were some single-story buildings, with a few traditional wagons tucked between them. From the open doorways of the wagons and the group of people gathered outside one of the buildings, faces turned to look at me. Conversations stopped. They all fell silent.

The only human sounds now came from a long building along the far side, where I could hear a clatter of pans and good-humoured chatter.

The three men came to a decision. The one from the woods walked over and gestured for me to start walking. The other two led the way to a small building, opened the door and stood waiting for me. Confused and hoping for somewhere to rest I followed them.

I leaned my bike against the outside wall. 'Will this be alright here?' I looked at them and regretted the question at once. I had obviously caused offence. Without comment, they ushered me inside, followed me in and shut the door behind them. It was an office.

The oldest of the three men walked round and took the chair behind the desk.

'Please, take a seat.'

I was so cold, wet, and exhausted. It was a relief to sit, even with three strange men regarding me as though I had dropped through a crack in the universe. The man behind the desk, wiry and weathered, who had to be the leader, projected a calm assurance. I removed my backpack and sat with it on my lap.

He turned to the one who had found me. 'Now, Camlo, you say you found her on the lane?'

Camlo – what a strange name – pulled a chair forward from the wall and sat down, leaning back in a relaxed manner. 'She was about halfway along, by the old chestnut.'

The leader turned to me. 'Can you tell me who you are, please? You say you were out on the road. You were looking for help and saw the lane. Is that right?'

'Yes, what's so odd about that? My name is Jess Hampshire. 'Why is that so difficult to believe?'

He turned away from me. 'Well, Camlo, Tobar, what do you think?'

Tobar, a tall man, probably in his thirties but with a streak of silver in his dark hair, had been studying me hard since we entered the room. He spread his hands. 'I think it's possible she's the one, her colouring is right. She could be one of us.'

The leader nodded. 'That's what I think, how about you, Camlo?'

'We must find out for sure if this is her. We can't take the chance.'

'You're all mad; I don't know who you are or who you think I am, but I am Jess Hampshire.' Now I was scared, what were they planning? How would they try to find out who I was?

The leader raised a hand, 'My name is Manfri. We're getting nowhere, I think we've heard enough for tonight ...'

'Too right it's enough, more than enough for me to cope with after the day I've had, I'm leaving.' I was on my feet and making for the door.

At a quiet word from Manfri, Camlo was on his feet. He reached out a hand and grabbed one of my wrists as I tried to pass. I struggled to wrench myself free. When I aimed a kick, he sidestepped effortlessly. I found myself dumped unceremoniously back on the chair.

There was a slight smile on Camlo's face as he stepped back and sat down again. Tobar was looking at Manfri from under raised brows. Manfri, seeming lost in thought, was sliding a notepad backwards and forwards on the desk.

'Are you trying to keep me here?' I started to root through my pack for my phone. Tobar reached out and took the backpack from me. He tossed it over to Camlo.

Manfri said, 'I'm afraid we can't let you make a call, Miss – whatever your name is – we have some things we have to discuss. You will have to stay here tonight. We can talk tomorrow. You know where to put our guest, Camlo.' He stood and walked to the door. Before opening it, he paused and glanced back at me as if puzzled.

Manfri and Tobar left, Camlo stood up. He took something from the cabinet drawer and put it in his pocket. 'Come on,' he said and led the way out into the cold evening air.

I was too tired to fight. The thought of being warm, dry, and sleeping overtook the desire to run. I would think what to do about this ridiculous situation in the morning. I followed Camlo out.

'Leave your bike.' Then after a moment, 'it will be quite safe.'

He took me over to a building at the edge of the site, where he opened a door, switched on a light, and ushered me inside. There was a chest of drawers with a large wall cupboard mounted over it, a small table beside the single bed, a larger table and two chairs against the opposite wall.

'Your bathroom is behind that door; you'll find you have everything you need.'

I nodded. I realised I was shaking. While I stood there, Camlo removed my phone and tablet from my pack, searched through the rest and returned it to me.

'Any chance I can have something to eat?' I hated asking for anything, but I was starving.

'I'll bring you something. Sandwiches alright?' I nodded.

He walked out, I heard him lock the door. He was soon back with a plate of sandwiches and a mug of tea, which he put on the table. On his way to the door there was a muttered, 'Goodnight.' The door closed behind him. I was alone. I heard a key turn in the lock again. I looked round the room. The window was a decent size, but there would be no escape there. I drew the curtains. If I was a prisoner at least I could keep some privacy.

Then I checked the sandwiches, they were chicken salad, generously filled. I tucked in.

When I had finished. With everything that had happened rocketing round in my head, I wandered into the bathroom. I dropped the wet, filthy clothes on the floor and stepped into the shower. There was shampoo and shower gel on the shelf. I used them both then used the shampoo to rinse the clothes I rescued from the floor. I wrung them out as well as I could and hung them over the shower-curtain rail. When I was dry, I crawled into the bed and despite everything, too shattered to care, I slept.

I woke slowly to the same dim light from the single bulb. My watch said that it was 8.30. As I came awake, the memory of the previous evening brought a tight knot of fear to sit under

23

my ribs. I sat on the edge of the bed fighting back the panic. I tried to think it through. I was a prisoner, but I didn't understand why. Why would these people think I was someone else? What had this other person done to make them act like this? Even more importantly, how could I possibly prove that I wasn't her without landing myself back with Phillip?

Thinking I had better be ready for whatever the day brought, I dressed in my spare clothes. I was still sitting at the table trying to make sense of my situation when a knock on the door made me jump. I heard the key turn in the lock. The door opened a crack and a woman's voice said. 'Are you decent?'

'Yes.'

The woman who walked in was a similar age to me. She was wearing jeans and a white shirt, her long hair tied back. She smiled, walked over, and placed a tray on the table.

'Hello, my name is Lela. There's breakfast and coffee on the tray. Did you sleep well?

She had left the door open; I could see a wedge of clear, bright daylight, partly obscured by the large man standing guard. I felt frustrated and angry. 'Why am I a prisoner? I want to leave.'

Lela looked from me to the man then back to me. 'You have presented us with a problem, I'm sure we can sort it out, but in the meantime, no, you can't leave. Sorry.' I was about to demand more of an explanation, but Lela had disappeared into the bathroom. She came out with my pile of wet clothes.

'These could do with a proper wash, and they will take an age to dry in there. I'll put them through a machine wash for you.'

'Thanks, that's kind of you.'

'It's no trouble at all.' There was another smile as she walked out. She locked the door again.

I paced the room to vent my frustration. Then I admitted to myself that I was starving. I sat at the table, took the cloth from the tray, and tucked into the cereal and coffee. When I had finished, there was nothing I could do but wait. It was going to be a long day.

Later, another young woman delivered a lunch of sandwiches along with more coffee. Her eyes were hard and cold. Even the way she walked across the room appeared threatening. She placed a new tray on the table, removed the breakfast tray and left without a backward glance.

I tried for ages to pick the lock with my nail file, it was too cumbersome, but I didn't have anything better. Eventually, I gave up on that and put the file back in my pack. Thoroughly fed up, I flung myself onto the bed and listened to the sounds from outside my cell. For most of the afternoon I heard only occasional sounds from the humans outside: footsteps as people passed by or snatches of conversation.

I could hear the distant call of pigeons from

the woods behind the building and from much nearer a blackbird's clear, melodic song. I tried to feel soothed by those sounds, but by the time I finally heard the footsteps that stopped at the door and the key turn in the lock, my fear, boredom, and frustration had turned to simmering anger.

It was the hostile woman again, accompanied by a tall, overweight young man. She stood by the door, glanced briefly at me, and said, 'They're ready for you.'

I picked up my pack to take it with me. I wasn't going to get separated from it. As I walked to the door, I looked very carefully at my guards. Neither was paying me any attention. I stepped outside and took a look around. There was no one else nearby.

The man took the lead. A jerk of his head showed that I should follow. I left a gap then started walking, the woman followed behind me. It only took a few steps to clear the end of the building. I took a quick look to my left. The woodland looked reasonably clear; this could be my best opportunity. I casually slipped my pack onto my back. Out of the corner of my eye, I checked the escort. Neither of them was paying any attention. She was checking her phone. I took a deep breath and ran for the woods as fast as I could, with panic powering me on, bruised legs pumping, fists clenched in determination.

As I hoped, my escort's lack of attention gave

me a few precious seconds head start before the shouting began. I could hear the alarm echoing around the site, shouted replies and running feet. I put my head down and concentrated on avoiding the undergrowth and uneven ground. I was making for the road and praying for a passing car that I could flag down.

I had judged the angle right. I found the track and the going was a little easier. I was still ahead of them but slowing, struggling for breath with a stitch stabbing at my side. There, closer than I expected was the road.

I stumbled out onto the tarmac, desperate to find help. A small red car was coming. I stood in the middle of the road and waved for the driver to stop. With a squeal of brakes, the car came to a halt. The door was flung open, I realised, with horror, that my escape had gone horribly wrong. The figure leaping out of the car was Camlo.

Chapter 3

I managed to turn, fear helping me move my weary legs. I made it to the verge. A few steps more and I would be into the trees. Then Camlo grabbed me from behind and we both landed full length on the bank. The weight of him crushed the wind out of me. Wretched and defeated, I let him pull me to my feet.

'You stupid bitch,' he shouted. He stepped back, fists clenched at his side, dark eyes blazing with anger. He took hold of my arm. 'Get in the car. I'm taking you back. There are things you need to hear. 'The grip he had on my arm was fierce. He dragged me to the car, opened the passenger door and shoved me inside, then stormed round and climbed in behind the steering wheel.

The chasing group had arrived, seeing that Camlo had me safely caught they started back up the track, stepping aside to let us pass. I took a look at Camlo as he eased the car over the treacherous surface. His mouth was a grim line, brows lowered, his face hard and withdrawn.

'You didn't have to be so rough.'

He turned to face me, then away, without any change of expression. We had now reached the camp. He drove in and parked beside the office. I noticed my bike was still resting against the wall.

'Wait. Don't move till I let you out.' When Camlo opened my door, I started to walk towards the office.

'No, this way, he didn't lead the way this time. He pointed me towards the largest of the buildings and walked behind me. As we walked inside, I realised that it was a meeting hall. At one end was a raised platform set with a table and four chairs. The body of the hall had a couple of rows of empty chairs.

Manfri was the only person inside. He walked over and clapped Camlo on the shoulder. 'Let's get ourselves settled. The others will be here soon.'

It seemed we were all going to sit at the table on the platform. I wondered what the hell was going on, why would they want me up there at a meeting, or was it a trial? My heart was beating hard and fast.

At the table, Manfri pulled out the second chair for me, he took the third one. Camlo sat beside me on the first chair. I noticed for the first time and with surprise that instead of the boots, jeans, and sweater of the previous night, he was wearing a suit. He caught me looking and turned his arms to show the mud smeared up the sleeves. I noticed that he wore a heavy gold ring.

'Oh dear, sorry, that will have to go to the cleaners.' I let my voice show that I really wasn't at all sorry. I couldn't read the expression in the dark eyes that stared, briefly, directly at me.

'I'll make sure you get the bill.'

The hall door opened. Tobar walked in, he came across and took the last chair on the platform.

'Everything set?' Manfri asked.

'Everyone who can come will be here.'

Sure enough, people started to filter in, looking round and choosing their seats, on their own and in groups. Most of them looked over to the table. Some to stare, others quickly looked away. Some of them looked hostile, others merely curious. I estimated the numbers at around thirty, including a few children. I saw Lela take a seat in the front row.

I clenched my hands in my lap and concentrated on keeping my breathing steady, determined to look calm. The seats filled, then, when the trickle of people dried up, a hush fell over the hall. All eyes turned to Manfri. When he started to speak, he had their total attention.

'Good evening, everyone. Many of you were here last night when we discussed the situation concerning this young woman. At that time, we agreed to keep her here until we can verify that she is who she claims to be.'

He turned and indicated me with a nod in my

direction. There was a rustle of agreement from the audience.

'We now have some new information that changes things, but first an explanation is owed.' He turned and spoke directly to me. 'There is a young woman who, for reasons we don't need to go into, is a danger to us. We thought you were her. That is why we kept you here; we needed time to find the truth.'

'Why on earth would you think that was me? Don't you know who she is? If not, why is she a threat? That's a stupid excuse.'

'She is one of us, who left our group some time ago when she was just a child. We haven't seen her since, we probably wouldn't recognise her, so we had to find out, for our own safety, if you are her.'

'Then why didn't he turn me away if he thought I was dangerous. Why bring me here and imprison me?' I glared at Camlo.

'For the same reason. The safety of the tribe. However, something happened today that changed things. Camlo, do you want to continue?'

All eyes in the room turned on the young man beside me. 'Thanks, Manfri,' he paused for a moment. 'For the benefit of our guest: as the rest of you know, I work at the hotel up the road. This morning a man came into reception. He didn't want to book a room. He took out a photo and started to question the staff, showing them the photo. He was looking for someone.'

The hall was silent. He spoke directly to me but clearly enough for everyone to hear.

'He had your photo. He was looking for you.'

Panic, I could hardly breathe. Had this been staged to hand me back, was this the easy solution? Hand me back to Phillip. Then if he accepts me as the woman he has been looking for, they needn't worry that I was the one making threats? I was halfway out of my seat, desperately looking round. Could I escape? One of my hands was gripping tight to the back of my chair as my eyes searched the hall for one of Phillip's men. A warm, strong hand covered mine.

'No, it's alright. I sent the man away. I told him you hadn't been there. You're safe.'

I looked at him, searching for reassurance, 'Really?'

He withdrew his hand as if stung by the touch, 'Yes, really.'

I sank back onto my chair, leaned on my elbows, and took my head in my hands. The hall was silent, no one moved. There were no whispered comments.

Manfri's voice was gentle. 'Who is looking for you? Why would someone go to so much trouble? Is it the police?

I remembered all the hurt, the humiliation, how pathetic and helpless I had felt. How I had learned to hide my anger and hatred

'I left my husband, because he is a monster and beat me, every time I made some small mistake or said something out of place. Before, when I tried to run away, he sent his men after me. They found me and took me back. I can't let them find me this time.'

A woman in the front row spoke up. 'Why didn't you go to the police?'

'Because no one would believe me, my husband is a powerful, influential man.'

There was a general murmur of acceptance they all understood about power and corruption.

Manfri had decided that it was time to wind up. 'I think this young woman has had enough for one day. I'm closing the meeting. Does everyone agree that we now know for sure she is not the person we thought she was? There were nods, muttered affirmations and then whispered conversation as they left the hall. One woman walked over to the platform.

'Well done, my dear.'

The atmosphere relaxed. In no time, the four of us were alone. Manfri laid his hands flat on the table. 'Well, I don't know about the rest of you, but I need a drink. I've got some beers in the office. Will you join us, Jess?'

I said, 'Yes please, I could really do with a drink.'

As easy as that, I moved from a day spent in fear and anxiety to going for a drink with the men who had imprisoned me.

In the office, we all took a chair. Manfri passed us each a beer from a cupboard in the corner. As he handed me mine, he said, 'You can use that room, we won't lock you in.' There was a glint to his eye and a smile hovered at the corners of his mouth. I smiled back.

'Thank you. I'll stay tonight. Tomorrow I will try and sort out what to do next. I have to phone the hotel where I had a room booked and apologise ...'

Camlo broke in. 'No, you don't. I know where you are.'

Of course, I should have realised. I had booked into the hotel where he worked. I looked at his face. From the time he found me he had only glowered at me, now the anger was gone. His expression was neutral.

Tobar said, 'So what were your plans before you stumbled on us?

'I want to get as far away from my old life as possible. Find somewhere safe and inexpensive to live and a job that pays enough to survive. Cash in hand if possible.'

'I take it Jess Hampshire isn't your real name?' Manfri asked, looking thoughtful.

'No, it isn't. I don't want to be that person anymore.'

'If you use a new name, you need so much more, a whole new identity complete with all the documents that prove that you exist.'

'Thanks, just as I'm feeling much better, you

had to say that. Actually, I have a bank account that my husband doesn't know about. That's my safety cushion; I plan to use it as little as possible though. That's why I will look for a job that pays cash.'

Manfri said, 'You could give that a try, but if you find a job like that at all, it will be menial, and the pay will be poor. Can you really live like that? You said your husband is an important man. What makes him so powerful that you have to go to such lengths?'

'He's a politician, a member of parliament. Phillip Pearson, you may have heard of him. He's hoping for a place in the cabinet at the next re-shuffle. His ambition is to go much higher, of course. Now I have broken away from him, he will be expecting me to tell the media, the police, anyone who'll listen to me what he's really like. He won't want that, at any cost.'

Chapter Four

Three pairs of eyes looked at me. 'Shit, girl.' said Tobar, what a mess.'

They exchanged glances. Manfri leaned towards me, 'Look, like I said you are welcome to use that room for as long as you like. Camlo, can you find Jess a job at the hotel, something back of house that will keep her out of sight.' He turned to the other two for their opinions. Tobar nodded in agreement.

Camlo nodded. 'I can do that, no problem.'

Manfri stood up and opened a drawer in the cabinet that stood under the window, placed a key on the table and slid it over to me, followed by my phone and tablet.

'Now, Camlo, would you give Jess a quick tour of the site, show her where the canteen and the laundry are.' Then to me, glancing at my mud smeared jeans, 'you might find that useful. Goodnight, we'll see you tomorrow.'

Outside in the chill air, lights already shone from some windows, a few figures moved through the shadows. By one of the buildings a woman was telling off a small boy, her son I assumed, for staying out past bedtime. All around, the trees, throwing dark patterns against the evening sky and scenting the air. It felt unreal to think that for a while at least, my home would be in a Gypsy camp.

I settled my backpack to a comfortable position, retrieved my bike and we started off. I stole a glance at Camlo. I couldn't make him out. Although the hostility had gone, there was still a chill to his manner. He avoided meeting my eyes. He was walking a little ahead of me, so I took the chance to look him over.

He was moderately tall, I guessed at around six feet, with an easy, relaxed walk. His dark hair was well-cut. Before he had rugby tackled me and got all that mud on his suit – as I had seen him when he leapt from his car to chase me – I had registered him as an attractive well-dressed man. I rather hoped he had another suit.

We stopped outside the long building. The one the clatter and chatter had come from the previous evening. He paused outside the door.

'Most of the families cook their own meals, but this place supplies a daily menu for when we fancy a change, a choice of two first courses and a dessert plus simple snacks and sandwiches, that sort of thing. Or you can come in for a coffee. There aren't all that many of us, so this place is quite adequate.'

He opened the door on a canteen. Tables and

chairs filled the area between the door and the back of the room where, behind a long counter, was a well-equipped kitchen with a professional cooker, a rack of pans, cupboards for storage and a large sink. One solitary woman was there, tidying away plates.

She smiled at Camlo. 'Everyone left early tonight, so I'm closing. Do you need anything?'

'No thanks, I'm just showing Jess around. She is staying with us for a while.'

I recognised her from the meeting. She smiled a little shyly and wiped her hands down her jeans.

'Good, we wondered if you would. My name is Mary.'

'Pleased to meet you, Mary.'

'Well, see you around.' With another smile, she left.

Camlo pointed out the group of small tables and armchairs that filled the end of the room. A large TV was mounted on the wall. 'This is the lounge area; it gets used a lot as a meeting place. Now I'll show you the laundry.'

'Before we go any further, I really want to know about all these buildings. Did your people put them up? They all have services, running water and electricity, here, in the middle of the woods.'

'They were here when we arrived. We have adapted the buildings to fit our needs, of course. One of the first things we did, after we decided to stay, was to find the owner and arrange to rent the site. We decided that we needed that kind of security, a safe refuge. He told us that the buildings go back to the early 20th century. At that time, a group of Arts and Crafts people had their workshops, studios and living accommodation here.

'A little later, back in the sixties, it was a thriving little business park. A machinery repair shop was the first to be established, then a bakery, rural craft workshops and a pottery. That is when they upgraded the services. Gradually the businesses all closed or moved away. The buildings had been empty a long time when we arrived and made our home here.'

The laundry turned out to be the next building. There were two commercial washing machines, tumble driers, even a dry-cleaning machine. I looked down at my clothes.

'Lela took my other clothes for washing this morning. As soon as I get those back, I can bring these here.'

'I expect they will already be back in your room. I'll take you there now.'

We started walking back towards my room. It was full dark now, and lights showed in several windows. I took care not to trip. When we got there, I leaned my bike against the end wall, took out my key and opened the door. I was about to thank him for the tour and ask about the job, but he had already taken a first step away. He stopped and looked back at me.

'Can you be ready for eight in the morning?'

Surprised and a little confused, I looked around my room. 'Um,' I looked across at the bed where the clothes that Lela had taken were laid, neatly folded, on the cover. On the bedside table was an alarm clock. 'It doesn't seem to be a problem, my clothes have arrived back, and I see I now have an alarm clock, so yes, I can.'

'Eight it is then, goodnight.' He turned and walked away, disappearing into the shadows. Suddenly alone, I switched on the light and shut the door. So much had happened in a few hours that my mind was trying hard to push it away. I was dropping with exhaustion. I would have a shower and sleep.

First, I set the alarm clock, sorted the clothes for the morning, then headed for the shower. A few minutes later, I switched off the light and crawled into bed.

I lay in the dark and wondered about the people who had taken me in. I didn't know much about Gypsies. It had surprised me that they still lived in a separate group and even some still living in caravans. I hadn't realised they had a language of their own. That must be what they had been speaking to each other when Camlo took me to the camp. They had obviously used it then as a way to keep the conversation private.

I drifted off to sleep feeling exhausted and warm and, unexpectedly, safe.

By ten to eight in the morning, I was ready and waiting. I sat on the bed feeling pleased with myself. In three days, I had turned my life around and found a place to live for a while. I had also found somewhere to work – assuming Camlo could arrange a position for me. All this would suit me well, at least for a while.

I was startled from my reverie by a crisp knock on the door. I grabbed my pack and stepped out into a bright morning. Full of optimism, I couldn't help smiling as I walked towards Camlo. I must have taken him by surprise because he almost smiled back. There was a definite tilt to the corners of his mouth.

'Come on, no time to waste. I want to get you settled before nine. I have an appointment then.'

'Do you think you really can arrange a job for me?'

'Oh, I think so. I manage the place. I hold the lease, on behalf of the tribe.'

It was said in an offhand manner, a little sarcastic and without any warmth.

He had his car ready and waiting. As I climbed in beside him, he started the engine. At the end of the track, he turned right. We sat in silence. Just as I was beginning to feel uncomfortable and wondering how far it was to the hotel, I saw the sign for it at the corner of a wide driveway. We can't have driven more than half a mile.

Camlo drove round to the back of the hotel and parked between the industrial size bins and the staff entrance. As he ushered me through the door, he said, ' Look, let me show you where everything is before you start work.'

He whisked me round the hotel explaining the layout and introducing me to the staff on duty that day. Inside the entrance was a small reception area. The girl on the desk, who was busy with a guest, raised a hand in greeting. A door off reception gave access to the service area. This consisted of several rooms, opening off a long passage. There was already a busy clatter from the kitchen, where breakfast preparation was in full swing.

'You'll meet the kitchen staff later. The breakfast service is no time to interrupt them.'

It wasn't a large hotel, two stories with six double rooms and six singles. We ended the tour in Camlo's office, a practical working environment with no frills. He perched on the edge of the desk. He seemed distracted, avoiding my eyes. I waited to find out what my role would be.

'Right, the only place I can offer to keep you safely back of house is housekeeping.'

I was confused. 'Do you mean cleaning rooms and making beds?'

'No, at least not unless we have one of the girls off sick, it covers a range of things, for example, sorting and itemising the laundry, making sure that the number of pillowcases that go off have come back. You will be looking after the stock levels of complimentary tea, coffee, shampoo, stationary, office equipment, that sort of thing. Basically, you will be responsible for making sure we have enough supplies of pretty much everything we need to run the hotel. Your first job each morning is to set up the trollies for the maids. They look after the cleaning materials, you load on the clean bedding, complimentary goods, teas, and coffees. Come on. I'll show you your room.'

Camlo strode along the corridor checking his watch. He stopped outside a door on the left, 'Staff restroom. There we can make tea and coffee and the kitchen supply us with sandwiches, cake, and fruit for lunch, we help ourselves and put the money in the honesty box.' Two doors, further on, another door was held open for me to enter.

'Have a look round. There's a schedule pinned up on the board. We haven't had anyone for a few weeks since Kizzy left us to work outside, so people have been mucking in. I'll come back and see how you're getting on after this appointment.'

He turned on his heel and was gone, just like that. I took stock. There was a desk, phone, laptop, and a pin-board with a long and comprehensive list of things to do. With days and, in some cases, times, all noted. I swallowed and sat down at the desk to study it. I had started my new job.

Over the next couple of weeks, life settled into

a routine. I enjoyed the hours I spent there. I got to know the other staff, meeting them in the restroom and chatting over coffee. There weren't many of us and most of them were from the camp, although a few came in from outside. Jason, the assistant manager, the chef, and his assistant. Camlo, as the manager was the solver of all problems.

I travelled to and from the hotel each day with Camlo. His initial cold attitude eased after a while, and he began to talk more freely. I soon found out that others travelled out of the camp to work. A minibus made the trip each day to the local town. It left early and returned in the evening. Anyone could grab a lift if there was space. A few, who worked in the other direction used the regular bus service. Others worked as casual labour in the local pubs and on farms. One of the men had taken on an abandoned workshop and was carving wood into rather lovely animals and figures, which he sold through a shop in the local town.

Back in the camp, I made a habit of spending evenings in the canteen. It was a welcoming place to meet the people living there and watch the communal TV. I followed the news, but there was no mention of Phillip Pearson's wife disappearing. I worried that this meant he was still looking for me.

Jenny, the one I had given the slip when I tried to escape that first day, when I was under suspicion, maintained a hostile distance. I would sometimes catch her looking at me, her eyes hard and cold.

It was Lela who became my closest friend. She came in one evening along with two others – Miri and Oshina – plonked herself down and started talking as though I had been there forever. We became the gang of four spending our evenings together, a fixture in the corner of the canteen. Sometimes Kizzy joined us, but she had a boyfriend in town and spent most of her time with him.

I told them about the things that happened at the hotel. They chatted about boyfriends, music, TV programmes and clothes. Sometimes they talked about their work. They never talked about being Romany and I never talked about my marriage.

One Friday evening, when it was only Lela and me watching the TV, she proposed a trip out on the minibus the next day, 'You have the day off, we can shop and have lunch, do say you'll come.'

'I'd like that. Are the others going?'

'Kizzy will be on the bus, she can't shop with us because she's working tomorrow. Miri and Oshina will be busy here.' I didn't notice the way Lela had hesitated before explaining about Miri and Oshina.

I looked forward eagerly to buying new clothes. Lela had given me a few items and, along with the ones I had with me when I arrived, I had been rotating them constantly. Now summer was arriving, and I was feeling optimistic about life for the first time that I could remember.

We had to be ready to leave early. The bus only made the journey once a day to be in Rotherton before the working day started. So regardless of what you were doing in town that was the time you left.

I should have had plenty of time to catch the bus, I set the alarm to wake me early but for once I slept through. I only just made it, leaving my room in a rush, grabbing my sunspecs as a last-minute thought.

Lela and Kizzy were already on the bus. They were calling for the driver to wait and waving frantically for me to get a move on. I leapt in, staggered through the seats, and sat between them on the back seat, out of breath and laughing.

It took the mini-bus half an hour to reach the drop-off point in town. We climbed out into an empty yard behind a car repair workshop. The driver disappeared inside, and the rest of the passengers scattered. We walked along with Kizzy as far as the café where she worked, left her there and headed for the shops.

Lela was eager to get started, 'Come on, let's go and spoil ourselves.'

It had been so long since I only had myself to please that I was tempted by gorgeous but totally impractical clothes. Lela took me in hand, by lunchtime I had a practical everyday wardrobe, and as a final treat, a dress, and a pair of pretty sandals.

'That will do for a start. Let's get some lunch now.'

'Shall we go to Kizzy's café?'

'No, we'll stop off there later. Right now, after a morning keeping you in check, I need a proper hot meal and a glass of wine, at least one glass of wine. They do a great lasagne in here. OK with you?'

I glanced at the place Lela was talking about. We were standing outside a small Italian restaurant. I took the lead inside, thankful for a chance to put down the bags and sit for a while.

She was right. We had an excellent lasagne and a decent glass of wine. As we were eating, I watched her, as confident and comfortable away from the camp as she was there.

I said, 'Does it feel odd that life in the camp is so different to this world?'

'Do you mean, how does the little Romany girl cope with all this sophistication?'

She wasn't offended. She merely seemed amused. I felt myself go scarlet with embarrassment.

'Sorry, that didn't come out right. It's just that though I'm used to living there now, at first it felt strange to me, that's all.'

'I was born there so it has always felt normal to me. Now drink some more wine and tell me about you.'

I was going to give her the sanitised, short version. I started off skimming through, but she asked questions and prompted. We ordered coffee and sat there until I had run out of words. I told her pretty much everything, my whole life story in all its drab squalor.

In the end, the dark eyes that had followed every emotion closed briefly. Lela asked for the bill. We shared it between us and left. We never spoke about it again.

I said, 'Right, this afternoon it is your turn.'

We stopped mid-afternoon at Kizzy's café for coffee and cake and to rest our feet. The café was quiet when we arrived, so Kizzy could spend a little time with us. She talked about the plans she and her boyfriend had for their wedding and that she would be staying in town that night, in fact, in a couple of days she would be moving in with him. We wished her well. Then there was a rush of fresh customers, and she was busy again. As we walked away from the café I asked if Kizzy moving out was a sudden decision. Lela laughed and said that everyone had expected it for ages.

By the time we climbed into the minibus at going home time, we were weary. We travelled home, both of us happy and relaxed, so when we arrived back in camp, we were slow picking up on the tension.

Manfri and Tobar were standing in the open space with a handful of others milling round.

When they saw us on the bus, they strode over and banged on the door for it to open. As soon as the gap was wide enough, Manfri pushed inside, eyes searching the seats.

'Miri and Oshina, they didn't come with you?'

Lela was confused. 'No, you know where...'

'Yes, yes, of course – I only wondered.'

He backed out and went back to the group outside. Lela jumped up and followed, dashing over to join them. I could see that she was asking questions. I climbed off the bus and hung back, waiting. I didn't like the body language, something was wrong.

The group got bigger and bigger. I could see the discussion, the arguments, the arm-waving, then at last the agreement. I couldn't join them. This wasn't for me, but I couldn't leave. I needed to know what had happened, Lela would tell me. At last, she came over, her face tight with anxiety.

'What's the matter? Has something happened to Miri and Oshina?'

Chapter 5

'Come with me, I'll explain while I get changed.'

I hadn't been inside Lela's place. Rather than live with her parents. She had moved to a place of her own in one of the buildings. It had, like mine, a bed-sitting room, and a bathroom; she had also added some extra furniture, including a small camping cooker on a stand. I made a mental note to do the same. I dumped my shopping on a chair and sat on the sofa while she talked.

'You know that this is a Romany camp.' She shook her head to stop me from interrupting, 'now, there's something you need to know and no matter how improbable it sounds you have to believe me. I know Camlo hasn't told you this because I've asked him and no one else would.' She paused. 'This place is also a gateway between two time zones.'

'What?' Had down to earth Lela really said that? Was she joking? 'Say that again, I thought you said …' I heard the disbelief in my voice as it tailed away.

She had been looking in the mirror taking off

her make up, now she turned to face me. The anger in her eyes shocked me. More than anger, I saw hurt and confusion.

'I wouldn't lie to you. I can't believe you think I would. I am letting you into the tribe's most guarded secret.'

'Ok, I'm sorry, really, I am. You took me by surprise, that's not something you hear every day. Why don't you tell me about it?' I knew Lela as a meticulously honest person, and she obviously believed it was true. What was more I couldn't believe she would lie when our friends were missing, possibly in danger.

'Our tribe arrived here twenty-five years ago. We were travelling in the year 1847. When we reached here, we stopped to rest for a while. The day after we made camp, two of our people walked down the track looking for work. As they stood at the side of the road, a car roared by. They had found themselves in a terrifying new world. We had walked out into 1997.

'It was such a shock. Imagine how it felt to jump forward one hundred and fifty years? It took a while for tribe to come to terms with what had happened, so much had changed. We had to learn how to live in a new century.'

While she talked, she stripped off the jeans and top she had worn during the day. From her chest of drawers, she took a different outfit. When she had finished changing, Lela was transformed by a long full skirt in dark blue, a white blouse and a dark red shawl. She rooted under her bed, brought out a pair of black lace-up ankle boots and put them on. Gone was the girl from the twenty-first century. In front of me I saw a figure from the 19th century.

'Wow, Lela. Why…?'

'There's much more to tell but that will have to wait. All you need to know at the moment is that they went back, two nights ago, the two of them and two of the men, Durril and Fell. It was supposed to be a brief visit, all of them travelling together.

The men wanted to visit the graves of relatives in a different village from where the girls were going. Miri and Oshina told them to go. Insisting they would be alright. They agreed on a time and place to meet. Then, when the men arrived, the girls weren't there They were all expected back this morning. 'Durril and Fell waited a long time, but eventually they came back for help. The girls wouldn't have got lost or forgotten where to meet. Something must have gone wrong. I'm going with Tobar to look for them.'

'Can I come? I want to help.'

'You don't understand. We're going back to where we came from, to the past.'

'Why not let me come then. An extra pair of hands and eyes could help. You took me in and gave me a place to stay. They are my friends too. If they are in trouble, I want to help.' I could see the indecision on Lela's face. Before she could answer, there was a knock on the door. Tobar opened it and stood in the doorway. 'Are you ready?'

'Jess wants to come.'

Tobar gave me a long, assessing look. 'There could be trouble. We have no idea what we are going to find.'

'I understand that. You can trust me to follow instructions, I can be useful.'

He turned to Lela, 'have you got another outfit?' She nodded. 'Five minutes, no more. Consider this a test.' He shut the door.

'Let your hair down and shake it out, take your make up off. What have you got on your feet? They will have to do,' I was wearing trainers. 'Put these on.' She chucked another long skirt, a black one, and a white blouse at me. With my heart pounding, tripping over the hem of the skirt, I managed to get them on.

'Good, now put this round your shoulders.' She passed me a blue shawl then she stood back and surveyed the effect. She grinned. 'Take a quick look in the mirror. Leave your watch and your phone and let's get going.' A glance in the mirror showed me another young woman I didn't quite recognise.

Lela opened the door. We walked down the steps and over to Tobar, who raised his brows. He took a torch from a pack, slung the pack over his shoulder and said, 'Let's go.

We walked through the camp along the

familiar pathways. Small groups of figures turned to watch us go. There were muttered good wishes as we passed. It seemed everyone knew where we were going.

The path we took wound away from the last of the wagons and the buildings, leaving them far behind. I wanted to test Tobar, so I waited until Lela had dropped behind to re-tie her boot. Feeling slightly as though I was betraying my friend, I said, as casually as I could, 'Do you go back often, to the past I mean?'

'Not often, once or twice year, to see friends.'

A confirmation from Tobar of what Lela had told me. I was on my way, actually going back in time. I found that very disturbing.

The night grew cold. I pulled the shawl closer and concentrated on the small pool of light from the torch, feeling grateful that the moon was helping to light our way. After what seemed like hours of walking, Tobar called a stop. He unrolled a groundsheet and laid it down.

'Let's take a break, try and sleep for a while.'

I felt relieved, it would be very welcome to sit and relax. Gathering my skirts, I sat down gingerly and wrapped my arms round my knees. After a couple of minutes, I rested my head on my arms.

I woke curled up on my side. Opening my eyes, I could just see Tobar standing close by, staring along the path. It was beginning to get light; I could see the faint outlines of trees in a world that was grey and misty. I shivered.

'Here, take a mouthful of this.' He passed me a bottle. I squinted at it in the gloom. 'Whiskey, great.' I took a large swig and breathed in the warmth, letting it flood through me.
'Thanks.'

Lela stirred, 'I could do with some of that.' She sat up and held out a hand for the bottle.

Ten minutes later we were ready to move on. The groundsheet was rolled up, replaced in its bag, and left hidden under some bushes ready to pick up on our return. There was a sharper atmosphere now, we were alert and tense. Tobar and Lela led the way confidently.

The path soon petered out into an area of open trackless ground. When we had crossed that, we stepped out at last, onto a road. The surface was compacted earth, rough with stones,
hoof prints and wagon wheel ruts.

Lela said, 'If we meet anyone don't say anything, your accent is all wrong, we'll do all the talking.'

The road led down through a small wood, entered a long wide valley, where it followed the curve of the low ground. At a fork in the road one lane worked back up into some more high country off to our left. The other wound onwards into the distance. Far away, along that road, I could see a cluster of buildings where a bridge crossed a river.

We headed in that direction. By the time we

were getting close to the buildings, I could see they were a few cottages and an inn, it was well into the day. It was warm and sunny, so the shawl that I had wrapped tightly round me I slipped off my shoulders and tied round my waist.

'This inn is where they were supposed to meet, you two to stay outside. I'll see what I can find out.'

While Tobar went inside, Lela and I stood on the bridge and looked down at the river, not speaking much just watching the water flow. When Tobar walked out, he brought us a tankard of beer each. While we drank, all of us leaning casually on the bridge, he told us what he had found out. 'The landlord says that he hasn't seen the women. However, he was keen to tell me that a stranger passed through yesterday and that was all I could get out of him.'

Was he was implying that someone waylaid them?' Lela clearly didn't believe that.

'I think that was his intention, we can't afford to dismiss the possibility. One other person interested me. A man at the bar took a real interest in the conversation, more than normal curiosity. When I asked him if he'd seen anyone, he shook his head and hurried away. Drink your beers. When he comes out, I want to talk to him, but not until he is well away from here.'

When we had finished our drinks and Tobar had taken the tankards back, we walked away without looking back until we were out of sight.

Then we left the road, stepping over the ditch that ran beside it then slipping through a gap in the hedge into the field. We worked our way back to a position where we could see the inn door through the branches. We would know if anyone left. Without comment Tobar removed the canvas bag he carried on his back and tucked it into the hedge.

We waited in hiding, eyes fixed on that door, for what seemed a long time. Eventually, the door opened, a man stepped out and began to walk towards us. Dressed similarly to Tobar in shapeless, shabby trousers, a collarless shirt, and a tweed jacket, but in his case he and his clothing looked ingrained with dirt. On his head he wore a brown, grease-stained trilby.

I was so relieved that something was happening at last that I took hold of Tobar's sleeve, shook it, and whispered, 'Look.'

Tobar raised a hand in warning and pulled us deeper into the shadows. Lela and I looked a question at Tobar, who said very quietly, 'yes, that's him.'

We watched him walk past and waited until he was a fair distance ahead. At a gesture from Tobar, we stepped out of the shadows, back onto the road and followed. Then, when we were well out of sight of the houses and the pub, Tobar lifted the pace a little and we began to close up on him.

'Try to look casual, don't alarm him.'

We were closing nicely with him when the road curved to the right. As we rounded the bend, we could see a cottage behind an overgrown hedge. The man must have heard us, he looked over his shoulder and started to hurry.

'Come on, don't let him get inside.'

Tobar was gone, pounding along at a hell of a pace. We lifted our skirts and chased after him. Tobar caught the man at the gate, catching hold of his jacket. The man turned and punched Tobar and the two of them fell through the gate. We arrived to see a flurry of arms and legs before Tobar ended up on top. He took hold of the man, then he stood, dragging the man up with him. Holding his shirt collar, he pulled him back onto the road.

We stood beside Tobar, Lela's face assumed a hard eyed glare that reminded me of Camlo, I just tried to look threatening. I don't know why we bothered; the expression on Tobar's face would have terrified anyone.

'We are looking for two young women who have gone missing. We know they were travelling on this road and that they were going to meet someone in that inn. I believe you know something about what happened to them, so come on, tell me what you know.'

'I don't know nothin. With who?'

Tobar wound his hand tighter in the collar and started searching the man's pockets. The jacket had nothing of interest, but when he took his hand out of a trouser pocket, his expression had grown even darker. He opened his hand and there, sitting on his palm, was a gold bracelet we all recognised.

Lela stepped forward and touched it gently, 'Miri's bracelet.'

'Where are they? What have you done with them?'

This man was an idiot. He decided to try a bluff, 'No, no, this belongs to my wife.'

Lela snatched it up. Tobar shook him again; squeezing his neck until he couldn't breathe, then he relaxed his hold to give the man a chance to speak.

'Look, it's an easy choice, either you talk, or you die.'

He still didn't answer, so Tobar tightened his grip again. The man held out until his lips were going blue. At last, he tried to speak, Tobar released his neck.

'The landlord, he made fools of you alright. He made me help him; I didn't want to.'

Tobar let him go. We all stood back to have a good look at him. He really was a pathetic creature. His clothing was threadbare, boots cracked and scuffed, and he stank. Lela and I stood guard over him while Tobar searched the cottage for anything else that belonged to Miri or Oshina. There was nothing.

We left him to his squalor, went back out to the road and started walking back towards the inn, Tobar striding along like an avenging tornado.

A desperate voice called after us. 'Don't let him know it was me as told on him.'

Tobar was leaving us behind. Lela muttered, 'Oh shit. Come on, don't let him get away. There's going to be trouble.'

We did our best to keep up. However, as we approached the inn Tobar slowed to a stop and pulled us off the road. 'We need to agree on a plan. Let me go first. You hold back until I'm inside, then you two check out the back. See if there's a rear entrance or a storeroom.' He didn't wait for us to agree. He started to walk away then, turning back, he said, 'and listen out, see if you can hear the girls.'

I said, 'Has he thought that through properly? He could be walking into all sorts of trouble.'

'He's worried sick about them and he's quite good at taking care of himself you know. We'd better do as he asked. Come on. It's time we were moving.'

As we walked along, we looked out for something that could be used for defence – or attack – if needed. I chose a lump of flint, a good, hard stone. The smoothly rounded outside surface fitted nicely in the palm of my hand, presenting a broken surface with razor-sharp facets. Holding it tight, I tucked that hand inside my shawl.

Lela found a large cast-off horseshoe by the

side of the road. She stared at it for a moment then bent, placed her shawl on the ground with the horseshoe in the centre. She gathered up the edges, letting the horseshoe hang as if in a bag. After a couple of trial swings she nodded, satisfied. We moved on.

Tobar stopped in front of the inn. He looked behind him to check we were on our way, then opened the door and disappeared inside. We walked past as though we had no intention of stopping, planning to double back and investigate behind the building. That was until we heard a crash and yelling from the bar. We turned and, plan forgotten, together we dashed to the door.

Chapter 6

'Drop the shawl, Jess.'

As we ran, I let the shawl slip to the ground. It sounded as though the third world war had broken out in the bar. In the seconds before we burst through the door, I remembered that I was back in a time before there had even been a first world war.

Lela got to the door first. She glanced back and grinned. I could see a bright fire in her eyes, so I gripped my stone and nodded. We went in yelling as loud as we could, the door banged back against the wall and the windows rattled.

Of the five men inside the landlord was the worst off. He was stumbling around, still brandishing a cosh, blood flooding into his eyes from a cut across his forehead. Three other men were working together as a team. They had Tobar backed into a corner, but he was far from beaten. He had a knife in one hand, and he gripped a tankard in the other. He was breathing heavily, balanced, and looking for an opening.

All three men attacking Tobar were wielding

evil looking wooden coshes. They started to turn to see what the interruption was. Seeing his chance Tobar lunged. Lela launched herself at the furthest man, swinging her horseshoe weapon, I hefted my flint and laid into the man nearest me, keeping a tight hold on it so I could hit with it over and over again.

I still believe that the surprise and the sheer ferocity of our unexpected attack were what saved Lela and me from serious harm. We managed to get a few good blows in before they got serious. I had managed to hit the face of mine, which was bleeding impressively. Then we were in real trouble. I partially deflected a couple of blows. They hurt like hell, but I didn't think he'd broken any bones. Then, of course, I dropped my stone.

I backed away, cursing my stupidity, and watching for the next swing of the cosh. I reached behind my back, searching for something, anything, hard and heavy I could use. My hand had closed round the handle of a tankard, when from the corner of my eye I saw Lela's guy catch hold of her arm, the one holding her weapon, now she was defenceless.

'No.' I bellowed it out as loud as I could, anything to divert his attention. For an instant, it worked. All three men paused to see what the noise was all about. Tobar swung his left hand and smashed his tankard into the side of his opponent's head. He reversed the knife, then; fast as light he threw it at the man who was still gripping Lela's arm. It buried itself in the muscle of his shoulder. The man yelled out, letting go of Lela and his cosh, twisting around, trying to reach the knife.

I almost left it too late. My man had turned back to face me, a triumphant grin starting on his face. His judgement of me was wrong, though. With my weapon lost, he thought he could pick me off at his ease, so his cosh was down at his side. I had seen Tobar wield his tankard. I would do the same.

He didn't even see my arm swing back, gaining extra power, then fast and as hard as I could, I brought it round and up, crunching it into his genitals with all my strength. As he folded round the pain, I lifted it again. Gripping firmly with both hands I brought it down on his exposed neck.

Lela hadn't wasted any time. She had wound up her horseshoe like a dervish and whirled it at her man, catching him on his remaining good arm, another one out of the fight. Tobar caught hold of the man he had hit with the tankard, then the landlord. With a grim smile of satisfaction and massive force he banged their heads together. They were still conscious but staggering and holding their heads, they had had enough. The fight was over.

We shuffled them into a huddle in the centre of the bar. Tobar reclaimed his knife and slipped it back into a sheath on his ankle. As he locked the door he said, 'We don't want to be disturbed, do we? One of you go and look around for some rope.'

I went. The first room had a sink and a couple of cupboards, no rope. After rooting around for a while I found some in the cellar. Back in the bar we tied each of them in a chair, with their arms tied behind them. We didn't bother with the one Tobar had knifed, we tied his legs together and left him helpless on the floor.

Tobar looked down at him. 'That arm isn't much use and Lela broke the other, he might get them free after a while, or they may have to wait for rescue. Now,' he bent over the landlord and slowly took out his knife again, 'Where are our girls?'

'I don't know nothin' about no girls.'

The knife passed close to the landlord's eyes and rested gently on his cheek. Tobar tilted it so that only the tip touched the skin and pressed gently. A single drop of blood trickled slowly down a cheek that began to quiver.

'I'll ask again for the last time, where are they?'

The man was too slow. The knife slid down half an inch, blood spurted, and he screamed.

He drew a deep breath. 'I knew you see. I knew they were supposed to be carrying, they're out the back, in the hut.'

We were out of the back door fast, racing across a scrubby field towards a ramshackle stone hut. Tobar got there first. He dragged open the door and we gathered to look inside. Before he could move Lela slipped past him into the hut. Tobar and I followed, afraid to look at what we had found. They were there, sitting side by side on a wooden bench.

I realised why one end of the rope I found had been newly cut. Miri and Oshina had their hands tied behind their backs. The rope passed from their wrists under the bench and then tied round their ankles. They couldn't stand or stretch out their legs. Filthy rags had been stuffed into their mouths.

Tobar cut away the ropes and removed the rags. Once he had freed them, we gently massaged their arms and legs to get the blood flowing again. They hadn't made a sound. Tears flooded down over faces rigid with fear. We put our arms round them until the fear dissipated and relief flooded in. We held them until the shivering stopped.

Tobar sat on a crate and waited until the girls were calmer. Then he took one of Oshina's hands and one of Miri's, holding them very gently. With their attention on Tobar, I looked them over. They had put up a fight. I could see bruises on their arms and legs. Miri had a nasty one on her left cheek, colouring up purple and green.

Tobar said, 'I'm so sorry, but I have to ask, did they get the stuff?'

Oshina shook her head. 'No, I don't know why,

what the delay is, but they haven't arrived yet. Not only that, but somehow, we missed Durril and Fell. We were waiting by the bridge, talking over what we should do, how much longer we should wait before giving up and leaving. The landlord and those other men came out,' she took a moment to control her shaking voice. 'Those men took us inside. They told us they knew what we were doing and asked us where we had hidden the stuff. They wouldn't believe that we didn't have it. They kept us in the cellar, then this morning put us here, tied us up, told us that if we told them where to find it, they would set us free.'

'So, where the hell have they got to?'

I was thinking, where was who and what stuff had Miri and Oshina been waiting to collect?

Lela said. 'What do we do next then, Tobar?'

Tobar sighed, 'We must decide if we wait or go home and send out a proper search party. Oh Christ, let's get a drink and think it over.'

Back in the bar, Lela poured us all drinks. As the group of angry and unhappy prisoners were still struggling to get free, we took the drinks outside. I retrieved my shawl. Tobar slipped away and returned with his bag. We stood together by the bridge.

I took a good swig of whiskey and stepped slightly away from the group. I was having trouble accommodating to the things I had heard, to the things that had happened. I wanted to know what was going on. Lela was my friend for god's sake, so were Miri and Oshina. In all our hours together, there had been no hint of – well, I had no idea what – I felt excluded. It brought home in no uncertain terms that I was an outsider. There was no doubt that they were seriously worried. I would keep my peace. Get back to the camp and then I would pack up and move on.

I stood to one side while the four of them talked. Miri and Oshina wanted to know how we had found them, so they heard the whole story. The fight was described in detail and much enjoyed by the girls. My part in it was praised, earning a grateful hug from each of them. The colour was back to their cheeks, they had their people with them, they were safe now.

After a discussion between the four of them, they decided to wait for the rest of the day. Then if the men hadn't turned up by dusk, we would leave. No one could understand how the men who had come back to alert the camp had managed to miss the girls. They concluded that when Durril and Fell came looking for them, they were already in the cellar.

We all settled down on a grassy bank by the river, where there was a good view of the road in both directions and waited. There was hardly any conversation. While they watched the road, I dozed in the sunshine.

Lela woke me. They were ready to leave, the

men they had been waiting for hadn't come and it was nearly dark. We gathered ourselves together and trailed away into the dusk.

For the first part of our journey back there was still enough light to see the road in front of us, but when we reached the footpath through the dense woodland Tobar took torches from his bag and passed them round.

'You go on. I want to make sure that no one is following us.'

He stepped off the path and into the deep shadows, immediately invisible. As we walked on, I tried to swallow my sense of unease. The night was pitch black now with the torches showing only wavering patches of light. The condition of the path made the going dangerous. The surface was uneven and broken by tree roots and stones, twigs, and years of leaf fall.

After a while, Lela raised a hand for us to stop. We had reached the group of bushes where Tobar had left the groundsheet on the outward journey. 'Let's wait here for Tobar. Is everyone OK?' We clustered together. Lela shone her torch over each of us in turn. They all looked pale. I suppose I did too. We were all exhausted but, yes, we were fine. We wrapped our shawls tighter against the cold and waited for Tobar.

The glow from his torch was the first sign that he was coming. I heard his footsteps hurrying along the path then suddenly he was there.

'Alright? Let's get moving.'

He pushed the groundsheet into his pack and slung it over his shoulder. There was no more stopping on the way home. Tobar led the way, striding out with grim determination. Miri and Oshina struggled along behind him, followed by Lela helping and encouraging them. I brought up the rear. The night grew colder.

From out of nowhere, a cluster of flickering lights bloomed on the path ahead. Tobar stopped dead and we formed a group behind him. I wasn't sure if it was for protection or to support him. Slowly he reached for his knife.

A voice shouted out, 'Put it back, you silly bugger, who do you think you are?' Half a dozen of them burst out of the trees, men from the camp. They had been watching for our return. It was too dark to recognise any of them, but I thought I heard Camlo's voice. There was laughter and relief and then we all walked back together. On the way, Tobar gave them a brief explanation of what had happened and one of them ran on ahead to spread the word.

As we entered the camp, we saw Manfri standing in the light from the open office door. He had been waiting for our return. He walked forward to meet us. He looked tired. Other people also waited. In silent groups or singly, almost hidden in the shadows. Manfri placed his hands on Oshina's shoulders and kissed her forehead, then Miri, Lela and finally me. His voice betrayed his relief. Rather gruffly he said, 'Get some sleep now. In the morning, we will all get together and talk, decide what to do. Goodnight.'

We stood there while he walked away, then quite overwhelmed that it was all over we drew together and hugged, my feeling of isolation momentarily evaporated, then we said goodnight and went off to our rooms. When I reached my door I turned to look around the camp. Everyone else had disappeared, the camp was deserted. I closed the door and locked it. Without stopping to switch on the light, I kicked off my trainers on the way to the bed. I almost fell onto the mattress. Curled up in my shawl, I fell asleep.

The alarm woke me at the usual time. I fought my way out of the tangle of shawl and the covers I had pulled over me during the night. I staggered into the bathroom and stood under the shower until I felt human. With a towel round my hair and finally awake, I sat on the bed and tried to order my thoughts.

The negative emotions of the previous day seemed foolish in the light of a new day. There was a lot I didn't know about these people that I might come to understand, if I stuck around. I instinctively felt that knowledge would bring commitment. I already shared some of their worries. If that deeper involvement wasn't what I wanted, then this was the time to walk away. It was decision time.

While I struggled with my thoughts, I started

to pack up my things, I didn't have a clue what I would do, but I would be ready to leave, just in case. Manfri had called a meeting, so I would go along and see if it helped me make up my mind.

I had almost finished when there was a knock at the door. Camlo, I thought, he always managed to make a knock on a door sound like a command. I called out, 'Coming,' then walked over and opened the door. Sure enough, it was Camlo. He was leaning nonchalantly on the wall, dressed in casual clothes, not for work.

'Is it time for the meeting?'

'Yes, what are you doing?' his eyes missed nothing; he had noticed my pack open on the bed, full of stuff.

I left it there and stood blocking the door. 'Tidying, what are we doing about work this morning?'

He was already walking away. Over his shoulder, he said, 'I have phoned in that we have a meeting and will be in later.'

I was getting used to his abrupt manner now. He was friendly enough in a cool, distant way. Quite different from the way he was with everyone else. Yet I saw more of him than anyone, even more than the girls and they were all good friends. I locked my door and followed him to the hall.

At the door, he stood to the side to let me go first. As I passed, he looked me full in the face. For a moment I felt he was about to say something, but then the moment passed. I went to sit with Lela, Oshina and Miri. Camlo followed behind and took the last seat in the row.

This time there were no chairs on the stage. Manfri and Tobar stood together and waited for the crowd to settle. Then Tobar took a few steps to the side and Manfri started right in.

'Thank you all for coming. You all know by now that Miri and Oshina were waylaid, beaten, and imprisoned on their trip this time. Luckily, they were rescued and brought home to us. For that we are all very grateful.'

There was a smatter of applause and mutters of approval.

'The important thing now is to consider the implications and what actions we will take. Let me run through what we know. Then we will have a free discussion. 'He paused. There was silence while everyone waited.

'I'm worried about our men. Why didn't they make the delivery? Do they have a problem, do we send people back to try and find them? Or, although I hate to say this, are they our problem, have they been careless and were overheard talking in the pub? Make no mistake; the landlord knew the girls should have been carrying the stuff.'

Beside me, Camlo stirred, he spoke out, 'Or maybe they had no intention of handing anything over and wanted to frighten us off. Perhaps they set everyone up. Did they know what the landlord was like, and they weren't careless, they deliberately let him hear them talking, gambling that he would ambush the girls. Maybe they realised he would be pretty pissed off that the girls weren't carrying, maybe not. Either way, Miri and Oshina were lucky to get out alive. How much information did the men have this time? Was it more valuable than the usual quota for three months?'

Now there was a rustle in the crowd as they absorbed that.

Manfri spoke directly to Camlo. It was clear to see he was worried 'Yes, it should have been a very profitable quarter.'

There were angry words now from the people in the hall. Some protests and arguments began to break out. Manfri raised a hand, 'Stop! If you have something to say, come up here and we will all listen.'

Plenty of them had things to say. I barely listened. I wanted to know what the hell they were talking about, so I glanced at Camlo. He was looking exasperated. When there was a lull, he got to his feet and climbed onto the stage.

'I'm sorry if some of us don't believe that we have been betrayed. I suggest we wait and see. Myself, I suspect we will never see either of them again. However, I think we're strong enough, we don't need those men anymore. So as far as I'm concerned, I say no to going back looking for them.'

He jumped off the stage and sat back down. I decided it was time for me to go; this wasn't any concern of mine. As I stepped past Camlo, he looked up and said, 'I've had enough too, fancy a drink?'

'Oh, please.'

We went to the canteen. There was no one else there, the others were all still at the meeting. Camlo said, 'grab a seat.' and disappeared into the back room. He came back with a couple of beers, then sat opposite me at one of the tables.

I lifted my beer. 'Are we really going to work this afternoon, after drinking this?'

'No,' he paused, looking distracted. 'I just phoned in and they're fine. We'll take the rest of the day off.

I waited. At least twice he made to start talking, but nothing happened. I had just about decided to give up and go home. I drained the last of my beer and started to get up.

'Don't go, I think we should talk. Another beer?'

Without waiting for an answer, he collected two more bottles and brought them back to the table.

I had sat back down, now I leaned back, staring expectantly. I had just about had enough.

'Try talking then.'

For the second time ever, the second time in one day, he looked directly into my eyes.

'I'm worried about you.'

'What?'

'You heard. I saw your expression last night when we came to meet you. You were trailing along at the back, looking closed off and angry. I almost expected you to continue walking, that when I called in this morning, you'd be gone. Then I find you're still here, but you're packing your bag. Can you tell me why? You and Lela, you're good friends, Miri and Oshina too. As I understand it, you did a good job yesterday.'

How very observant of him. I had recognised his voice among the others, I hadn't seen him, yet he had registered how upset I'd been.

'Did a good job? If by that you mean I did my best to help find the girls and fought side by side with Lela and Tobar, then I may have 'done a good job.' Did I have any idea what the hell was going on? Not a flying f... clue.'

I noticed how hard my hand was gripping my beer bottle. I put it back on the table and forced myself to sit back in my chair.

'Don't get me wrong. I am very grateful that you all let me stay here and found me something useful to do, but there's all sorts going on here, illegal, and dangerous things that I do not understand and of course that makes me uncomfortable.'

'Lela hasn't explained anything to you?'

I shook my head.

'What do you talk about then?'

'The usual girl things, men, films, TV shows,

clothes, work, men. She probably thinks you blokes, the ones who run the place, have filled me in.'

There was a brief silence while we both paused for thought. After a moment, Camlo pushed back his chair and stood.

'I think we need to talk somewhere where we won't be disturbed. This place will get crowded when the meeting breaks up. Would it be alright to use your room?'

Well. It looked as though I might be going to get some information at last. 'Come on then.'

I led the way, letting us both into my room. I spirited away my half-full backpack. The table against the side wall that served as a dining table/desk had two chairs. I pulled out one and sat, Camlo took the other.

'Where would you like me to start?'

'Start with the only thing anyone told me, that you all arrived here by accident, one hundred and fifty years out of your time. Lela only told me that as she was getting ready to go.'

'Right, well, you know that is true because you have been there yourself. We could never pinpoint the exact spot but somewhere between here and where the path meets the road, time changes. I think it's likely to be close to here.'

He leaned back and gazed into space, somewhere over my right shoulder. 'We were all gathered, several families of us. It was winter and there wasn't much work available. That was always a hard time for us, so we had grouped together to support each other.

We had been warned that the local village didn't like such a large group of Romanies nearby. One day, we had word that a large gang of men were on their way to attack us, so to avoid trouble we moved on. We chose roads we had never travelled before, attempting to escape them. On impulse, we followed a path through the woods that was so narrow we only took it because we were desperate. We lost the ones who were chasing us and just kept moving. The path went on and on. Then, when we thought it would go on for ever, we found this clearing. The old people and the very young were exhausted, so we stopped to rest, we set up camp here.'

'You were part of that group? You must have been very young.'

It took him a while to answer that, 'Yes. The wagons struggled to get through, it was rough going. To make it easier for the horses, most people walked. There were a lot of places where everyone had to push, to keep the wagons moving. I was only one year old, so my parents took turns carrying me. My mother wasn't well. She had recently had a miscarriage. She was confused and frightened. A month after we arrived, she died.'

'Oh Christ, Camlo, I'm so sorry.'

He dragged his eyes back to the present. The focus returned and he looked at me, his brown eyes large and dark.

'It's alright, let's get this done, now where was I?'

'You had made camp here.'

'Some of our people started to investigate the area. To find out where we were.'

'Lela has already told me the story of the young men who strolled down to the end of the lane and a car drove by. How it scared them to hell.'

He nodded. 'Anyway, to skip quickly through the years, a few people, families and individuals, went back to the old life. Most of the people decided this new world offered more than the one they had left behind. They would stay, except it wasn't that easy. To find a place in today's world you must belong. You need all the paperwork and a history, to get a bank account, a driving licence, virtually everything.

'Eventually, we found people who can supply all of that, birth certificates, passports and national insurance numbers, everything to give our people an identity.' Camlo was looking at me to see if I understood.

'That must be expensive.'

He nodded. 'So, we made plans. We used today's easy access to information: the internet. We researched the things that people gamble on, the results of horse races from back then, plus other events that provide a profitable bet.

'We reached an agreement with two of our

men who wanted to return to the past, that they would place bets using the knowledge we passed on to them. We carefully worked out a schedule of dates to place the bets. The first time we also sent them some of the old money we still had from when we arrived. Always spreading the bets so not too much would be taken from any individual bookmaker.

'They collected the winnings, kept some back for the next round of bets and an agreed percentage for themselves. With the rest, they bought things that would sell profitably back here, jewellery, pieces of China, paintings, things that are now valuable antiques. At first, they would bring them back here and then we agreed a rota of meeting places, where someone from here would collect the goods. They would bring them back here to be sold, converting the old money to today's currency.

'After a while, this became quite profitable, so we expanded the operation. We have now bought identities for most of us. This means we can work and pay our way in this world. Now the men have gone missing. I think they must have taken the last returns and scarpered.'

'They should have delivered the latest batch of goods, desirable objects, whatever, to our girls?' I asked.

He sat back, 'That's it. Sure, it is most probably illegal, but it has been necessary. That's the whole story.' He started to stand.

'Would you like a coffee before you go?'

Camlo stayed for coffee, and we talked it through a bit more until we both felt comfortable that I understood. The question when it came was casual and conveyed no particular interest. 'Will you be leaving, now you know?'

'No, not now.'

There was only one question that still needed an answer. I asked it as Camlo was on his way to the door. 'You lost your mother but is your father still here?'

He stopped in the doorway and smiled at me, his first real, warm smile. 'Of course, didn't you realise? Manfri is my father.'

Chapter 7

I spent the rest of the day cleaning my room and thinking through Camlo's story. I tried to understand how they must have felt, those families, moving on to avoid trouble. Looking for somewhere safe to stop for a while, until, at last, they found this place. It must have taken so much courage, finding their way in this time. A process they still hadn't completed 25 years later.

I realised I had been standing by the window, staring out at the camp for so long the minibus had arrived, bringing back those who worked in the town and a few people who had been shopping. I watched them as they separated to walk to their homes. Camlo had said almost all of them had identities paid for by the betting scheme. I couldn't find it in my heart to disapprove.

They had missed the meeting but would be brought up to date by friends and family later. The canteen would be crowded and noisy tonight; I wanted to avoid that, so I crossed to the cupboard where I kept my emergency store of crisps, biscuits, and cake. When I had demolished most of that, I settled down with my book and spent the evening reading fiction that was in no way as strange as real life had turned out to be.

When my alarm dragged me from sleep in the morning, I lay for a while wondering if I would open the door to the new Camlo, the one who had talked openly and honestly and even smiled. Or would the surly, distant, and remote version I was used to be collecting me for work.

When I heard the familiar knock, I opened the door. Camlo was facing away, his attention on Tobar, who was shouting, something from outside the office. Camlo called back: 'I'll bring some back this afternoon.' Then he turned to face me and smiled.

'Good morning, Jess, are you ready to find out what the maids did to your department yesterday?'

I hadn't thought of my little job as a department, I grinned back. 'As long as they didn't throw all my neat piles of towels over the floor and leave dirty coffee cups on the shelves, how bad can it be? How about you? How much can your assistant manager have screwed up?'

'Oh, Jason is well trained. He can cope.'

We set off down the track. I had something I wanted to say that had niggled at me into the night. 'There is something that worries me. I am sure it is something you have considered. I wonder what you plan to do. Do you mind me asking?'

He flicked his eyes in my direction. 'Well, if I knew what you're talking about, I may be able to answer you.'

'It's those men, the ones who betrayed you all. They must realise that everyone now knows what they were doing. Would they still want to continue, independently?

We were almost at the hotel. Camlo was silent until the car was parked, then he switched off the motor and looked at me thoughtfully.

'That is something I have considered, on balance I don't think so.' We sat for a moment in silence. He sighed, 'Let's get on and start the day.'

He paused at the door to my room, restless, as if he had something else to say.

While he was hesitating, I said, 'You don't look convinced.'

'I think it would be clearer in my mind if I talk it through with someone, I'll clear my emails and come along, I'll bring coffee.'

I quickly sorted the most immediate jobs, laying out the two cleaning trolleys, adding fresh linen, the toiletries, and drinks. I lined them up in the corridor, ready for the maids to collect. Camlo arrived soon after carrying two coffees.

'Are you free to talk for a while?'

'Yes, come in.'

We settled ourselves down in the chairs. I could see Camlo was about to start, so I held up a hand to stop him.

'Why me, am I really the person you should discuss this with? You made it clear enough when I arrived that you considered me an intruder.'

He started to shake his head. I continued, 'I think we have got past that now. I appreciate that you took the trouble to explain everything to me. Do you think that gives me the right to an opinion?'

I thought, for a moment, I had gone too far, that I had put too much trust in this new comfortable relationship. Camlo was motionless for a moment. His eyes were large and dark with long lashes. They caught mine and held them for a moment. Just when I thought I really needed to start breathing again, he sat back and smiled.

'As a matter of fact, I do. We didn't get off to a great start, did we? I'm sorry for that, I do tend to react strongly sometimes, having a stranger walk up the track so soon after receiving those threats. Well, it spooked me. The thing is we must be very careful, a few of our group still have no identities. This makes them stateless people, stateless people who happen to be Gypsies.' He shrugged. 'We were threatened with violence by that woman but calling in the authorities could cause us trouble too.'

'I'm beginning to understand how insecure that must feel.'

Camlo nodded slowly.

I had another thought. 'Will it make a lot of difference, losing the money you made trading through those men?'

'Well, the hotel is running at a profit, the good thing is most of us are working, I think we will be able to acquire the last few identities soon even without their input. That isn't what worries me. I want to talk it over with you because you recognised the problem.

'Everyone else is so overjoyed at getting the girls back safely, they haven't thought it through. I'm worried that I might be letting my imagination run away with me. The thing is, to get the information needed to go independent they would have to come through the camp. That would mean real trouble, we don't take kindly to traitors. Tell me honestly what you think?'

My answer to this was important. I took some time to think, staring into my coffee cup before I said, 'I don't think you need to worry. They don't have a clue how to deal with living here, they wouldn't know how to get hold of that information, you told me they hated it here. Besides there's only two of them to – how many of you are there?

For a while, Camlo was miles away, engrossed in his own thoughts. He brought himself back to the present. 'I had better get on. Thanks Jess. That was a great help.'

The door closed behind him. I took a deep breath. Where did I stand with this guy? In a couple of days, it seemed that I had moved from unwanted pain in the arse to first choice confidant. How did that happen? Over the next few days everything returned to normal. One quiet night, when the diners had finished and gone from the canteen. Lela casually mentioned that she and Ruslo were going to the cinema the next evening.

I smiled at her, 'Is this a new romance?'

Rather indignantly and blushing Lela told me that they had been friends since childhood, Ruslo was just a friend, not a boyfriend. The other girls, struggling to keep a straight face, agreed that friendship was definitely a barrier to romance.

When I met with the girls the next evening, we discussed the blossoming romance. They told me – falling over their words in excitement – how they had been expecting the two of them to get together for ages.

I wasn't sure which of the young men Ruslo was, until Lela brought him to the lounge area the day after their date. Then, of course I recognised him as a familiar face. He seemed shy, he was a little taller than Lela, with thick unruly hair and a smile that lit his whole face. I could see how happy he was making my best friend. I was pleased for her.

Walking back to my room, not thinking of anything in particular, I found Camlo drifting into my thoughts. I had an involuntary image of him, as I had seen him one evening laughing with Manfri. There had been such warmth and happiness in his face. I stopped where I was, resisting the emotion that I didn't want to admit, even to myself. I knew I shouldn't be so fanciful, I wasn't a teenager after all. The man was my boss and that was that. The truth of it was I was attracted to him. Only natural, I told myself. He was a very attractive man. Any woman would recognise the truth of that. I walked into my room and put the kettle on.

That Friday, after I finished dinner, I took my coffee to join Lela who was on her own in the lounge area. We chatted for a while, about her date. When I asked if the others were coming in, she said that Miri and Oshina were on a trip back to the past, not to the pub where the horror happened but to a place where they had friends. 'To banish the ghosts, you know.'

I reached out and took her hand, giving it a squeeze. 'I know, very well.'

She looked down at the floor for a moment, then lifted her head and smiled. 'I know, let's have a group night out. Invite everyone available, get together a gang of us, we'll ask if we can have the minibus. Are you up for it?'

'What a good idea. You had better organise it but count me in.'

A few evenings later, a group of us had gathered at the minibus: Lela, Miri, me, Ruslo, Kem – a young guy who obviously fancied Miri

– and Camlo. Oshina had caught a cold and was feeling too ill to come.

Lela had volunteered to drive. She stood swinging the keys, 'Well, where do we all want to go?' No one had any strong feelings about that, so we ended up going for a drink at a pub a few miles away that was popular with the younger generation from the camp.

As we pulled into the pub car park, Ruslo said, 'There's a lot of cars here tonight, must be something on.'

As we climbed out of the bus, we could hear music. Miri said, 'Great, they've got a group in, get a move on so we can get a good table.' We hurried into the pub and the guys went to the bar for the drinks while the rest of us managed to claim the last table and find the extra two chairs we needed. With a bit of a squeeze, we all managed to fit round the table.

The group were playing a selection of rock and pop numbers. The crowd were enthusiastic, clapping and cheering their favourite songs. As the evening wore on, the bar became a solid crush of bodies. We had given up any attempt at conversation and were just listening to the group.

It all went downhill when Ruslo, trying to get through to our table with some fresh drinks, got nudged in the back. This sent him staggering into a large guy sporting a shaved head. A whole pint of beer spilled over a lot of soft flesh; a football shirt stretched tight, shorts that didn't quite reach the shirt and fat hairy legs.

Fat man let out a bellow, turned on Ruslo and, swearing aggressively, gave him a shove. Ruslo apologised and got back to our table as quickly as he could.

'I didn't fancy mixing it with that bloke. He could smother you to death.'

The big guy wouldn't let it go. He and his two mates moved over closer to our table.

'Oi you, where do you lot come from then? Not English, are ya?'

He could easily make himself heard even over the music. There was a moment's pause while we wondered if it was wisest to ignore him or to answer.

'Yes, we are English, thanks. Look, let me buy you a drink as a gesture of goodwill.' Kem smiled and started to rise.

'Nah, I wouldn't take nuffin' from you lot. You all look bloody foreign to me. Illegals, are ya?'

'No mate, English as you are.'

That was Camlo, sitting back in his chair, relaxed, not the slightest bit aggressive.

We were left in peace after that, big guy and his mates moved away. They got themselves into a huddle over by the door. Our group went back to watching the musicians. I was still concerned, surprised that they had given up on their entertainment quite so easily. Camlo caught my eye and nodded over to the group by the door. He raised his brows in a question.

I said, 'Yes, I think so. We should go, now.'

We passed the word round. So that it wasn't obvious we were leaving, our men would walk towards the bar. We would gather our handbags and walk towards the bar door as though we were going to the ladies; conveniently positioned next to the outside door. We would chatter and giggle in a suitably girlie way as we passed the big guy and his mates. For extra authenticity, Miri would call out, 'make mine a double' before walking through the door. If the plan worked, there would be no reason for them to realise we were leaving. At the last moment, our men could change direction and follow us out. We would nip into the minibus and away. Good plan, we thought.

It didn't work out that way. As we approached the group of men by the door, a little unsteady on our feet and way too relaxed to be making a run for it, they must have thought they could have more fun with us than the men. As we passed through the door, they swung into the passage behind us. One walked ahead and blocked the entrance to the ladies. A meaty arm went round my waist, pushing me forwards. We were all being forced out of the pub.

They didn't waste any time. As soon as we were through the door, I was pushed against the wall. He had my skirt up round my waist, one hand found its way inside my pants. With his other hand, he was fumbling with his shorts. I brought my knee up hard and heard a satisfying grunt. That only made him angry. He called me a fucking cow, drew back an arm and came in with a punch to my ribs that made me gasp and cry out.

Then he was gone, dragged away from me by a shadowed figure who took him down with an attack of pure savagery that left him a curled-up mess on the ground. In the dim light from the pub, I could see blood running into the dust from a cut over one eye and from a smashed mouth. As I looked, he pushed out a couple of teeth along with a gout of dark blood.

I realised I was still standing there with my skirt tucked into my pants. I pulled it out and smoothed it back down with hands that were shaking and looked round for the others. The rest of the attackers had disappeared. Lela and Miri stood like statues, still too shocked to move. Ruslo and Kem were talking softly to them. Kem had taken Miri's hand and was gently rubbing her arm. Ruslo had an arm round Lela's shoulders, her head rested on his shoulder.

The car park was suddenly quiet. The only sound the muffled music from inside the pub. I turned to face Camlo. He was standing close, using an outstretched arm to lean against the wall. His breathing was uneven, his face down. I couldn't see his expression.

'Are you alright? I'm so sorry, Jess, we should

have realised. When we saw them follow you out – we were still too far away – the crowd...'

'I'm fine.'

Camlo lifted his face, and, for just a moment, there was an expression in his eyes – then he was back, the self-contained cool guy who takes charge and copes with problems. He laid a comforting hand on my back. 'Come on, let's go home.' He raised his voice to include the others,' Gather up anything you've dropped. I'll drive back.'

We all climbed into the minibus in silence. By the time we were halfway home everyone was talking at once, us women laughing it out and saying how awful the men were and how none of us thought they could have managed it anyway. The men, well Ruslo and Kem, boasted of how they had fought off the attackers. Harmless bravado that made us all feel better. Only Camlo remained silent.

Back in the camp, we gathered by the minibus to say our goodnights. Anyone listening would have thought the evening had been a triumph. I suppose it had been, in a way. Lela and Ruslo walked away, arms around each other. Miri and Kem almost kissed, then didn't, shyly said goodnight to each other and walked their separate ways.

Camlo said, 'Would you like someone to come and look at your ribs?'

I smiled at him. 'No, it's alright, Camlo, I've

taken worse punches than that.'

'Many times?' his hand reached out and touched my arm.

'Many times. Goodnight Camlo, see you in the morning.'

In the morning he was his usual bright self. Usual for the new Camlo, that was. We chatted aimlessly, all the short distance to the hotel. With ribs that had bruised up nicely but weren't too uncomfortable, I bustled around and completed my usual morning stuff, so, feeling like a cup of coffee, it occurred to me that Donna might like one too. Working on the reception desk, she often missed out on coffee breaks. I would go and ask her.

I left the service area and started walking along the corridor to reception. I was almost there when Camlo, who was in reception, standing just in view, saw me coming. He walked at a leisurely pace towards me. Then, as soon as he was close he put on a turn of speed. Without saying anything, he grabbed my arm, opened the linen store door, and swung us both inside, shutting the door quietly behind us.

I opened my mouth to ask what the hell he was doing and got a finger to my lips in warning. He put his mouth close to my ear.

'That guy, the one who was looking for you, Mr Pellow, he's just checked in. Donna has put him in room five.'

Chapter 8

That would mean him coming along to the lift. Down the corridor where I was on my way to reception. I would have walked straight into him.

'Why, what the hell is he doing checking in here? Oh god, he must know I'm in the area.' I was panicking. I had not forgotten, but my previous life had slipped out of the foreground of my mind. My life now was so different, like living in a new world.

Camlo said, 'No, at least I don't think so. He said he liked the look of the place when he was here before. He brought a woman with him.'

Then perhaps I was still safe. Feeling weak with relief, I did what felt like the most natural thing in the world. I sagged against Camlo and rested my head on his shoulder.

For the space of a breath, I felt his body tighten and try to pull away.

'Sorry, oh, I'm so sorry. I didn't mean to do that.' I stepped back and looked up at him thinking; don't go back to hating me, not now.

Instead of pushing me away, Camlo slid his

arms round me and pulled me close again.

'You're trembling. Are you that scared of your husband?'

I nodded into his shoulder. 'I planned my escape so very carefully, for such a long time. I can't go back.'

I raised my head and looked up into his face. He lifted a hand and cradled the side of my face; his thumb stroked my cheek.

'If I ever get the chance, I may just have to kill him.' Then his hand slipped round to the back of my head and lifted my face closer to his. He paused to look into my eyes and then, at last, his mouth found mine.

I believe whole galaxies may have formed, lived, and died while Camlo kissed me that first time. I know that what began as a gentle, sweet thing became fire and flame and powerful desire. And yet, when we surfaced, both of us a little unsteady, we were still in the linen store and only a couple of minutes had gone by.

We stood a little apart, a little embarrassed. Camlo took my hands in his and we leaned our heads together, just our heads. I don't think either of us could trust ourselves to closer contact.

I found what didn't sound like my voice. It wobbled alarmingly. 'I never thought – where did that come from?'

He squeezed my hands. 'If you only knew – but you were so – I didn't think you would ever be approachable, but I understand why now.'

'You scared me you were so cold.'

'No, you had this thorny barricade round you with great big no-go signs.'

We looked at each other and laughed. There was nothing I wanted to do other than stand and look at this surprising man, but there would be plenty of time for that. Camlo let go of my hands, slid his hands up my arms and held me by my shoulders. 'There's so much I want to say to you, wasted time to make up for, but I had better get out there and see if it's safe to move you. Wait here.'

His lips briefly touched mine, then he left and the door closed behind him. I stood and tried to make sense of what had just happened and what had been said. Had I really been giving keep off signals? Probably. I lifted my fingers to my lips and lived, again, the feeling of that kiss. Suddenly life had found a whole lot of magic.

Camlo opened the door. 'Come on, it's quite safe at the moment. He's taken his woman to Brighton. He asked Donna for directions.'

I started towards my office, but he steered me in the opposite direction.

'Why are we going this way?'

'Because I'm taking you home, that's why.'

It was weird, sneaking out of the staff door, with the boss, during the working day. We crossed to his car like a pair of kids sneaking out of school, watching the driveway in case Pellow came back for some reason.

I felt safer once I was in the car. Suddenly curious, I said, 'What did she look like, the woman he brought with him?'

'She is short and plump with an absolute mess of ginger curls.'

That caused me to think, hard. 'You have got CCTV in reception, haven't you?'

'Yes, in all the public areas.' He turned his head to check my expression. 'You think you may know her?'

'I can't help wondering. Could I see it sometime?'

Camlo stopped the car by the office to let me out. 'I'll copy this morning's recording and bring it home tonight.' Then softly, 'I have to get back, will you be ok until I get home, you won't worry?'

I shook my head. He turned the car and was gone. I stood and listened to the sound of his car as it bumped away down the track. I could still hear it when it pulled onto the road and accelerated away. I turned to find Tobar standing close behind, watching me. He smiled knowingly.

'Getting on a bit better now, are you?'

I grinned at him. 'You're getting very nosy in your old age,' I patted his arm as I walked past him, back to my room.

As soon as I had closed the door behind me, I rooted through my backpack for my phone, brought it out and switched it on. Apart from keeping it charged, I hadn't even switched it on for ages. There it was. The message I expected to find. It had come in fresh that very day.

Maureen, you evil bitch! Maureen Punter or Mo as she liked to be called, one of my group of 'friends' which meant ladies selected, vetted, and approved by Phillip as suitable company for me, each of them the wives of associates. One or two had been alright. I had liked them. We had sometimes managed to drop the rest of the group, especially Maureen, and let our hair down a little.

I read the message: 'Hi Lucy, I haven't heard from you in such a long time. Phillip says that you had to go to Eastbourne and nurse your mother. That she is extremely ill, and you may be away for a while. The rumour is that you have separated. I don't believe that, of course. I know a happy couple when I see one. Well, whatever the truth, he's pining for you, poor lamb.

Anyway, Dennis is away on business for a month, so I'm taking a little holiday. I would love for us to get together, have a good old chat, and catch up. I'm staying near Brighton at the moment. I'm at a bit of a loose end so I could meet you anywhere. So, looking forward to hearing from you, love, Mo.'

I stared at the screen long after I had read the message. Then I switched it back off and placed it carefully on the table.

I stayed in my room as I didn't put it

past Tobar, because he missed nothing that happened, to spread the word. There were few secrets in the camp. What happened had been such a precious moment, but I needed to be sure that I hadn't imagined meaning and promise where there was none.

I watched from my window as the time for Camlo to come home approached. At last, I saw the car swing into the camp and stop in the usual place. I saw him climb from the car. There was a quick glance over to where I stood, back from the glass so he wouldn't see me waiting, then he gathered an arm full of stuff from the boot and strode away out of sight. He was going home.

Ok, plenty of evening yet. I would settle down with a coffee and my book, no problem. Except that I stayed where I was, watching through the window, all freshly showered and in my favourite dress.

Ten minutes passed, a quarter of an hour – I just happened to notice the time by the clock on the bedside table, it wasn't that I was counting the minutes – seventeen minutes and there he was, hurrying, hair all damp. He had changed into jeans and a t-shirt.

I was going to count to ten before answering his knock on the door, but he saw me, and his smile was so vivid that I had the door open even before he reached it. I stepped aside, Camlo walked in and closed the door behind him. My pulse was racing; I think we both felt awkward.

We stood there like a couple of shy teenagers.

Someone had to speak first. I searched desperately for something to say.

'Good afternoon?' at least it was polite. The words, 'Did you mean to kiss me like that?' retired to the back of my brain, disgusted.

Camlo nodded.

Oh well, business then. 'Did you bring the stuff?'

He looked down at the pile in his hands. After a moment, he put it on the table.

In a voice deeper than I had heard from him he said, 'Important things first, come here.'

Surfing on a wave of relief, I took that one step that took me right up to him. I saw the joy in his eyes, I felt the strength in his arms as they wrapped around me. I lifted my face for another heart-stopping, lingering kiss. When the kiss ended, I clung to the feeling for just that little bit longer. I ran my palms from the back of Camlo's neck over his shoulders, down over the muscles in his chest; I could feel his heart beating. I snuggled closer.

'Jess, please, we have things to sort, plans to make.'

He was right, of course. 'Would you like a coffee?' safe ground, I thought, I can play it cool.

'I'd like to toast you with champagne, but that will have to wait. Yes, I'd like a cup of coffee.'

Camlo pulled a chair up to the table and set up his laptop while I made the coffee. 'I don't know how you like your coffee.' We shared a grin, both of us thinking how much we still had to learn about each other.

'Black one sugar, please.'

I carried the coffees over to the table. 'Right, what have we got?'

'I've got this set to start as they walk into reception. Ready?'

I sat down beside him. 'Ready.' Camlo pressed start. I saw Pellow walk into reception, Maureen following behind. Not the manners that Maureen would expect from a lover, but Pellow was an arrogant bastard.

'Is that who you thought it might be?'

'Mmm, I want to watch them, see how they behave together.' Pellow managed booking the room, explaining how much he liked the place. So, when he wanted to take his special lady somewhere special, this was his first choice. I saw Camlo come into reception and try to look busy with a pile of forms.

Pellow and Maureen played at the happy, loving couple. He gave her a hug, she simpered at him. I watched them taking the room key and moving away. Camlo had already disappeared to scoop me into the linen store. I glanced at him and found he was watching me.

He said, 'Now it shows footage from the corridor outside their room.'

In no way were they a couple. They were already bickering over sleeping arrangements, she said he should sleep in the car, he said they would put a rolled-up towel down the centre of the bed if she insisted, but she was safe anyway because he was more selective than to bother her. They opened the door and disappeared into the room.

That was the end of the recording. I picked up my phone and turned it on, found the message and handed the phone to Camlo. He read it through twice, then handed it back. I turned it off and put it back in my pack.

'They know you're in the area, not where exactly, but that you are not far away. Did you see him at all, on your way here?'

I nodded, 'I was in a shop, and I saw his car go by.'

'And that was the same day you found the camp,'

'Yes. I was sure he hadn't seen me, so I carried on, I almost made it to the Hotel, but then, well you know what happened.'

'I shouted at you.' He was looking at me intently, tenderness and amusement clear to see, in his eyes and on his face.

'Yes, I was hurting and sore and soaked through and then this fierce gypsy leapt out of the trees shouting and swearing.'

'Fierce Gypsy, eh? Sheer surprise, for all I knew then, you really could be the one posing a threat.'

'And, and after all that, I got locked up for a whole day.

103

'If Pellow hadn't come asking about you, you could still be locked up.'

'Oh, thanks.' But he wasn't listening; he went quiet and sat back in his chair. I was going to ask if he'd thought of something, but he cut me off with a raised hand.

'Dash cams, I bet he had dash cams, angled to the side. He could check the footage later just as we did just now with the CCTV.'

That was a shock. 'I planned everything so carefully. I watched him drive past and I knew he hadn't seen me, I never thought about dash cams, how stupid of me.'

'Don't say that, no-one can think of every single possibility.'

He had laid a hand over mine where it rested on the table. I looked at the long brown fingers, capable hands. He had gone quiet again. 'I have to ask, she calls you Lucy, is that your real name?'

'Yes, I used to be Lucy.'

That is so pretty.'

'Don't you like Jess?'

'I love Jess. I just wanted to know. I want to know everything about you.'

Overwhelmed by the intensity of the expression in his eyes and struggling to breathe, I said, 'Cam, would you like to – stay. I turned away, embarrassed. Oh hell.'

'Yes, I would, you know that.' He reached and gently turned me to face him, traced a fingertip from my eyebrow down my cheek. 'But I don't want to rush; I want to make it special. I have some work to finish tonight but will you come and walk with me first? I'd like that.'

He took hold of my hand and led me out into a soft, summer evening. Several Romani were taking the air, gossiping with friends, or sitting quietly outside their doors. I didn't look to see, but I could feel eyes turning to watch us pass. A few called out a greeting.

' See, we won't need to tell anyone about us. The word will be all round camp by morning.'

'Already is, probably, Tobar noticed me watching you leave and listening until I couldn't hear your car anymore. He enquired if we were getting on a little better, with one of his knowing smiles.'

'Did you?' then, 'Tobar is a wise old devil.'

'He can't be all that much older than you. Ten years or so?"

'Good guess, it is ten years. Tobar was eleven when we came through.'

We had left the camp behind. The quiet of the woods closed around us, rich with the scent of sun-warmed earth.

I looked up at the figure beside me. 'That makes you twenty-six.'

'I'll be twenty-seven next month, on the fifth, how about you?'

'Twenty-four, my birthday is September the fourteenth.'

'You're so young to have coped with so

much. What about your parents? You haven't mentioned them.'

'I was told my parents died in a car crash when I was a baby. I had a succession of foster parents. The less said about most of them, the better. Then the couple I had been with for three years, a couple I had been quite happy with, sat me down and told me they were very sorry and would miss me, but as government support had ended, I had to leave. I crashed and burned. I was a mess.'

I told him the story of my marriage. How the impressionable young fool I had been then was so easily lured into a loveless hell, how Phillip had done his research and chosen the perfect victim.'

Camlo had stopped and wrapped me tightly in his arms while I told my story. I clung to him, holding him close. We stood like that while, unnoticed, clouds rolled across the sky and a chill breeze whispered through the leaves. Eventually, Camlo let go and said in a voice rough with emotion, 'So, Cam will be your pet name for me forever now, I like that. He took my hand again and we strolled back home. Quickening our pace as it began to rain.

We arrived at my door just as it really began to pour. He collected his laptop and stepped back outside, then he turned and looked back at me. There was a sadness to his smile that I couldn't bear. I followed him out, put my arms round him and looking into his eyes quietly spoke his name.

Camlo kissed me as the rain soaked us through then took a reluctant step back, 'Goodnight Jess.'

Overwhelmingly happy, I said, 'Goodnight, Cam.' I stood and smiled at him until he responded to the joy on my face, the warm smile I had waited for replaced the sadness. I blew him one more kiss and went inside.

Chapter 9

I towelled my hair, changed into dry clothes and was brushing my hair when I realised, I hadn't eaten since lunchtime, I would go and get some food. A peer through the window showed the rain had passed over. As I closed the door behind me, Lela and Miri came rushing up. There was nothing subtle about Lela. She threw her arms around me, making me struggle to breathe.

'Jess, Jess, I'm so happy for you. It was so obvious right from the start that you two should be together. What the pair of you thought you were doing for so long, God knows. Can I be your bridesmaid?'

'Me too,' said Miri, bouncing gently behind Lela.

'Have you forgotten that I am already married, technically?'

'That can be sorted, no problem, all we need to do is get you a new identity, then the new you will be a single woman. Easy.'

'Anyway, you're a fine one to talk. You grew up with Ruslo, and how long did it take you two?'

I made for the canteen, Lela came along with me, but Miri walked away saying she had promised to meet Kem.

We collected our meals, salad for me and cottage pie for her. Once we had seated ourselves at a table, Lela said, 'I want to hear all about it, which one of you finally broke through whose protective shield? How did it happen, for goodness sake?'

I gave her a basic outline out of sheer self-defence. She almost choked on her cottage pie. With eyes wide with delighted disbelief, she said, 'The linen store, really? There's not a lot of room in there, so what then?'

'It's a bit complicated, but I suppose I sort of started it by leaning on him. Don't ask.'

'Good move, Jess, I bet he couldn't resist that.'

I shook my head at her in exasperation. I knew she was teasing.

'Was it good then, that first kiss? I've always thought that Camlo would be rather good at sex. I expect to hear all about your first time.' She grinned at me. We finished our meals in silence, then we returned our plates, collected coffees, and went to watch the TV. She reached one of her dainty hands to touch my arm.

'Seriously, Jess, I couldn't be happier for you.'

I looked at her, a little thing, full of life – and tough, I knew that from fighting beside her – and behind those guileless brown eyes was huge heart and a keen intelligence. I was glad to have her as a friend.

The next morning, I was up and ready for work in plenty of time. I stepped out into a perfect morning. Bright sunlight filled the camp, the day was already warming, drying the paths still wet from the evening's rain. I went and stood by Camlo's car and waited. At first, he didn't see me, he came hurrying round the corner with his arms full and stopped dead when he saw me standing there.

'What do you think you're doing, woman?'

Torn between anger and happiness, he scowled at me with his brows drawn together in a frown, but the light in his eyes gave him away.

'I'm coming to work. There's no reason for me to hide away here. If I stay put in my room, how can anyone know I'm there?'

He opened my door for me, a way of agreeing without having to say so. As we started off, he conceded. 'As long as I can get you in the hotel and out again safely.

He glanced towards me and caught me watching him. I said, 'Yesterday was quite a day.'

His smile was wide, 'I came up with a couple of ideas last night.'

'Really, any of them concern me?'

'Maybe, now be prepared to duck down if I give the word.'

I saw Pellow's car in the guests' car park as we pulled into the staff parking area. There was no one around. Most members of staff were already working. The part-time people would arrive later. Camlo insisted on peering through the door before letting me in, just in case either of them, Pellow, or Maureen, was lurking in the corridor. Once we reached my room, we both relaxed, sharing a relieved grin.

'I'll bring along coffee and lunch later, stay in here.'

He left it until after the maids had collected their trolleys. Then he arrived with the coffee, a round of my favourite sandwiches: brie and grape, and a fresh cream éclair, another favourite.

'Thanks, I really like these.'

'I know, I noticed you buy them in the staff room last week.' He had brought coffee and sandwiches for himself as well, so it seemed he was staying for a while, but instead of settling in a chair, he stood by the boxes of tea and sugar sachets, shuffling them around, his back to me. I had noticed him doing that before when struggling with a decision, fiddling with something.

'Don't you like the way I organise those, or would you be more comfortable counting sheets in the linen store?'

He turned to face me. There was that smile, with raised brows and eyes full of mischief. Then the smile faded. Serious once more, he picked up a chair and placed it close to mine where he could face me. I moved my chair around, facing him. It seemed he had something difficult to say, something that I needed to understand.

After staring over my shoulder for a while, his focus moved to my face. His eyes held mine. 'How would you feel if something not exactly fatal happened to your – to – what did you say his name is?'

'Phillip.'

'If something not fatal happened to Phillip, which meant you would never have to worry about him again?'

My answer here was important. Camlo didn't want me to see him as an amoral thug, looking to commit murder as an easy way out of a problem. Nor did I think I should tell him I would rather see Phillip dead.

'Overjoyed, is this one of your night-time ideas then?'

'Yes, I was going to spend some time thinking it through; then I thought that I need to find out how you feel about it as soon as possible.'

I took a swig of coffee, pushed his towards him across the desk as a reminder to drink it and broke open the sandwiches. 'Come on then, let's have it.' I chewed on a sandwich and waited.

'Well, it's not without some risk.' I shrugged. Encouraged he continued. 'I think you should respond to that message from Maureen, say you would be delighted to get together with her and would she like you to come to her. Now, this is where we will have to be adaptable. If she says she will come to you, then we will re-jig. I think it most likely that meeting here at the hotel will suit them very well, as she is already here, plus he is conveniently available to walk in and overpower you. Only you will have your own personal army of hunky Romanies ready to leap in and save you.'

He paused for a bite of sandwich, more confident now.

'Oh, do I know any hunky Romanies? Where are we going to find them?'

After a fleeting grin, he continued. 'We sweep in and neutralise them. Now, maybe Phillip will have come down to join in the fun, if so great but if not, we lure him down with a message from Pellow or maybe from Maureen. I have a variety of ideas for this bit. Anyway, if he comes, we'll have him, but if he wants to wait in London, we go up there and get him.'

There was another pause, to finish his coffee.

I said, 'I think we should go and get him. What then? We have Phillip, Pellow, and Maureen, we've taken them prisoner. What comes next?'

Camlo swallowed a mouthful of sandwich. With a wicked grin he delivered his coup de grace. 'We take them on a long, long journey and then we leave them. We leave them one hundred and fifty years ago.'

I sat there, too stunned to speak for several seconds.

'Brilliant, just brilliant.'

'I'm pleased you think so. Personally, I'd rather just kill the bastard, but I wouldn't like you to think I'm some sort of savage.'

I ignored that. I knew he was a kind and caring person, I had also seen the condition of that human ape, curled up in agony on the pub car park gravel and I had no issue with what he had done there at all.

'What other ideas did you have, all alone in the night?'

'Well, there were a lot of very personal ones concerning you, of course, but there was one, a last flourish to finalise our trade with the past. I think we should take a comprehensive list and cover a much larger area of the country. Using all the old money we have left we could clear enough to buy the last people their lives.'

'Good idea, especially as none of it will slip into someone else's pocket.'

He shook his head impatiently. 'I tried to tell them we were getting ripped off, but they couldn't accept that members of our tribe would betray us like that. I couldn't even persuade them we needed proper paperwork from them. Anyway, when we get back this afternoon, I'll arrange for some of the guys to be available, then you can arrange your meeting with your old friend.'

I could see how relieved he was. He had shared his ideas with me, and I had approved them. He heaved a huge breath and let it go slowly. He stood, then pulled me to my feet so he could hug me.

'I'll see you later. Keep your head down. OK?'

'Don't worry. I know how to take care of myself.'

After a swift, tender kiss, Camlo left. I settled down for a peaceful afternoon, feeling relaxed and confident. Nothing could be easier. All I had to do was stay put until the end of the day.

Not quite. The peace lasted half an hour if that. The bloody fire alarms went off. A raw screaming racket loud enough to echo round three counties. Now what the hell do I do? I heard urgent voices and hurried footsteps. Undecided, gripping the edge of my desk, I peered out of the window. On that side of the hotel there was an open grassy space between my office window and the trees. Could I climb through the window and hide in the trees until it was safe?

Camlo opened the door and hurried in, all brisk efficiency.

'Sorry, Jess, but you have to evacuate to the main car park and join the rest of the staff there.'

'Is it bad then, the fire?'

'We're not sure yet. It's in one of the bedrooms, God knows how it started. I can't take any chances, there are procedures.'

'Do I have to? Why can't I go somewhere else? You will know that I'm safe.'

He shook his head, avoiding my eyes. 'No, sweetheart, I would know, but no one else would.

I can't risk someone going back in to find you because you aren't with the others. In case this gets bad.' I could see how much he hated to do that.

'OK, no problem, I'll just blend into the crowd. I go out of the staff entrance and round to the front, right?'

'Right, I must go and check all the rooms. I'll see you later.'

We walked through the door together. Camlo turned and headed for the centre of the hotel and the bedrooms. I headed for the staff entrance, feeling decidedly jittery about being so exposed. With the alarms still jangling my nerves, I made my way round to the front of the hotel, to the car park. A group of staff members were gathered in a tight little cluster. I joined them, working my way well into the group. Donna seemed to have taken charge; she was busy checking names off a list.

'At last, Jess, we were beginning to worry about you. Relax everyone, we're all here except for Jason. He's helping Camlo check the rooms.'

The guests had also gathered together in a group. Some talking, while a couple of others stood aloof. There was no sign of Pellow or Maureen. I began to relax. If they were away from the hotel, perhaps everything was going to be alright.

Then Maureen appeared. She stood apart from the other guests, checking her watch constantly.

I stepped behind the tallest staff member, the chef, and peered at her through the cluster of bodies. Maureen walked up the drive to the entrance where she stood and looked along the road.

She's waiting for Pellow, I thought. It looks as though he's overdue. I hope to Christ, we get sent back inside soon.

I often wondered if I was cursed with bad luck. True to form, everything happened at once.

Jason, the assistant manager, walked out of the main entrance shouting for attention.

'The fire engine will be here any minute, so will you all come off the car park onto the path and move well clear of the entrance please.'

In the confusion of a crowd all trying to find a direction and getting in each other's way, I found myself at the back of our group. Over the shuffle of feet and the loud, excited chatter I heard a car drive in through the entrance. Without turning I knew.

Instead of slowing, the engine roared. Somewhere Maureen was shouting. I tried to run but there were so many people in my way, in the panic of the moment I missed the curb, tripped, and fell.

Brakes squealed behind me. Struggling to get to my feet I heard the footsteps. I knew that despite my very best efforts, the security of the camp and the newly found love of my new life, none of those things would help me now.

There were shouts of protest, but nothing could protect me from the hands that dragged me to my feet and across to the car. Pellow practically threw me into the back seat and climbed in beside me. The other one, Phillip's other tame thug Cotton, was driving. He hit the throttle; the car slewed, tyres throwing up gravel and then straightened, heading for the gates.

As we roared away, I scrabbled around and managed to get a view through the rear window. I saw Camlo. He had forced his way through the crowd and was giving chase. It was pointless. We left him in our dust, turned a corner and, he was gone. I will never forget the expression on his face. I was lost to him now, I had lost everything.

I knew where we were going – back. His men were taking me back for Phillip to do whatever he wanted with me, and I didn't care.

Pellow probably watched me, carefully, all the way. I turned my back and ignored him.

When we turned into the drive, Phillip's car was parked in front of the house, along with one other car, so he had a visitor. I hoped they would stick around for a while and buy me a little time.

The garage door was open, the space inside waiting for us. The door clanged down behind us, leaving the garage a dimly lit space. Full of menacing shadows.

From the driver's seat, Cotton said, 'What do we do now then, take her in?'

'We wait here. The boss don't want to risk her

making a row before they're gone.'

Nothing more was said, and no one moved for what seemed an age. In my mind I may not have cared what would happen when Phillip finally came to collect me, but that good old instinct, the fear of pain, kicked in, squeezing tight round my chest, and setting my heart beating, so hard I could feel the pounding of it in my throat.

Eventually, I heard the visitor's car pulling away. My heart rate moved up a notch. I could feel the sweat trickle down between my breasts. The daylight that streamed through the door to the kitchen when it swung open was blinding after the gloom.

Pellow gave me a shove, 'time to move.'

I didn't move, so he got out and walked round. He opened the door, pulled me out of the car and on out of the garage. Phillip was waiting, holding open the door. I swear that man had the most evil eyes in the world, killer's eyes.

'Welcome back, Lucy. I hope you enjoyed your little jaunt because now I have got to punish you. I'm sure you understand that I really can't let you behave so badly.'

He moved his free hand and I saw, looped between his fingers, his latest and favourite toy, the heavy leather belt. He liked it because it didn't break bones, with all the inconvenience that entailed, but it left pleasing great long welts of swollen bruised flesh. Soaked with water, it struck with a loud, crisp crack and best of all, despite my efforts to stay silent, it hurt so much that after the first couple of lashes, he could make me cry out with every strike.

Shit, shit, shit. I could hardly stand; my legs had turned to mush.

'Upstairs. Now.'

Desperately afraid, I shook my head. Phillip nodded to Pellow, who picked me up and carried me. From below, I heard Phillip say, 'Chuck her on the bed, I'll be right up.'

Thrown onto the bed, I tried to slip off the other side and into the en suite, but Pellow was too fast for me and anyway, Phillip had arrived. As well as the belt, he was carrying a coil of fine rope and the kitchen scissors. The belt had been soaked, the leather darkened and dripping.

'Now Lucy, we need to get those clothes off. Do you want to take them off, or shall I cut them off?'

I scrambled to the top of the bed and sat with my arms clamped round my knees.

'Oh, for Pete's sake, cut some lengths of this for me while I sort her out.' He passed Pellow the rope and scissors. Phillip grabbed an ankle and pulled me down the bed. He took the first length from Pellow and tied my ankles together, then moved to the side of the bed and took the second rope. He tied one wrist tight, I fought to keep the other free, but Pellow caught it and held it. They tied my wrists together.

I tried to curl up on my side to protect myself. I

knew what was coming next. Phillip had chosen an old-fashioned metal bedstead. In no time, the ropes were tied to the rails at the top and bottom. I was secured, stretched out like a kebab.

Chapter 10

Taking his time, making sure to scrape the sharp point of the scissors across my skin, Phillip began to cut away my clothes, starting at an ankle. When he reached the edge of my pants, I said, 'Please, send him out.'

'But Pellow has performed outstanding service. He deserves a treat.'

I gave up. I closed my eyes until Phillip had finished cutting, then I had to open them to be prepared for the first lash. The shreds of my clothes were spread out then wrenched from under me. I could feel myself trembling, arms and legs twitching with terror.

'I think we'll do the back first.' I saw the salacious look they exchanged. They manhandled me onto my front. I twisted my head to try and see the first strike coming, but I had chosen the wrong side.

'No, don't let her move, hold her head still.'

He was making me wait. So, I listened. I thought I heard him swing the belt, I was wrong, but my bladder had given way. I felt the wet spreading under me and sobbed with the humiliation. I heard them laughing at me as the belt struck for the first time. I didn't make a sound. That one had struck across the centre of my buttocks; the next one hit in the same place. Despite my gritted teeth, I grunted.

Before, when he had used the belt, four or five lashes had been enough for him. This time I lost count. My world was a blaze of pain and, at every single strike now, I cried out.

Then the time came when they wanted to start the real fun. 'Turn over.'

I couldn't move, so they did it for me. Ignoring my cries of pain, they grasped handfuls of flesh and turned me over, bouncing me around until I was positioned just right.

'I'll just go and re-wet this.'

While he was gone, I tried to gather some reserves of courage to face what I knew would be the worst bit. If he struck as many times and as hard on the tender bits of me, belly, and breasts, as he had my back, how could I possibly survive that?

He is going to kill me. This time he really will keep going until I'm dead. Somewhere in the centre of my being, I knew the belt was only the beginning.

Oh, Christ, oh Christ, oh Christ almighty, he's back. Only now I would see the belt coming.

He stood there, swinging the belt, building up momentum. I felt my whole body spasm time and again. From somewhere beyond all self-control came a screeching wavering wail that became a scream of terror. I stopped to breathe then; having abandoned every shred of reason the scream tore itself out of me again and again.

They must have loved it. Through all my tears and swollen eyelids, I could see them laughing again. They decided to end the delay. 'Where shall I start, across the breasts do you think?'

I threw myself about to the limit of my movement, writhing and jerking, but the belt found me. I screamed, louder and longer than ever. Phillip started to swing back for the next strike.

It never came. The door crashed open to reveal Camlo. Motionless for a moment, then, with a roar of fury, he charged into the room. There were others following, but my eyes only saw him. He took Phillip down, going down with him and pounding him into the floor.

Camlo rose to his knees and then staggered to his feet. Phillip was beaten, but Camlo hadn't finished. Picking up the belt from the floor where it had been dropped, he set about the bastard with renewed enthusiasm. Again and again, he lashed out, head, body, and every time the belt landed, Phillip cried out.

'What are you making all that noise for, you useless piece of shit? You're fully dressed.' Camlo threw the belt down and lashed out with his foot, connecting with Phillip's head, changed direction and landed several more on his body. He seemed unstoppable until Manfri laid a gentle hand on his shoulder.

'Enough, son, leave him now. Jess needs you.'

As Camlo turned to look at me, his fury drained away. 'Find something to wrap Jess in, something soft.'

He bent and picked up the scissors from the bedside table and cut me free. Then he finally allowed himself to look me in my face. 'I heard the scream. We have to move you. I'm so sorry.'

The wave of relief when the torture ended was like being dragged from the fires of hell to the shores of paradise. I was me again.

'I know. I'll be alright.' My voice was barely even a croak. 'CCTV – in the office, it backs up to the laptop.'

'I'm on it,' said Tobar, 'where's the office?'

'Two doors down, on the right.'

As he left, Manfri reappeared with a pile of soft towels. 'I'll leave you two alone now. I'll only be outside the door when you're ready.'

The door closed and we were alone. 'Camlo walked over and looked down at me. I looked for something to cover myself with, mentally shrugged because there was no point anymore, so I decided the moment demanded a little humour.

'It's not the way I planned it, you know, the first time you saw me without my clothes. I planned candlelight, so much more flattering, and champagne. I would be wearing something flimsy.' I choked on the words and shut my eyes tight against the tears. Camlo knelt by the bed and wiped away my tears with the tip of one finger.

'Who needs candlelight and champagne?'

I swallowed hard, 'Can you help me up? We should go.'

So Camlo took my hands and helped me to my feet. 'Stand there, I'll wrap you in the towels, make you respectable for the journey home.' He stepped behind me with a towel. I braced myself. There was total silence, no movement. I turned to see him struggling to control his face.

'I don't know how to do this. How can I do it without hurting you even more?'

'I know, collect the towels together. They can pad me out for the journey. How did you get here?'

'In the minibus, not the most comfortable ride, I'm afraid.'

'With lots of padding, it will be fine. What I need next to my skin is something silky. I walked carefully to the wardrobe and took out a silk dressing gown. Camlo helped me slip it on. It felt cool and weightless on my skin. We started towards the door. My mind clicked back into operation, 'Where did Pellow go?'

Manfri, waiting at the top of the stairs said, Tobar dealt with him.'

Satisfied I began to move again.

'How are you managing with walking?'

'Fine.'

'No, how is it really?'

'It hurts, but I can manage it. Getting down the stairs will be the tough bit.'

'Painkillers, have you got any?'

'In the kitchen, there should be a packet behind the flour in the left-hand wall cabinet. I'll take some when we get down there.'

We took the stairs slowly; each step down pulled on painful muscles and skin. I found it helped if Camlo walked in front, I could use him like a Zimmer frame and that way, he couldn't see my face. I was calmer now, although a spasm of trembling stopped me until I had control again.

At the bottom of the stairs, Camlo went into the kitchen to look for the painkillers. He brought back a box of tablets. He also brought a glass of water for me to take them with. I looked at the water, took out a double dose from the offered tablets and put the packet in the pocket of my dressing gown.

'Don't think me ungrateful, Cam, but if you look in that cupboard, yes, that one, there will probably be a bottle of whisky.'

He took out the whisky, 'You intend to take powerful medicine with alcohol?'

I gave him a hard stare. 'Damn right I do.'

'In that case.' he handed it over, took it back and removed the top, then gave it back. I took the tablets with small sips then swigged down a mouthful for good luck.

The others arrived. Tobar walked up to us with Phillip's laptop nonchalantly tucked under his arm and then Manfri joined us. He had been checking the house. 'Everything is secure, all external doors are locked apart from the front door, all windows closed and locked. Now, let's discuss how we do this. When we arrived, we didn't want to arouse suspicion, so we parked a few houses down, doing our best to look like a bunch of workmen, slamming the doors, loud talk, carrying this.'

He brandished a large, well-worn canvas bag.

I said, 'It looks just like a tool bag, good cover.'

'That's because it is. We didn't know if we would have to break in. So, now it is the end of the job, I suggest one of us collects the mini-bus and drives in casual as you like to pick up the others. The important thing is to load the bodies fast, we don't want a nosy neighbour wondering what's going on.'

'Perfect.' I managed a smile, loving each one of them. Tobar took the keys and strode off.

'God, I've just thought, Cotton, the other one, he drove us here. I don't know what happened to him. He could talk. We won't be safe.'

The two of them exchanged pleased looks. Manfri opened the lounge door. With a sweep of his arm, he showed the three thoroughly trussed bodies, mouths covered with industrial tape, lined up, side by side. Manfri and Camlo dragged the bodies to the front door, ready for loading.

The minibus arrived and pulled up close to the door. It was the work of seconds to load the bodies. The tool bag was thrown in and then it was my turn.

They both helped, but I was sweating by the time I made it to a seat. A nest of towels made me as comfortable as possible.

Manfri said, 'Let's go,' and we drove slowly away from the house where I had learned about pain and hatred.

Camlo leaned close and said, 'You've forgotten about Maureen, haven't you.'

That gave me a jolt. 'Oh Cam, there was her as well! Yes completely. Did she get away? How do we find her?'

He jerked his head towards the back of the bus. 'If you could check the number of bodies, you would find there are four.'

By twisting my head and peering towards the back I saw that the bodies were laid in front of the rear seats and covered with old blankets.

'How the devil did you manage that?'

'I called Manfri as I walked back to the hotel, gave him a brief outline, and asked him to come with the bus and wait outside the gates. I nipped round and into the back door, gave it a couple of minutes, then I walked out of reception calling her name. When she came to find out what I wanted, I told her that Mr Pellow had called and left a message. She had to meet him along the road and bring her phone. I told her he insisted that the matter was urgent.'

He stopped talking. The bus had driven over a speed bump and the unexpected lurch made me gasp. I held out my hand for the whiskey, took three large swallows and gave it back. He watched my face until I was relaxed again, then he continued.

'She set off right away. I found Jason and told him that I had urgent business, and he was in charge, then I set off after her. She was out on the road, looking up and down for Pellow. She saw me coming and turned to speak to me. While she was asking me about the message, Manfri pulled up behind her. I grabbed her and, together, we bundled her into the bus.

'We went back to the camp. I had a hell of a job holding her down on the way. We collected some rope and other useful stuff and picked up Tobar. She was happy to give us the address, thinking we would let her go, we set the sat nav and here we are, easy.'

'I thought I would never see you again. I was sure Phillip was going to kill me. You should have seen the look in his eyes, Cam.' I helped myself to the whiskey. I was allowed a few more large swigs before he took it away. A few minutes later, I started to sing to myself, in a world of my own. Then having something important to say, I snuggled close to Camlo.

'Do you know that you are a very beautiful man?' He laughed and squeezed my hand gently. 'And, and, and – this is a secret – I have to tell you; you mustn't laugh though. I love you, Camlo.'

He didn't laugh at all, which I decided was really good, so I closed my eyes and dozed.

The next time I opened my eyes the movement had stopped. Someone was saying, 'Jess sweetheart, wake up, we're home.' I opened my eyes and saw a pair of dark eyes.

'What are we doing now?'

'I am taking you to your room where I will try and make you comfortable. Then I am going to get someone who will take care of you until I get back. Manfri will wait at the bus. Tobar is collecting one of the horses and the flatbed wagon. When we have loaded up, it will be goodbye twenty-first century and hello to the nineteenth.

'I don't want you to go without me.'

'Tough, you can't possibly come along in the state you're in and we dare not keep them here. I have already agreed that I won't be going back on the last fundraising trip, when I get back, it will be to stay.'

'Alright, but before you go, let me take a last look at Phillip. I want him to see me victorious, that I'm alive and happy. I want to see him defeated and humiliated.'

Without a word, Camlo helped me walk to the back seats. He pulled back the blankets and, there they were. Cotton just looked confused. He wasn't the brightest of the bunch. Pellow glared up at us, still full of fight. I looked at Maureen, my good friend. She started to make noises from behind her gag, shaking her head. Perhaps she was trying to say that it was nothing to do with her. Too late for that, dear, I thought.

As for Phillip, he wasn't angry and there was no way that he would beg. He laid there; his dead lizard eyes open wide, full of hate. I think he was confident that at some time, he would be released. That we wouldn't kill him and that then, with all his power and all his money, he would come and find us.

So many words passed through my mind, in the end all I said was, 'For so long, I have wanted to look you in the eye and send you to hell. Tonight, at last, that is exactly what I'm doing. The guys are taking you away soon. Enjoy your new home.'

Camlo had just helped me out of the bus when Tobar arrived back, with a sturdy black and white horse hitched to a flatbed wagon.

I couldn't believe my eyes. 'Where did that horse come from?'

'We keep a couple in a field behind the hotel, now come on; you need treatment and lots of rest.'

We stepped into my room, unbelievably it looked just as I had left it, only a few hours earlier.

'Tell me how you feel now.'

'The burning and the stinging are easier. It's just very tender now.' I had been going to say, 'fine,' but decided that I couldn't lie to Camlo.

'OK, wait here, I'm coming back.' He was through the door before I could stop him. I wanted to ask him to stay, stay with me until it was time for him to leave with the others.

He was soon back, a quick knock and he walked in. Behind him was a woman I had seen around camp but had never spoken to. 'Jess, this is Gillie. She is going to look after you.'

I said hello, suddenly nervous. I didn't want to have to explain what had happened to me. I really didn't need some overly sympathetic woman holding my hand and doing the 'there, there dear' bit.

I wasn't going to get that from this woman, however. Tall and erect, almost stately, I put her age somewhere in her fifties, with a calm face and a steady gaze from kind brown eyes.

'Camlo has explained your injuries. I have a jar of salve here that will help. Remove your dressing gown, please.'

I slipped my dressing gown off. Camlo took it and hung it carefully on my coat hook while Gillie looked me over.

'You need to go now Camlo, the others are waiting for you. I'll take good care of her.'

He stepped over and cupped my head in his hand, an echo of our first kiss. This time the touch of his lips was pure tenderness. I watched him all the way to the door, the door closed, and he was gone.

Chapter 11

Gillie was rooting in a bag, she brought out a jar that she put on the bedside table.

'Stand still for me, I will begin with your breasts.'

With a touch that was assured but gentle Gillie smoothed on the cream. It felt cool with an aroma reminiscent of green plants and sunshine. Standing back to survey her work she gave a slight smile of satisfaction.

I said, 'Is that some magic Gypsy recipe?'

She smiled. 'No, it's a perfectly ordinary herbal balm. She sorted through the towels that Camlo had dumped on a chair. She selected one, rolled it and put it on the bed just under the pillow then piled some more, neatly folded, a little lower. Good, now if you lay on your front, just a little lower, that's right.'

I positioned myself as instructed and it was surprisingly comfortable, the arrangement of the towels took the weight. She began on my back. I felt my flesh flinch a few times when she found the most tender places, it didn't put her off, her fingers continued to smooth their way down my back.

'He was a sadistic bastard, your husband.' That was all she said until my back was finished, then, 'Does that feel any better?'

'Yes, it does thank you – Gillie?'

'What?'

'I don't know how long he'll be away.'

She brought a chair and set it down beside the bed. 'He told me he thought it would be at least four or five days, they want to travel a long way before they leave those people.'

I turned my face away. It was what I had expected.

'He will come back to you as soon as he can, Jess.'

'I know.' I turned back to look at her. 'How do the people in the camp feel about Camlo being with me?'

'They like you, so they are happy for you both. Apart from Jenny and that puppy dog follower of hers, Don. Of course, she wanted Camlo for herself. Now try to get moving as soon as you can. I will be back tomorrow. If you feel like venturing out just leave me a note, I'll leave the door unlocked if you don't mind.'

I thanked Gillie, she covered me with my duvet, and she left. It was quiet in my room and outside in the camp there was hardly a sound. I drifted off to sleep.

The alarm woke me at the usual time. Trying

to turn it off I knocked it onto the floor, so I wriggled to the edge of the bed. 'Bloody hellfire.' I muttered. I stretched out a hand, trying to reach the clock, slipped, and was spread-eagled, supporting myself with my arms when Gillie walked in.

Calmly, she heaved me back on to the bed. 'What kind of early morning exercise do you call that?'

'Stupid clock fell on the floor.'

'Of course, it did, lay still and let me see your back.'

And so it went, not the most comfortable five days of my life but with Gillie's regular treatments, twice a day, I improved rapidly. I wanted to be as healed as possible for when he returned.

I made it to the canteen on the next day. Lela appeared soon after Gillie left, demanding an account. I told her she was a ghoul, but she pestered me until she had the full story. Then I showed her the damage and that shut her up.

Anyway, after all that I was hungry and thirsty so with Lela hovering like a mother hen we went for lunch.

I found the armchairs in the lounge area the most comfortable place to sit and so spent much of my time there. I counted the days. I told myself not to think in terms of the possible four days, feeling it was safer to concentrate on five. I had plenty of company; I got to know most of the people in the camp. They would come and sit with me and chat. Most of them asked when I expected Camlo back and I would tell them he thought the trip would take about five days.

The closer we came to the end of those days the stronger the feeling, at first a vague unease, becoming a deep-down fear, that there was something wrong. So, I wasn't surprised when day five came and went and there was no familiar knock on the door, no triumphant voice calling my name from across the camp. No Camlo.

That was when I began to hide away. Apart from quick trips to the canteen to collect a snack to take back with me, I spent all my time in my room. I didn't want to deal with the inevitable questions. How many times would I be able to trot out a confident, 'Yes he is later than expected but I'm sure he will soon be home.' I couldn't bear the thought of the silent sympathy from kind people who deserved more than the snappy reply which was all they would get.

Lela came often, sitting peacefully, hardly speaking. We would read or listen to music. And Gillie came. The first few times to check how the healing was going. Then one day when she visited, she stood awkwardly in the middle of the room.

'Do you mind if sometimes I come and wait with you?'

Something in her face made me pull out a chair for her. I said, 'Tea?'

'Please.'

I made it and placed it on the table, she sat down facing the window, I sat opposite. 'What is it, Gillie?'

'It's hard, waiting like this. Here we are the two of us. You're waiting for your lover,'

I interrupted her, 'Not yet.' She dismissed the distinction with a wave of her hand.

Who are you waiting for Gillie?'

'My son.'

'Tobar?'

She nodded. That was the only time we spoke about the waiting. She would tell me stories of the old life and I told her everything about my life with Phillip. She listened, properly, her only comment was, 'You can't let any of that affect your life with Camlo, Jess.' I had smiled and said, 'of course not.' A throw-away phrase and I should have paid it more attention.

It was the early afternoon of day ten. I had waited for the end of the Saturday lunchtime crush in the canteen before scurrying along to pick up a sandwich. I stepped out of my room and sensed a change in the air.

I looked round, there was nothing any different that I could see but people were gathering, looking towards the path, the one that Camlo and the others would use when they came back home.

Then Tobar walked slowly into camp. Gillie ran over and hugged him, and a small crowd gathered round. I stood, unable to move, straining to see if anyone else was coming but the path was empty.

Some of the group around Tobar turned to look at me, words were passed from person to person and then the eyes that had been on me turned away. I felt my pulse begin to pound.

I heard the wagon before I saw it, the clink of the harness and the horse's hooves on the sun-dried grass, slowly the wagon emerged from the trees.

Camlo was driving with his elbows on his knees, eyes cast down. Manfri walked beside the horse's head and on the seat beside Camlo was a young woman. She looked lithe and vibrant, even from that distance. She leaned close to Camlo, spoke to him then kissed his cheek and hugged him. She had a thick tumble of hair that she tossed back as she leapt from the wagon and embraced several of the crowd.

My mind was trying to tell me that he had given her a lift, that nothing was wrong here. Then from just behind me I heard that bitch Jenny saying, loud enough that everyone close by could hear, 'Oh look, he has brought Rose back, I knew he would one day, he has always loved her.'

Silence, in a wide circle round me no-one spoke or moved. Was that the silence of agreement? What should I do? I could walk over and wait confidently for Camlo to greet me with one of his radiant smiles or I could take the initiative, put my arms round him, kiss him and claim him as mine. Instead, I stepped back inside my room and closed the door quietly. With my heart pounding, eyes blind with tears, I staggered round my room, collecting up my belongings, only the essential stuff and crammed it into my backpack.

I put on my cycling gear then I peered out of the window. It seemed the whole camp had gathered round the wagon now, the area just outside my door was deserted. Clutching my pack and cycle helmet I slipped out of the door and collected my bike from where it had been stored behind the building.

Nobody noticed me start off down the track, or at least nobody called out to me. The sounds from camp faded to silence by the time I was halfway to the road.

When I reached the road I turned right, the direction I had been travelling when I had tumbled from my bike those few months ago.

At first, I just peddled, concentrating on the mind-numbing monotony of the movement. As I passed the entrance to the hotel, I had a momentary vision of Camlo kissing me in the linen store. I clenched my teeth and closed a door in my mind, vowing to keep that memory locked away for ever. I would have to decide what to do, where to go – eventually. Then it came to me from out of nowhere, I didn't have to hide anymore; no-one was hunting me.

I slowed my pedalling; needing to think that over.

Phillip wasn't hunting me anymore, but he had now been gone for ten days so had he been missed? Parliament wouldn't be sitting yet, still on the summer break but Phillip worked constantly, there would surely have been the usual meetings, the consultations with his private secretary. Were the police even now looking for him? And if they were would they wonder about his wife, was she with him? Or would they wonder if I was responsible for him disappearing?

I could go back of course. Phillip hadn't broadcast that I had left. He had been counting on getting me back. It was probably better to be there, if the police weren't already searching, I could report him missing myself then just wait it out. I couldn't convince them that I was innocent if I wasn't there.

One thing for sure, I couldn't continue to be Jess Hampshire.

Had I stayed with the Romani things would be different, but that time was gone.

With my head reeling with problems and possibilities I started off again. Soon the late summer light started to fade, a chill wind had sprung up, pushing against me, making progress slow.

When I reached the village I withdrew some cash from the cash machine outside the shop, left the bike in the pub car park and then walked on far enough to be out of sight of the village. I rooted in my pack for my mobile, turned it on and called a taxi, explaining where he could find me.

The wait by the roadside seemed to last a lifetime and standing still in the cold evening air chilled me. I wrapped my arms round myself to conserve a little warmth. The taxi came at last, cruising slowly round the corner, looking for me.

'The nearest train station please.' I said as soon as I was inside.

'That will be Worthing. Will that be alright?'

I said, 'That will be fine.' Then, satisfied, I settled back in the seat. The taxi pulled back onto the road. I was on my way. I ignored the pain, like an iron band round my chest that threatened to choke me, telling myself it would go in time.

The taxi dropped me off and I bought a ticket to London Victoria.

There was only half an hour to wait so I spent the time scrolling through my mobile, checking for and deleting Maureen's message and the ones that Phillip had sent. The curses and the threats. Once I was on the train and safely on the move I sat and watched the country passing away behind me. Taking a last, long look. I had been so very happy there.

Victoria station was one mad crush with people scurrying in all directions. It had been so long since I had experienced anything like it, I found it overwhelming, nevertheless I managed to grab a taxi and scramble into the back.

I had a moment of panic on the way. What would I do if the place was crawling with police? I asked the driver to let me out two roads away from the house.

After the taxi drove away, I stood on a silent, deserted street, gathered my courage around me and walked towards the house. At the corner I stopped and took a small step forward, then again and again until I could see all the way down to the house.

No police cars in fact no sign of anyone. It was time to stop messing about. I took a deep breath and walked confidently past the gardens and driveways all the way to what was, again, home.

At the door it took a while to find the keys, I unlocked and walked slowly inside.

With the hall light on and the door closed I leaned back on the door and closed my eyes. So far, so OK.

Slowly I walked round the house, getting used to being there, especially getting used to Phillip not being there, ever again. Room by room I walked round the walls first, drawing curtains, straightening pictures. Then the rest of the room, touching and moving the furniture, banishing ghosts.

I took everything that was mine out of Phillip's bedroom. I had always thought of the room as his, not ours. My room would be the light bright modern room at the other end of the passage. I put everything away, filled drawers and the wardrobe then stood back and looked round, yes, I could sleep in here. Then I made myself go back and clear away the remnants of rope that were still attached to the bed. I cleared away into the laundry bin the rumpled mess from the mattress and made the bed up fresh and clean.

I should eat, I didn't feel like it, but I would. I trailed down to the kitchen and had a quick look in the fridge, Phillip obviously hadn't been cooking for himself, there was some milk, which went straight down the sink, some butter which was fine, some cans of beer and two bottles of champagne.

Well, I wouldn't get fat on that. There was no bread and anyway nothing to make a sandwich. I gave that up and checked the freezer. I found a pizza and decided that would do nicely. I would shop the next day.

While the pizza cooked, I checked the voicemail. There were a few messages that didn't need replies and one from his secretary. 'Just checking in from Italy, the kids are driving me mad so feel free to call me back if anything important comes up.'

Well, maybe no-one had missed him yet. I went up to the office. After a search through his desk, I found his diary. He had always kept a paper back-up. Tobar had taken his laptop, so this was now the only record of his schedule. I flipped through. There had been half a dozen meetings scheduled but he had cancelled them, probably so he could be on hand if his men found me.

I dropped the diary on the desk and took a deep breath. Maybe, just maybe I could make this work. Down in the kitchen the oven timer started to ping. I went and turned the oven off, put the pizza on a plate and put the pizza, a bottle of champagne and a glass on the kitchen table.

For a moment, the memory of laughing and chatting with Lela in the canteen back at the camp forced itself into my mind. I poured some champagne and turned on the kitchen TV.

Chapter 12

That night, well it was too long. In the dark all the memories came forcing themselves between me and sleep. When I looked into the mirror the next morning, at red eyes lost between puffy lids, I went to the freezer and took out a bag of frozen peas, wrapped them in a tea towel and spent a while on the sofa in the lounge with the peas resting on my eyes.

By the time I had showered, dressed, and applied some make, up to a casual glance I looked quite normal. It was time I went food shopping. I took my car and made sure to chat with the woman at the checkout. After I had put the shopping away, I texted several acquaintances. 'Hi...how about a catch up, love to hear from you.'

I lunched with three of 'the girls' I told them that yes, I had been away, looking after my mother and very sadly she had died. When I said that I had needed time to mourn so had shut myself away they were very understanding. Phillip? Oh, he had gone off walking in Scotland, he would be back in a day or so. Maureen? No, I hadn't seen or heard anything from her.

I gave it two more days. I was seen around, I talked to anyone and everyone, I shopped. Then I phoned the police. 'I know you are very busy, but I am worried, my husband should be home from his walking holiday.' I don't know what response most people would have had. Because of who he was they were round almost immediately. I played the worried – but not yet too worried – wife. They were sympathetic.

They asked if I knew where he had gone in Scotland or which hotels he had booked. I told them that no, he hadn't told me anything.

Time went by and no trace was found of Phillip Pearson, he seemed to have disappeared from the face of the earth. I was offered comfort and asked if I would like to talk to someone. I bravely told them that I could cope, thank you.

Privately I wondered if the people in the camp had watched all this drama, it had been on the news for several days, then there had been a disaster in the Philippines and the world moved on. If they had seen it what on earth had they made of it. How about Camlo? Would he and his new – no, re-discovered – love see this, and would he wonder if he had ever known this woman. This Lucy Pearson.

I still cried my heart out in the dark of the night.

Although the police assured me that the

search for my husband was ongoing and would continue until the truth was revealed they gradually disappeared from my life. I thought that there was probably a small cupboard somewhere with all the files from the case, which was sometimes opened and trawled through before they were put back and locked away again.

I was growing restless. I had grown used to getting up in the morning and working for a living and the house was so large and so empty. My days were empty, oh I had a social life, it was important not to hide away but I was only going through the motions.

I waited it out until after Christmas before making a move.

I spoke to a solicitor. Until it was known what had happened to Phillip or until enough time had passed to declare him legally dead, I couldn't sell the house, but I could rent it out, I wanted a fresh start, away from London and the past.

The house rented easily, in early March, on a day of weak, damp sunshine I said goodbye to the people I knew and moved to Guildford. I rented a small house near the university and started to job hunt. Although I had been married to a public figure as far as employment went I had very little experience, people weren't falling over themselves to offer me a job.

I was eventually taken on, in a jewellery shop, not one of the big multiples on the high street but a small independent tucked in a side street. Sophia's Gems was owned by Sophia Martin and her brother George.

They were proud of the business they had built between them and were keen to teach me. Having worked in the past in shops where goods were picked up from the shelf and taken to a cash point, the jewellery business turned out to be completely different.

By the end of the first week my mind was reeling, there was so much to remember.

They were politely curious about me, about what had happened to my husband and how I was coping with the tragedy. For a few days we were all carefully polite, until the morning we had the customer from hell.

She came in oozing attitude and asked to look at gold bracelets, Sophia was dealing with her and with great tact avoided telling the customer that she had an enormous wrist. Instead offering, if madam found one that she wanted, to have it extended to fit.

The customer had never been so insulted, was this perhaps a ploy to get extra money from innocent customers, why weren't the bracelets made a reasonable length in the first place? She demanded to try every bracelet in the shop and then left with a toss of her head.

Sophia walked quietly into the back room. There was no-one else in the shop, so I followed her in. She was leaning against the wall swearing, she certainly had a colourful vocabulary. Beaming approval, I gave her a round of applause. The ice was broken, and we went out to the shop to tidy the cabinet where all the bracelets had been hurriedly dumped.

She said, 'Do you fancy going for a drink after we close?'

'I'd really like that, thanks.'

When we had closed, we walked to the nearest pub and found ourselves a table, after we had downed our first drink, looking slightly embarrassed, Sophia said, 'When you started here, Lucy, I thought you were perfect for the shop, but I wasn't sure we would get along. I'm glad you're so normal.'

It became a regular thing, one evening a week slotted in between Sophie's busy social life and the rare occasions when I went to see some of the old crowd in London, to see and be seen. Sometimes George would come along too and the three of us would gossip and laugh over a couple of drinks then go our separate ways.

On my way back to the house one evening in May, after one of our evenings, fighting the rain and a gusty wind that was trying to steal my umbrella, I passed a car that was parked along the kerb, half a street away from home. I wouldn't have noticed except for the flare of a match inside the car that drew my eye. There were two men in the car. I thought they must be waiting for someone.

They were waiting for someone. They were waiting for me. As I stopped at my door to unlock it two men stepped up beside me.

'What do you want? Why are you here on my doorstep at this time of night?' I despair of myself sometimes; I will never know why I didn't make a run for it. Instead, I stood there and allowed them to snatch the keys from my hand and manhandle me indoors. They hustled me into my sitting room, sat me down and drew up chairs either side of me.

Now I could see them properly by the lights in the sitting room, I realised they were Chinese, or from one of those countries in Asia. My instincts told me it was particularly important to keep everything low key, I wasn't going to antagonise these guys.

'Why don't you tell me what you want?'

The big man said, 'What else, your husband of course. We need to know where he is.'

'But I don't know, I have no idea if he is dead or alive, the police are still looking for him.'

'Oh, they say they are but there's no effort being put into it, our sources say the case has practically been abandoned. You see there is no proof that he is dead, no body, nothing, even after all this time, so you see we believe he is hiding.'

'Ridiculous, what would he be hiding from.'

The short skinny one snorted. The big one shot him a look and said, 'He's hiding from us of course.'

I was beginning to get a bad feeling about this. I thought; don't ask him why, Lucy.

'Why on earth would he hide from you?'

The little one said, 'Because he was scheduled to make a delivery to us three months ago,'

'What? Are you off your heads? Phillip? Delivery of what?'

'You don't need to know that.' He stirred in his chair, beginning to get impatient. 'How often does he contact you? We think you moved here, away from London, to make it easier for him to get in touch.'

'Look, if he was alive and if he found me, he would kill me. He hated me as much as I hated him.'

That surprised them, they were beginning to realise things were not as they had expected.

'So, you're saying he's definitely dead? Did you kill him?'

I sighed. 'No, I didn't, unfortunately. You will have to excuse me. I have had a little too much to drink so I'm not making much sense of this, but I need the loo and a cup of coffee. Would you guys like one before you go?'

The big one gave an exasperated shrug the two of them exchanged a few words then the little one said, 'White one sugar, twice,'

He followed me into the kitchen and watched me as if I was going to poison the coffee. I put the coffees on a tray and carried them back to the lounge. He followed me to the loo, waited outside and then back again.

The atmosphere had changed, the big man was tired of getting nowhere. He gave an abrupt order and the little one walked into the kitchen, bringing back a wooden chair. By the time he had put it down I had been grabbed, I didn't struggle, what would have been the point. I let them sit me on the chair and start to tie me down with the plastic ties the big guy took from his pocket.

'Look, I have only just made that coffee, will you leave one hand free until I have drunk it?'

They exchanged a look. 'Only until then.'

They spoke together in snappy tones. Whatever they had expected from the situation they were now reassessing. They kept looking at me. Was I lying to them? They weren't sure. I drank my coffee and left them to it.'

They stopped talking, exchanged a last long look and nodded, then they both sat round and regarded me.

'My associate is going to search your flat; you and I are going to continue our conversation.'

The short one started with my bag, he had found my mobile and was scrolling through my messages. The big man gestured for him to leave the room, so he left, taking phone and bag with him.

'So, to be quite clear, you say that you have no contact with your husband, that in fact as far as you know he could be dead.'

'That's right.'

'You don't think that if we let it be known that we are holding you prisoner and if he didn't contact us, we would kill you he would make contact?'

'You could do that? How?'

The look on his face told me not to ask questions like that.

I sighed. 'He would wish you luck and tell you to get on with it.'

'Alright, I'll move on. Do you know anything about the arrangement we have with your husband?'

'Absolutely nothing. I am surprised though that he would get into something criminal, he was – is, whatever – a deeply unpleasant man, although he disguised it very well. He didn't really need money, he had more than enough. The thing that drove him, consumed him above anything else was his political ambition.'

I stopped there. I had struck a nerve. There was a hint of reaction in the big man's face. It really was time to shut up.

I dropped my head. I wouldn't give in to fear but I needed to appear defeated and compliant. There was a long silence before he got up and left the room. I could hear the pair of them ransacking my bedroom, one of them used the bathroom then they both came back into the lounge. Ignoring me, I was useless to them now, every inch, drawer and corner was searched, they finished side by side in the middle of the room.

The big man took a bottle from his pocket; he took the cushions from the sofa, pulled the curtains off the rails, and dumped them together in the corner then poured over the contents of the bottle. The fumes grabbed at the back of my throat.

'If you have anything to tell us you had better say it now.'

I just stared at him.

After the briefest of pauses he bent and lit the corner of a cushion then the two of them calmly walked out. I heard the door slam after them.

Chapter 13

I stared in horror at the greedy flames that were already taking hold, making little runs along the carpet, pausing to flare up and gather strength then off again. Then there was the smoke, thick and black, swirling round the room. How the hell was I going to get out of this alive? I tried to force my shocked brain to think. Was there anything in the room, that I could reach, that I could cut the ties with?

I had asked the big man to leave a hand free so I could drink my coffee and he had forgotten to secure it. I could reach the cup. I took a firm hold, lifted it, and then brought it down hard on the corner of the table. Nothing, the damn thing hadn't even cracked.

'Come on you bastard,' I shouted at it, 'pretend I put you in the drainer and you toppled over. You would bloody well break then.'

I brought it down again with all my strength and it shattered. I was left holding the handle with a shard of jagged china attached.

My eyes were beginning to stream, I had to

stop to cough and wipe my eyes on my sleeve. Then I concentrated on sawing through the tie round my left wrist. It was getting very hot in the lounge now. I had to free my ankles and get out fast. One ankle was free, now for the last one. As I began to cut, a billow of thick smoke, moving on a draught from the fire, obscured my makeshift knife, I felt rather than saw it slice into my ankle, but I didn't care, I was free.

I staggered out of the lounge and closed the door behind me. What should I do, run out right away? But my bag, with my phone, all my papers, passport, and purse with my cards, they were all in the kitchen. I had to get them.

Closing the door was holding back the flames for the moment, so I took the chance and went into the kitchen. My bag lay on the table with the contents spilled around it. Choking from the smoke and struggling to get air into my lungs, hardly able to see through my streaming eyes, I picked it all up and stuffed it into my bag then with everything safely inside I made my way to the front door, propping myself up on the wall all the way.

The cold air outside hit me like walking into a freezer. As I took out my phone and dialled 999 a part of my mind asked where my coat had gone.

Once I had the fire brigade on their way, feeling I had done everything I could, I sat on the low wall that divided the front garden from the pavement. A small crowd had gathered, a woman came over to me. I saw her lips moving and tried to make sense of her words, but she was fading away from me.

I thought I was dreaming, why did I have this thing on my face. I was on my back and the bed was bouncing. I opened my eyes. Ambulance, this was an ambulance. I reached up and moved the thing from my face.

'Hello dear, don't worry, you are on your way to hospital. Can you tell me what your name is?'

'Where is my bag?' Was that funny, rough sound my voice?

'Here it is, quite safe.' I took it from her and held it close. 'Who are you?

'Lucy, my name is Lucy.'

'Good, now let me put the mask back on, you have inhaled too much smoke, so we are taking you in to hospital, we're nearly there now so don't worry.'

I felt awful so I closed my eyes, and the mask came back. I could breathe with that thing on, so I relaxed and drifted away again. Images came and went, cold air again, being lifted, the sound of rolling wheels. Then being lifted again and warmth and far away voices.

When I woke up, I felt much better. The mask had gone I looked around and saw that I was in a small ward with four other beds. My bag was on the chair beside my bed, I looked alright, but I had to check. I pulled it onto the bed and opened it, everything was there. I laid it on the bed beside me, under my hand.

I slept. Later someone came round and gave me a list of options for lunch, evening meal and breakfast the next morning.

I said, 'Do I need to choose all these meals? I feel fine now I should go.'

'Not until the doctor has cleared you. Look, choose anyway. If you leave before mealtime we can always cancel.'

So, I chose meals and waited for a doctor to come and tell me I could go. Go where?'

Eventually a doctor came along. He asked a couple of questions about how I was feeling now and was shown the results of tests that I hadn't known had been done. He closed his tablet and smiled. 'I'm glad to say that there is no sign of permanent damage. You will need to take it easy for a few days though. Your ankle is healing nicely too. Now I have two policemen who would like to speak to you, so we are going to take you somewhere a little more private.'

With one more smile he turned and left. A porter arrived with a wheelchair, when I protested that I could walk, he said, 'Just humour them love.' He wheeled me into a nearby room where there were two men sitting in armchairs. They welcomed me in and introduced themselves as Inspector George Young and Simon, no further details offered. I was invited to join them in the third armchair. A tray with a cafetiere, milk, sugar and cups sat on a table between the chairs. The aroma of coffee was almost too much to bear.

I accepted a coffee and consumed by curiosity waited for them to explain what they wanted.

The inspector confirmed my identity again and then moved on to the important stuff. 'Now Lucy, tell us what happened in your house last night, who was there with you and how the fire started.'

I had already decided to be completely honest. I gave them everything from the moment I saw the men waiting in the car to when I called for the fire brigade.

'They claimed that your husband had contracted to provide them with – what? Goods or information?'

'They didn't specify, I think it was more likely to be information, I have been giving it some thought and that would be my guess.'

'You thought the men were Chinese.' I nodded. 'And no names were used?'

'No.'

There was a long pause before Simon carefully placed his cup back on the tray and said, 'Why do you think you were left with one hand free, and no attempt was made to prevent you from shouting for help?'

I hadn't given that too much thought. Now I did. I stared at Simon as a small light bulb sprung to life in my mind.

'I think it was deliberate, they were showing

me that it didn't matter to them if I died or if I escaped, I could shout for help, get free and tell everyone about them and they wouldn't care. They feel safe, they feel too powerful to have to worry.'

The policeman said, 'Hold on a minute, don't get fanciful, they probably just forgot.'

Simon shook his head and spoke directly to the Inspector. 'Nothing else about their behaviour was that careless. I agree with Mrs Pearson.'

Then he spoke to me again. 'I also think there was an element of threat to you. I want to take you somewhere safe, into protection. As soon as the doctor discharges you, I will come for you.'

'Can you do that?' I turned to the Inspector. 'Can he?'

'Yes, he can.'

They both rose and said goodbye, Inspector Young shook my hand and wished me the best of luck, he opened the door and they both walked out.

After they had gone, I waited for the porter to take me back to the ward. The wait became so long that I began to panic. Eventually the door opened, and the porter came in and behind him walked Simon.

'I have seen the doctor, Lucy. Can I call you Lucy?' I nodded. 'You have been discharged, is there anything else you brought in with you?'

I had my bag with me, I was keeping it close.

'No, only this.' He turned to leave. 'Is it possible to go to the house?'

He stopped at the door and looked at me, 'No, I'm sorry Lucy, we looked but there was nothing left to bring.'

'OK.'

I told the porter I had no need of the wheelchair, and I walked out of the hospital with a man I had only just met, who had the power to arrange things and it wasn't at all OK.

We left through a back service door, climbed into the back of a large van, and sat in the gloomy interior on makeshift seats.

'Where are you taking me?'

'I'm afraid I can't tell you that.'

I clutched my bag close, my arms wrapped tightly round it and I told myself that I had everything I needed inside there, but the house had contained other things that I wished I could have. Not the expensive clothes and shoes that I had brought from the London house or the jewellery but the outfits I had bought on shopping trips with Lela and the birthday cards from her, Miri and Oshina.

I did have, zipped away in an interior pocket of my bag, a small photo of Camlo taken when he was a young boy and given to me by Gillie. It was my most precious possession and had been the first thing I had looked for as soon as I'd had a private moment.

'I should let my employers know that I won't

be in. They will need to find someone else unless I will only be away a little while.'

I let the end of that hang there like a question, testing for his reaction.

'I can do that for you, don't worry we will take good care of you.'

I felt very lost and very alone, bumping along in the back of that van. Once or twice, Simon spoke in his radio to someone else. They must have been travelling in close formation to us. He would ask if there were any suspicious cars and whoever it was would report back to him.

I should feel glad, grateful that they were going to keep me safe, but I could have done that. They wanted information. That was the core of all this.

We changed our vehicle at one point. The van stopped and the driver came and opened the back doors. We were in a quiet corner of a garden centre car park. We climbed out then as soon as the van doors were closed the driver got back in put it into gear and left.

Simon guided me into the back of another, smaller, anonymous van with a different driver and we resumed our journey.

When we stopped, the driver climbed out and I heard his footsteps as he walked to the rear and a garage door opening. Then he was back and reversing the van. At last, the rear doors opened, and I was ushered quickly out and through the garage. The door slammed shut behind us.

'Come on through to the lounge, I expect you could do with something to eat and drink, and I'll introduce you to your protection team.'

I followed Simon into a cosy room where two people waited, a man and a woman. They introduced themselves and explained that they would work alternating shifts of twelve hours, then they withdrew to the kitchen.

I stood overwhelmed and bewildered in the centre of the room. 'What happens now? How long will I be here?'

'That depends, I will bring some files over to go through with you. If you can identify the men and we can deal with them you may not be here too long, we want to feel that you will be safe before we relocate you.'

'Relocate me, what do you mean? Please explain.'

'A new name, a new life, a new place to live.'

'Does that have to happen? If you deal with the men, why do I have to go on hiding?'

'You won't be hiding. You will be living a different life and you must realise why.'

Yes, I did, they couldn't guarantee Lucy Pearson would ever be safe.

'What happens about the London house, my bank account in my own name?'

'Everything will be taken care of; you have nothing to worry about. Leave it all to us. I'll say goodbye now, have a good rest, and tomorrow we will start tracking them down.' He paused in the doorway, 'we are preparing your new life now. You can choose a name if you like.'

'I'd like that.' I told him the first name that came into my head.

He repeated the name. 'I'll make sure of that for you.' He closed the door behind him.

I stayed where he left me, swallowing down the loss and the panic, I felt the weight of my bag, still clutched in my arms, most of the contents identified me as Lucy Pearson, they would be useless to Jess Hampshire, and I probably wouldn't be allowed to keep them anyway.

I sat in the nearest armchair, I felt bone weary, too much had happened, and my chest still hurt. Was that the smoke or tension and anxiety. I closed my eyes and leaned back in the chair,

The door opened, the woman who had said her name was Susan said, 'Duncan has gone now. You can't have eaten, are you hungry?'

I realised that I was starving. 'Yes, and thirsty.'

'How about a Chinese takeaway?'

'Great.'

We chose some dishes from a takeaway menu and Susan phoned it through.

'While we wait what would you like to drink?'

'Coffee please, which is my bedroom?'

'Come on I'll show you,'

She took me up the stairs, there were two bedrooms – mine was the one furthest from the stairs – and a small bathroom. Susan left to make the coffee while I checked out my new bedroom.

I sat on the bed for a moment and opened my bag. I looked at the photo of Camlo, all tousled hair and huge dark eyes. I smiled at the way I had automatically chosen the name I had used back then.

I put it carefully away and rifled through the rest of the contents. Cash, I could keep that, passport and driving licence – I held them in my hand. Could I keep those, secretly keep something of that life, a sort of insurance? With those I could still be Lucy Pearson if I needed to be.

I told myself I was being paranoid. Even so I slipped them under my mattress. I would claim I had left them in the house and like everything else they were lost and gone, as an afterthought I took Camlo's photo out and put it carefully in my passport before hiding them again. Feeling a little better I went back downstairs. I left my bag on a chair in my room.

The takeaway arrived, Susan and I sat at the kitchen table to eat it, threw away the containers and washed the plates and cutlery. Then I made myself comfortable in front of the TV. Susan browsed a magazine for a while, then said, 'I'm shattered, I'm for a shower and bed, goodnight.'

I listened carefully and when I heard the shower running, I got up from the armchair and walked carefully to the front door, it was locked. I tried the back door and the windows. All of them were secure. 'Well, I'm safe enough then, locked in but safe.'

Chapter 14

When everything was quiet upstairs, I went up to my room. My bag had been moved and of the carefully arranged contents one or two had been put back the wrong way round. Next, I checked under the mattress, everything was still in place and as far as I could tell undisturbed.

When I climbed into bed despite feeling tired to my bones, I lay awake for a long time, so much had happened that I needed to make some kind of sense of and the more I struggled with it all the less I understood. Eventually I must have drifted off because my next conscious moment was hearing a door bang downstairs. I didn't rush down, I showered and dressed and then I went downstairs and got myself some breakfast. Susan had gone and Duncan was in place. He had slumped into a chair in the lounge and apart from saying good morning to me I might just as well not be there.

Simon arrived at ten and we settled down with a laptop and the pile of files he had brought. He sent Duncan out of the room, and we got started.

For almost an hour I leafed through photos to see if I could spot the men who had come to my house.

'Who are these men, Simon?'

'People we have reason to keep an eye on, please try and concentrate, try the next page.'

Some of the photos were taken from passports, some from newspaper or magazine articles, a lot of them looked as though they had been taken out in the street. I saw a few that might have been the short man, he hadn't made a strong enough impression for me to be sure, but I was positive about the big man, none of the shots were of him.

After an hour or two Simon closed the files. 'That will do for today, we will try again tomorrow. Now tell me what you know about your husband's fellow MPs, can you tell me who he respected and who not. Did he consider any of them to be dangerous?'

'I don't think he respected any of them, he pretended to of course. He was motivated by ambition, so he considered most of them to be dangerous to him.'

'OK, now try to think, did he ever say anything to you or to anyone else about one of them having something to hide, had they done or said anything that your husband could profit from?'

I looked at him. 'You think it was something like that he was supposed to deliver to them?'

He stared at me. His face expressionless.

'Yes, it would be. He would do that for the next step up the ladder. If he had something to discredit...well it would have to be a minister.'

'So can you recall anything?'

'You will have to give me time to think.'

'I'll be back tomorrow.' He stood to leave, collected his stuff together. 'Bear in mind that your husband may have wanted this to further his career but whoever those guys were, they weren't the slightest bit interested in that, they wanted something much bigger. Even if he never mentioned what he knew. If he spoke of anyone in a way that implied more, we can take it from there.'

I nodded and watched him leave the room. Then I took a handful of magazines and sat in an armchair pretending to read them while I thought the whole thing through. After a while Duncan poked his head round the door and asked if I wanted some sandwiches for lunch.

'Please, that's kind of you.'

'It's nothing.'

He brought me in the sandwiches and some coffee then sat in front of the TV and turned it on. That suited me it gave me space to think. Someone was anxious to acquire information about an important British politician. It would have to be bigger than the usual minor misdemeanour or incompetence, those things happened all the time.

I put down the first magazine and picked up

the next. I decided to concentrate on trying to remember anything Phillip had said that implied knowledge of a marketable secret. It didn't help that I hadn't been there for some months. I spent hours mulling it over and still my mind was a complete blank, I had nothing.

Susan arrived back and we ordered in another takeaway. I found a rack of wine and had a glass of red with dinner. Susan declined, 'just in case,' she said. After dinner I poured myself another and took it up to my room.

My bag hadn't been touched this time and the rest of my stuff was still safe. I got ready for bed and lay back thinking of nothing at all. There was a cobweb hanging from the ceiling and I watched it swaying in the breeze. Sighing I leaned up on an elbow to sip the last of the wine, put the glass back on the table and flopped back down, ready for sleep.

I was just drifting off, comfortable and warm, when I remembered walking past Phillip's office door, back a few weeks before I left him. He was on the phone to someone and laughing, the laugh he always used when he was sucking up to 'one of the top guys' I heard him put the phone down, then, because I was tip toeing slowly away so he didn't hear me, I heard him comment, speaking his mind when the other person was safely off the line. His voice was full of contempt, there was no-one in the office with him, so he didn't hold back.

'Oh, Dicky boy, you evil piece of shit, move over, I'm bringing you down. Thanks a million.'

I would tell Simon in the morning. It made no sense at all to me because I couldn't think of a single man named Richard who Phillip would want to remove. All his ambition was directed into his political career, so this Dicky had to be a politician. The name might ring a bell with Simon. Pleased to have something to tell him in the morning I turned over, relaxed and was soon asleep.

The day began as a re-run of the day before: I got up, showered, and dressed. I found myself some breakfast and sat at the kitchen table to eat while Duncan sat opposite me engrossed in his laptop. I made us both coffee and took mine into the lounge.

Then when Simon arrived, we settled on opposite sides of the dining table and Simon stacked a fresh pile of files between us, ready for me to sift through, pages and pages of photos.

'Well Lucy, did you think of anything?

'Mmm, I think so.'

I told Simon what I had overheard. He sat still and quiet for a while then said, 'I need to make a call.'

He left the room and walked out into the garden where he paced up and down talking on his mobile before coming back in and sitting at the table.

'Right, let's get started on the photos, Lucy.'

'You think you know who it is?'

'I think there is something there that is worth looking into.'

'OK, and are you going to tell me who it is?'

'No, I'm afraid that information is confidential, here have a look through this first file.'

'Oh I see, even after I have been ambushed in my home by a couple of thugs who tried to kill me by burning my home down around me. I have lost everything or so you tell me. I have no way of actually knowing that because you hi-jacked me from my hospital bed and brought me here, god knows where 'here' is, and airily informed me that I will be given a new name and a new life. This man, the one I told you about, I assume that he has done or is planning to do something illegal, wicked, immoral and/or damaging to the country, therefore he could be yet another danger to me and you have no intention of telling me who he is? Well, you look through the photos. I've had enough of this.'

I was on my feet, leaning over the table, fists clenched on the tabletop.

'Well, what a fierce temper you have Mrs Pearson, I'm sure it will stand you in good stead in your new life. Now, I must insist that you continue looking through these files, if only for no other reason than that those men may find out that you are still alive.' He said it quietly; I hadn't even ruffled his smooth urbane expression.

The threat was clear. I sat back on my chair. 'You bastard.'

'Yes, quite. Now begin with these.'

I looked through the files, photo after photo and I tried, I needed to identify them so that this frighteningly powerful man could deal with them and, just in case, so that I would always recognise them. I didn't need Simon to tell me who Dicky was anyway, as I wound up my tirade his identity presented itself in my mind as fierce and clear as my anger. The name wasn't Richard at all. He was David Ingrams Kaufman, our recently appointed Secretary of State for International Trade and President of the Board of Trade.

When I had worked my way through half the pile Simon called in Duncan.

'Pop out and get some sandwiches, I think we could all do with a bite of lunch, oh and bring back some decent coffee that instant stuff is disgusting.'

It was while we were waiting for Duncan to come back with lunch. I flipped open yet another file. This one was different, instead of a random collection of odd sizes, taken in all sorts of places; these were much more uniform and posed. I looked up at Simon.

'Are these official shots?'

I was back to being Lucy now and the atmosphere had become more friendly, I was behaving myself after all.

'Yes, we always make sure to have a good clear image of anyone connected to each foreign embassy.'

I turned a few more over and stopped. There, facing out of the page was the big man.

'Him!'

I passed him the photo and turned over a couple more and there was the other one, the short skinny man. I drew in a huge breath and smiled at Simon as I pushed that one across the table to him. 'And him.'

We both beamed at each other, all animosity forgotten in our mutual relief.

'That's great, Lucy. Look, I'll crack on with this after lunch and see how preparations for your new life are coming on. With luck you may not need to be here much longer.

Duncan arrived back with lunch. He took himself into the kitchen while we ate where we were. Simon left as soon as he had finished, and I spent the afternoon watching the TV and trying to think in terms of living life as Jess Hampshire and wondering where that life would be.

Things moved surprisingly fast. I was amazed to see, on the ten o'clock news that very night, the announcement that two workers from the Chinese Embassy were being deported, accused of spying, they had fifteen days to get out of the country.

As for Diky: David Ingrams Kaufman. I never

knew exactly what happened there. I suspect that an accommodation had been agreed. There was no scandal, and he didn't resign, so the government continued, and the economy continued, on an even keel. Unexpectedly at the next election the Secretary of State for International Trade resigned his seat to spend more time with his family.

I moved out of the safe house two weeks after identifying the Chinese, well when I say moved out what happened was that Simon arrived early one morning, he breezed in and plonked a document case on the table.

'Here you are Lucy, everything you need to be Jess Hampshire. How long will it take you to be ready to leave? I have transport outside waiting for you.'

'Give me five minutes.' I dashed upstairs, into the bathroom first then the bedroom, where I quickly stuffed the two changes of clothes, I had been provided with into a carrier bag, topping it up with the rest of my meagre possessions. Then I retrieved my hidden items from under the mattress and put them carefully into the pocket I had made by carefully slitting the stitching of the lining at the bottom of my handbag.

One last look round the room then I walked out of the room and down the stairs. Simon was still waiting in the kitchen.

'Ready Jess? I'll bring the case. We're leaving through the garage I'm afraid.'

I shrugged. I understood the need for secrecy, if I didn't know the location of the safe house, I could never tell anyone.

Simon paused at the garage door. 'See you later Duncan.'

'Sure, cheerio.'

I didn't bother to say anything to him, we had hardly spoken in the time I had been there. I followed Simon and climbed into the open back of the same windowless van I had arrived in. Simon rapped on the partition, the engine started, and the journey began.

'Can you tell me where you are taking me?'

'Certainly, we are going to Plymouth.'

'Ok, what exactly will happen, will I have anywhere to live? We're halfway through June and Plymouth will be overflowing with people.'

'You have a lease on a small flat, paid for six months and an interview in two days in a café in the Barbican. All the balance from your old bank accounts is in your new account and the rent from the London house is being paid into it. Oh, and the house is now in the name of Jess Hampshire so you can sell it if you like. If your husband does ever turn up alive, he will be out of luck.'

More than a little overwhelmed I sat back and thought it through. I wasn't being abandoned, in fact I would be financially secure, and I had a home. I hadn't been to Plymouth for years, not since the foster parents I had had when I was eleven had taken me there, I had good memories from that visit.

The journey took a long time, I knew that meant nothing, we could have been five miles away and still taken as long.

In the end the van stopped, mid-afternoon in a street of detached houses, Simon and I climbed stiffly out.

I was handed the document case.

'Your flat is the ground floor of number twelve. The owner is expecting you. If you walk down the road that way you will find it leads to the Barbican. We wish you a happy life Jess Hampshire, there is an emergency phone number in the case in case you ever need help.'

We shook hands and I thanked him then I stood on the pavement and watched the van drive away. The rest of my life lay, a blank page, in the opposite direction.

Chapter 15

Come on then Jess Hampshire, let's get started. I turned, walked up to the door of number Twelve, and rang the bell. From inside I heard a scuttle of footsteps, the door was opened by a small brisk woman.

'Hello, my dear you must be Jess, come in we have been expecting you.'

I walked in through the door and looked around. Doors numbered 1 and 2 led off from the hall where we stood. A small side table for mail left just about enough room for me, the woman and the man who stood behind her.

'My name is Margaret Trent, and this is my husband John, I'll show you the flat and then if everything is to your satisfaction, we can get the contract signed. If it isn't what you want the deposit will be returned.'

She led the way through the door with the number 1 on the door and showed me round a kitchen and a lounge that looked over a small, neat garden.

'My husband takes care of the weeding and

grass cutting so there is nothing you need do out there.'

We moved on to the bedroom and bathroom which were on the road side of the flat. Everything was clean and in good condition.

'Yes, thank you, I am happy to move in. Do you have that contract with you?'

Mrs Trent laid the contract on the small table in the hall, and I signed it without reading a word of it. The husband looked at my pathetic bag of belongings.

'Is that all the luggage you have Miss Hampshire?'

'No, these are just a few essential bits. I'll go and bring the rest now I'm sure I want to live here, thank you.'

When they had finished, finally, and left, I had a more thorough look round. It had occurred to me that this conveniently arranged flat might be an extension of the safe house, that they might be remotely monitoring me. A quick look under tables and behind the picture on the lounge wall revealed nothing. I decided I didn't care anyway. I shoved the clothes into a drawer and had a good look at the contents of the document case. It really did contain everything I would need, bank cards, check books and passport, even an employment history and all the necessary paperwork. Good, because I had to go and buy almost all the things I would need for my new life.

Leaving the house behind, I started by walking the way I had been shown to the Barbican. There I found a street guide and followed the directions to a shopping centre. The funny thing was that the moment when reality hit home, that I was now a new person, was when I put my Jess Hampshire bank card into the cash machine and carefully punched in the number. My heart was thumping as I took the cash and walked away. I hadn't known how it would actually feel. Would I feel lost and abandoned? Now it had happened I felt liberated, I could do this.

I shopped as I hadn't done for years, with a sense of happy abandonment, and went back to the flat loaded with bags. When it was all arranged in drawers and the wardrobe, I realised I was hungry. I walked back into town to find somewhere to eat.

The next day was spent making the flat homely. I found a handy supermarket and stocked up on food then moved some of the furniture. Last of all, when I was ready for sleep, I sat on the edge of the bed and put my photo of Camlo into the pretty frame I had bought for it and placed it on the bedside table.

That was when the grief of losing him crashed down on me again, as fresh as at the start. I had held it at bay all this time, while I fought other battles. Now I had relaxed and there it was, crushing the breath out of me and twisting my gut. I curled up around the pain, clawing the bedding around me and let the tears flow.

My interview was scheduled for 11am the next day. When I made it to the bathroom mirror early in the morning a blotchy face and swollen eyes looked back at me, yet again. Sighing I went to the freezer and found my fallback method of dealing with swollen eyes, a bag of peas which I wrapped in a tea towel, then I lay back on the bed with the bag of peas resting over my eyes.

I found the café in one of the narrow lanes and looked it over before going in to meet the owner. It was a in a historic, stone building, like most in that part of Plymouth. The window carefully presented to look as though it had been here for the lifetime of the building, charming, set out with pretty china displaying tempting cakes.

A bell tinkled as I walked through the door, a smiling waitress greeted me and asked if I would like the table by the window. I said that I had an appointment with Mrs Rainbird.

'This way please, have you come for the job? Oh, I hope so we really need another pair of hands. Good luck.'

She knocked on a door, opened it and smiled me through.

'Mrs Rainbird? I'm Jess Hampshire.'

The woman who greeted me from behind a desk was smart, in every way, from the beautifully cut and styled hair and the clothes that could have been straight from the catwalk to the shining intelligence in her eyes.

Despite having browsed through my supposed CV, I stumbled over some of the questions she asked me but when I looked her in the eye and said that I needed this job and would work hard for her she smiled and asked me when I could start.

I often wondered about Mrs Rainbird, the interview had felt as though the decision had already been made and my job application had been a formality, but I never saw her again, I asked Susie, the waitress who had greeted me that first day, how often Mrs Rainbird came to the café.

'Never been here before, the café is owned by a multiple, so we get whichever manager is available. Daphne manages the café on a day-to-day basis.'

I spent the months of that high summer working in that café, serving the cream cakes and speciality teas to a constant flow of tourists. I worked with Susie who was funny in a quiet, unexpected way and her dry observations made many an afternoon fly by.

On my days off I explored the city or sat on the Hoe, looking down at the sea and watching the boats. Then I would walk back to my new home, sometimes I would cook myself a proper meal, often I couldn't be bothered to do more than cheese on toast, and I would eat it in front of the TV.

As the summer faded, business at the café

began to slow and I wondered how much longer my job at the café would last. I planned to look for something else, to last me through the winter but then the weather revived into a glorious late summer, and I put off the job hunt.

On one of those golden afternoons, I had taken a tray of cream teas out to the courtyard at the rear of the café. I served the customers, smiled, and told them I hoped they enjoyed their teas. I turned to walk back inside and then I saw at a table in the corner of the courtyard, staring at me with disbelief were Tobar and Gillie.

I wanted to run away but I stopped at their table.

'Hi.'

'Jess?'

I shrugged. 'Yes.'

'We thought you were dead, the reports said you had died in that house fire.'

'It's a long story.' This was difficult, what could I tell these old friends? I made myself look at them and found that I wasn't getting any warmth from them. Why were they looking so angry?

'How is Camlo?'

Tobar came right out with it, 'Why Jess? Can you explain that to me? You waited for him until he came back to you then you walked away and left him.'

'He came back with another woman!'

'Camlo brought Rose back to us because her

husband had died, that's all.'

'What?' Oh Christ, how had I got everything so wrong, misread the situation so completely, so disastrously? Was that possible?

I stared helplessly at them. They were standing now, getting ready to leave.

'Yes, Camlo went to visit his childhood friend, Kennick but he was too late, Kennick was dead, and Rose was alone, so he brought her home.'

'But she said Camlo had always loved her, Jenny said she knew Camlo would go back for her one day. She said…'

They hadn't heard, they were already walking away, rejecting me and my pathetic excuses.

I stood there in the centre of the courtyard, trapped in that golden afternoon while my mind flashed back a whole year to relive that other afternoon. I saw it all again, Manfri's grim expression and Camlo, his head down, not ashamed to look for me but heavy with grief for a dear friend. I saw Rose, not vibrant with the triumph of love regained but desperate for the comfort of the tribe.

What had I done? I started after them. I took three steps before the futility of it hit me. A year, it had been a year.

'Excuse me dear, two cream teas please.'

The elderly woman was standing in front of me peering anxiously into my face.

'So sorry madam, I'll get that for you right away.'

I served her the cream teas then stepped back into the kitchen where I took off my frilly apron and put it on the side with my order pad and pen. I picked up my bag. Susie caught my arm as I walked to the café door.

'Jess? Where are you going?'

'Sorry Susie, something awful has happened, I have to go.'

Outside I looked round. There was no sign of Tobar and Gillie. I started walking back to the flat.

I hurried round the corner and past the Mayflower steps. The pedestrian swing bridge was closed to let a boat through and a small crowd was waiting to cross. As soon as the bridge opened again, I hurried across with the others, not really planning, driven by instinct.

Once inside the flat I took my brand-new suitcase from the top of the wardrobe and packed. I took the document case with my new papers from the drawer, found the driving licence and put it in my purse. I checked every corner of the flat, I wouldn't be leaving anything behind. Camlo's photo went into a pocket in my bag.

I called and ordered a taxi and waited by the door, impatient to be gone. When the taxi arrived, I asked the driver if he knew where I could get a reliable second-hand car then told him I wanted to go there but would he take me to my bank first.

I chose a modest unremarkable car that I was assured was in good condition and was only three years old. I had a short test drive, and it ran well so I paid with my card.

Then I drove away from Plymouth and headed east.

I had no idea if I could ever put things right. With Camlo. With any of them but I would give all my strength, all my life to it.

Chapter 16

I checked my watch, it was already four-thirty, I was still struggling out of Plymouth and the rush hour would start soon. I settled down and concentrated on driving. My mind kept intruding on my concentration, nudging me with questions: What are you going to say to Camlo when you see him. Will they even let you into the camp? I swallowed back all those thoughts, if I allowed them in, they would paralyse me, and I had to keep going.

A large part of the journey would be on the A35. It was a road I knew quite well and had driven several times when I had been on my way to or from Phillip's constituency.

After an hour and a half, I stopped at a service station for petrol and as an afterthought I had a burger and chips. Three hours later I was driving a lane close to the camp, creeping along fighting the panic in my gut, I had no idea what I was going to say or how they would receive me.

'Come on Jess, if you don't try now, you may as well give up for ever.' It really didn't help, talking to myself, I still felt sick. I paused at the turn onto the track, took a breath, gripped the wheel, and started up the track. I did it on dipped lights, I didn't want to blaze my way into the camp. I pulled out of the woods and stopped in the area outside Manfri's office. There were no lights on inside, it looked dark and deserted.

There were lights on inside the canteen but no-one walking about or standing in twos or threes talking. It was as quiet as I had ever seen the camp. I got out of the car and closed the door. I didn't know where to go so I stood there thinking and fighting the urge to get back in and leave before they knew I was here.

A door opened somewhere in the dark and I heard the sound of footsteps coming closer. Oshina came round the corner and stopped, she peered at me unsure in the dark. 'Jess? Bloody hell girl. Stay there.'

She hurried away, to find someone I supposed, so I stayed there by my car and waited. She came back with Gillie. They stopped a few yards away and Gillie said. 'It's OK Oshina, you go and eat. I'll see to Jess.'

So, I was something to be seen to. I waited. Gillie came closer and stood with her hands on her hips.

'What are you doing here Jess?'

'I need to see Camlo, to try and explain.'

'You can't, he's gone.'

She sounded so sad, I crumpled against the car.

'Gone?'

'No, he's not dead, he went back. He waited for you until the news of your death and then because there was no hope, he couldn't bear to be here anymore.'

'He could have looked for me. I was in London for a while.'

'Look come to my place. We can't talk here.' She led the way. Once we were sitting in comfort she sighed and sat back regarding me without expression.

'Yes, you were in London, picking up your old life without the inconvenience of a husband. We watched you for a while, you were having a great time spending money and socialising.'

'Don't you see if I hadn't been there, behaving like an innocent wife, if I hadn't been the one to report my husband missing, they would have assumed that I had disposed of him.'

'He did eventually decide that he would go and speak to you, but you had gone, no-one knew where. Then the news reported that you had died in a house fire. That was what finally broke him.'

She stopped speaking, she sat back and calmly assessed how her words had destroyed me. 'What happened Jess, did you decide it was time to move on yet again? Did you set fire to the house and walk away?'

That did it, now I was angry. 'No Gillie. Two Chinese government agents who had a shady deal with my husband came to find out why they hadn't received the goods. I couldn't tell them anything, so they tied me to a chair, poured petrol onto the soft furnishings, set fire to the place, and walked out. I managed to get out, but I was taken to hospital with smoke inhalation. That wasn't the end, oh no, someone from our security services whisked me away from hospital and kept me in a safe house until I had helped him all I could, until I had identified the Chinese men, then he gave me a new identity, arranged a job and a place to live and took me to Plymouth.'

I sat back, shaking with anger and despair. I had never been more broken.

Gillie stood up and went into her kitchen, coming back a few minutes later with two coffees.

'Here, drink this.' We sat in silence, each with our own thoughts. 'Even so, you left. I thought you two would last, after what you had been through and I know you waited, I felt your desperation, yet at the very time he came back you disappeared, that's what I can't understand.'

'I was desperate, and I had such a strong feeling that something was wrong, every day it got stronger, I couldn't sleep, imagining what might have happened. Then, there they were coming back along the path out of the trees. I saw Manfri first then the wagon with Camlo, slumped as though he was ashamed, and that lovely young woman looked joyful. I misread their body language, just as I was thinking that there was a connection between them Jenny dropped her poison, she said that she always knew he would go and bring her back one day, that he had always loved her.'

She didn't say, 'And you believed her?' I saw it in her eyes, and I heard it in my head.

There was only one thing I could do. 'I would like to talk to Manfri, would he see me?'

'He hasn't been good since Camlo left. I'll see if he will talk to you. Wait here.'

Gillie was gone ten minutes and while I waited, I planned.

The door opened and Gillie stood in the open doorway. 'Come on then. I have told him what you said to me, don't expect too much though.'

When I walked into Manfri's sitting room, followed by Gillie, he was sitting in a chair. He didn't get up, only glancing up at me. He looked shrunken, a shocking change from the man I remembered.

'Gillie told me your story. What do you want?'

'Hello Manfri.' There was no point in putting off the moment. I would go in at the deep end. 'I would like to borrow the wagon and the horse, please.'

That raised a spark of interest. 'Why would you want my wagon?'

'I want to travel back. I want to find Camlo, tell him everything, what I did and why and then I am going to beg him to forgive me and come home.'

He stared at me. 'Can you harness a horse, drive a horse and wagon?'

'No, not yet.'

'Well, there you are then, no, of course you can't borrow them.'

'You could teach me.'

'I could, but I won't.'

'Fine, I'll find someone else who will, then I'll come back.'

'We have no idea where he is. It could take years to find him.'

'I had better get started then.'

I was through the door and striding away when I heard Manfri shout after me. 'Come back you stupid woman.'

Surprised I went back and stood at the door, ready to leave again, if he thought I was going to stand around to be verbally abused he was wrong.

'You can learn on the way if you're going to search for Camlo I'm coming too. Can you be ready to leave tomorrow?'

'I'll need some clothes, right for the time.' I didn't push my luck by smiling at him.

He nodded. 'We can supply those, your old place is empty, sleep there. How about you Gillie?'

'Oh, I'll be coming, try and keep me away. I'll go and tell Tobar I will be away for a while.'

Manfri gave me the keys to my old home, we said polite goodnights and went our separate ways, I walked up to the familiar door, I recognised the way the key felt as it turned in the lock and when I walked inside the place felt instantly welcoming.

'More than the people are. Can't expect anything different I suppose.'

I had spoken that out loud and surprised myself with the sound of my voice, so I made sure only to think and not say out loud: Stupid woman, get a grip. Of course, the people here would feel resentful.

When I got into bed I lay in the dark and told myself that I could do this, I could find Camlo and talk to him and he would understand.

I hardly slept that night and in the snatches of time that I did sleep I dreamt and woke up gripping the duvet. Then at last it was morning and Gillie arrived with three outfits for me. Three skirts, three blouses and a shawl.

'You will have to wear your own shoes, Lela and Oshina have smaller feet than you. I have brought enough to last a while. We have no idea how far Camlo has gone.'

Gillie was already in period dress, she stood just inside the door and waited while I put on a dark blue skirt and a black blouse. The shawl was black and heavy, it would be warm. My boots, practical walking boots, looked right with the outfit. I was ready.

'Come on then, she said and walked out. I looked round my room and followed locking the door behind me and slipping the key into the bag that held my spare clothes.

'Did Lela or Oshina say anything?' I asked Gillie's back as she led the way.

'No.'

Manfri was waiting in the wagon, sitting with his elbows on his knees while the horse helped himself to the long, lush grass growing on the bank by the path.

He looked me up and down.

'You'll do, climb up then.'

Both of us climbed up onto the bench seat along with Manfri, he clicked his tongue at the horse, and we started off. After a while the wooden seat became uncomfortable, I shifted position, it didn't help. Curious, I said, 'Are we there yet?'

'As far as we can tell we have been there for half an hour now. We think the past starts half a mile from home.

When we stopped for some breakfast: sandwiches and water, Gillie rooted in the back of the wagon among our bags of supplies and came back with a blanket. She folded it and laid it on the bench. The ride was a little more comfortable when we started again. After what had been a mild overcast start to the day, it was warming with the sun breaking through the clouds.

We came down out of the woodland and the landscape opened out with rolling farmland spreading all the way to a wider horizon. I looked around, yes, I remembered it all from the time I had been here before. Thick dark clouds hung low in the distance, threatening to chase away the sunny day. At the fork in the road, we took a different road to the one I had travelled before.

'Where should we begin looking?'

'The first place I think we should try is around three more hours from here, if he isn't there, it will be too far from the next place to carry on today. We will rest the night and try again tomorrow. Right, swap seats with me and I'll start teaching you how to handle Moonlight.'

Moonlight was a gentle soul and wandered on quite happily with an amateur on his reins, but I concentrated hard and felt I was getting the hang of it when Manfri stirred in his seat and said, 'That group of buildings down there, take Moonlight onto that patch of open ground on the left and stop him there.'

Moonlight had the manners to respond to my signals and he pulled off the road and onto the area of scrub grass. We climbed down, stretching out the kinks in our backs and Manfri showed me how to take the harness off Moonlight, feed and water him. Only then did he let us turn our attention to finding out if Camlo was nearby or if anyone had seen him.

I looked across the road to where there were half a dozen houses and an inn. Manfri came to stand beside me.

'We'll go and ask in the inn; if he has been here or passed through, they will know.'

This is just the first place we've come to, what are the chances?'

We have to look, every place we go. Not feeling discouraged so soon I hope?' I knew he couldn't resist that cutting comment. I had stirred him into action but I felt allowing me to come along was by way of a challenge. They were both being civil, that was all.

'No, I will keep looking until we've found him, I won't give up.' I wrapped the shawl tighter round me as we crossed the road. The light was fading, the sunlight had gone, and the dark clouds were rolling in bringing a cold wind with them.

There was warmth and light inside the inn, a handful of customers looked up as we walked in. I was walking in behind the other two, so I was well positioned to observe their reactions. There was a welcoming smile from the bartender. He called out, 'Manfri, it's been a long time, how are you?'

From the two men at the bar the reaction was neutral but the three men sitting round a table near the window stopped their conversation and turned hostile stares on us.

Manfri led the way to the bar and ordered beer all round, offering the other customers a drink as well. The two at the bar accepted but the three by the window refused.

'What brought you this way then, Manfri?'

'Passing through, Bob. I thought I would call in and say hello, as it's been a while since I came this way.'

Bob cocked a sceptical eyebrow at Manfri. 'And I stand here all hours serving ale for the good of my health. I see you are travelling with company. I recognise Gillie of course but I don't know the young lady.'

'Of course, you two haven't met, Bob this is Jess, Jess Hampshire.'

Bob smiled, 'Pleased to meet you, Jess.' Then he moved away, pouring drinks.

A little later another customer arrived with his dog. Both the man and his dog were drenched. The dog shook himself and wet all of us at the bar.

The man said, 'Pouring out there, set in for the rest of the day by the look of it.'

When Bob had finished with the new customer, he came back to us.

'So why are you here? And don't try to tell me you are only passing through.'

'Have you seen Camlo?'

Bob looked long and hard at Manfri. 'He was here, about a month ago, I think. He didn't look good, I wondered if he was ill.'

I had been holding back, letting Manfri talk, but now I couldn't help myself,

'Did he say which way he was heading?'

'He didn't say but I saw him walking off down

the road, he was heading off that way.' Bob indicated the road leading onward, the direction we were heading. 'It's a long stretch of open moor before you'll find anywhere to find shelter. You are welcome to pull into the barn for the night, it will only set you back the price of a bowl of Molly's stew each.'

Manfri took a long swallow of his beer then turned to peer out of the window, a gust of wind lashed rain against the glass. 'Three bowls of stew then Bob and thanks, we'll move into the barn and be back.'

As we stepped through the door the wind caught at my shawl, whipping it away from my body, I pulled it close. We struggled over the road and quickly harnessed Moonlight to the wagon. We encouraged him back across the road and round the back of the inn, Manfri dragged open the large barn door, fighting the wind and slipping in the mud. As soon as the door opened wide enough Moonlight pulled the wagon into the dim interior.

Again, all three of us worked to settle Moonlight for the night, I watched Manfri and Gillie, and followed what they did. Once we had the harness off, we rubbed him down with handfuls of straw and settled him with water and a nosebag of food. Then we stood back and looked at each other in the faint light from cracks in the wooden boards of the walls.

We were soaked, the water had run off us

making puddles on the floor. I scraped the hair away from my face and helped Gillie pull a tarpaulin from the wagon. Wrapped inside and wonder of wonders actually dry were blankets. With the tarpaulin laid out in one of the stalls and a pile of blankets ready for us we walked back through easing rain to the pub.

The three hostile customers had gone so we settled at the table by the window where they had been sitting and Manfri signalled to Bob that we were ready to eat.

When the stew arrived, a large bowl each with a plate of course brown bread, it finally brought home to me just how hungry I was. The stew was good with lamb, root vegetables and pearl barley in rich gravy.

The bar was warm and smoky from the log fire, by the time the last of the stew had been mopped up by the last crust of bread our clothes were nearly dry. We moved closer to the fire and ordered another drink which we made last until we were dry, warm, and sleepy. Then Manfri paid and we went out to the barn where we wrapped the blankets round us and lay down on the tarpaulin to sleep.

Gillie woke me the next morning. Manfri was already up and harnessing Moonlight to the wagon. We folded the bedding, put it into the back of the wagon and climbed up on the seat. Gillie took the reins and Manfri opened the barn door, we drove out into the yard and the early light.

Bob opened the pub door and stood watching as we drew up to him, we thanked him for his hospitality.

'Take care old friend, I hope you find Camlo.'

He raised a hand to Manfri then his eyes sought mine and held until I looked away. Further down the road I looked back, he still stood in the open doorway, as I watched he stepped back in and closed the door. I wondered if Camlo had told him about me.

The day was chilly and overcast but dry. The road led up a gentle incline until we were travelling open moor, sudden gusts of wind blew my hair over my eyes and caused Moonlight to toss his head. The clouds, thick grey, shot with ochre, hung low, casting shadows when shafts of bright sun broke through.

Towards lunchtime the road started to drop into a wooded valley curling round a thicket of trees. There waiting, standing side by side blocking the road, were the three men from the pub.

Chapter 17

Gillie said, 'Help me turn the wagon.'

Manfri grabbed the reins and stopped the wagon. 'No, there's not time, let's try driving through them.' He flicked the reins and yelled, a startling sound that Moonlight responded to by bounding forward, picking up speed, the wagon bouncing behind. Gillie and I grabbed hold of the seat while Manfri leaned forward still shouting encouragement and we flew towards the three men.

We almost made it. At first, they reacted by pulling back away from the charging horse then the closest man leapt forward and grabbed the side of Moonlight's bridle and held on making the terrified horse squeal in pain as the weight of the man on his bit dragged on his mouth. The others got the idea and as moonlight skidded to a stop all three of them rushed the wagon.

Gillie was pulled from the seat and thrown down on the road. I tried kicking out and landed a good one before hands trapped my ankles and pulled. My back and head bounced off some hard bits of the wagon before I landed on the road.

For several seconds I lay winded and struggling for consciousness, then I rolled up onto my knees and pulled myself to my feet by taking hold of one of the wagon wheels.

Gillie was already on her feet and trying to pull two of the men off Manfri who was curled up on the road. They had beaten him down to the ground and were now kicking him.

To my surprise I found I could move. I ducked under Moonlight's head and joined Gillie. She was thumping the back of one of the men, then she stood back and started to kick him on the back of his legs.

The other man drew back a foot ready for another kick at Manfri. I ran at him and luckily caught him at the point of least balance, I gave him a hefty push and he toppled over. As he tried to get up, I followed with a kick between his legs that doubled him over.

I had forgotten the last man; he was up on the seat of the wagon with the reins in his hands.

'C'mon lads.'

His voice was rough with an edge of desperation. The other two scrambled to the wagon and had barely got on board before, frightened and confused, our horse headed off down the road.

We had already helped Manfri to his feet. He was shaking and breathing hard. Gillie said, 'Keep hold of him.' She chased off after the wagon and managed to get onto the open back. She quickly pushed the bags with our belongings off the wagon and with her arms wrapped round the blanket bundle and the tarpaulin she sat down on the edge and smoothly slipped off, at the last moment the tarpaulin caught on something in the wagon and Gillie lost her grip on it.

Manfri and I hurried to help her, we collected our bundles and the blankets, then the three of us stood and watched the wagon disappear round the next bend with our tarpaulin trailing in the dirt.

Gillie said, 'Come on Manfri, let me look at you. She examined the bruises and swellings that were coming up on his face, then got him to lift his shirt while she felt round his ribs. He hissed with pain as she ran her hands over his right side.

'That will do Gillie, I'm alright.'

'I think you might have a rib that is either cracked or broken but I can't tell, as a precaution I'll bind that for you. Can you walk?'

'Course I can.'

'Well then, when I have bound your ribs, you can prove it as we have to walk now. We will have to find somewhere dry to spend the night. Sit yourself on the bank now.'

With Manfri perched on the roadside bank Gillie searched the bags for something to wrap him in pulling out from his bag a shirt and bringing out her first aid pouch. The shirt she cut and tore into wide strips.

'Now sit still while I do this.'

After spreading on a pain-relief cream Gillie bandaged Manfri's chest.

'Now you have finished fussing around me how about you Gillie?'

'Oh, I'm fine, you know me Manfri.'

I had been standing to one side, holding Gillie's pouch, and passing bandages and pins, now she took them back, tucked the pouch into her bag and after helping Manfri to his feet the two of them started off down the road.

I watched them as they walked away, I wasn't feeling so good, but we had to keep moving so I turned away and picked up my bag of belongings then followed them down the road. Gillie looked round and realised I wasn't quite with them.

'Come on Jess, keep up.'

I put on a spurt, closed the gap, and fell in step beside them.

Towards the end of the day, we reached a small town, a straggle of houses, shops and businesses spread along the road. Several people stared at us as we walked by. Manfri said, 'Look, they have a hotel, shall we see if we can get a room? I could do with a comfortable sleep tonight.'

I was so weary I didn't care how many people I shared with. The idea of a real bed was enough for me. They had a room and didn't seem at all worried about whom or how many would sleep in there. Manfri paid and we took the offered oil lamp and climbed a flight of steep narrow stairs and found our room at the end of the corridor.

Inside there was one large bed. We put our bags in the corner and Gillie said, 'I would love to have a wash.'

Manfri left the room, returning after a few minutes, 'I asked for some hot water.'

There was soon a knock on the door and a maid walked in carrying a huge jug of hot water. She poured it into a bowl on the table and left.

Manfri said, 'You two go first.' He sat with his back to us and began to sort his bag.

There was a lump of hard soap in a dish beside the bowl and a small thin towel beside the dish, but it felt the height of luxury to wash away the dirt from the road, even if the same clothes went back on.

When we had finished, we took our turn to sit and look away, I found my comb and started on my wind tangled hair. When I caught my breath and put a hand to where the comb had hurt my head, Gillie said. 'Let me see.' She separated my hair. 'You have a small cut and a bump. Where it bled your hair is matted, give me your comb.' Gently and with a great deal of patience she combed out the dried blood. 'How have you been feeling today, Jess?'

'I felt a bit giddy and nauseous for a while, but it wore off, I'm alright now.'

The care Gillie had shown and the hand that she laid on my shoulder, the first sign of warmth from either of them since we had met again, surprised me with the strength of my reaction. My eyes filled with tears. I lifted my hand and brushed them away hoping she hadn't noticed.

Manfri had finished. 'It's time we slept, settle down and I'll turn out the light.'

So, the three of us, Gillie in the middle, me nearest the window and Manfri closest to the door pulled up the blankets and slept away our second night spent in the past looking for Camlo. The image of him in my mind as sleep closed in was of the man who had kissed me in the stationary store.

When I woke in the morning, I was alone. A little alarmed I left the bed and went to look out of the window at the street below. In both directions early shoppers moved in and out of the shops. I could see a bakery, a cobbler, and a funeral parlour opposite the hotel.

There were people carrying bags and baskets, on their way to where a market was setting up further along the street. Wagons loaded with produce were unloading at the stalls. I couldn't see Manfri or Gillie. I opened the window and leaned out for a better view,

The door opened behind me, and they both walked in.

'Ah, she's awake. Good morning, Jess.'

I closed the window. The greeting had been delivered by Manfri, with a smile. I smiled back.

'A good morning to both of you, I wondered

where you were.'

'I went to buy us some food and Manfri has been asking around about Moonlight and the wagon. Let's sit and eat some breakfast.'

We sat on the edge of the bed and Gillie took bread and cheese from a bag, she tore chunks off the loaf and handed them round. Manfri produced his knife and cut helpings of cheese. There was silence while we chewed, the bread was dense and crusty, and the cheese was very good.

When we had finished, I said, 'You were asking about Moonlight, tell me you asked about Camlo too?'

'Yes of course I did, no-one seems to have seen him here but here's the thing, I think our first priority must be to find our horse and wagon, we need them to travel any significant distance, I'm sorry Jess but you must see that makes sense.'

I saw the practicality of being able to travel as widely and comparatively quickly as possible, which meant finding Moonlight, but every day not focussed on finding Camlo would tear at my nerves.

'I do see, and I agree, let's find our horse.'

We left the hotel and turned in the direction that we had travelled the day before. Gillie stopped at the market. 'We lost our tarpaulin so I want to see if I can find a replacement.'

While Gillie rooted through the piles of fabrics, blankets, and old clothing on a long table, Manfri and I moved on. He bought some matches which he put in his pocket and a cast iron saucepan that he tied to his bag and slung over his shoulder.

'Can you manage that with your ribs?'

'Yes, my dear, they're not so bad this morning, I don't think it is more than a bruise but Gillie, well she has a caring soul.'

He glanced towards where Gillie was deep in discussion with the stallholder and for a moment his eyes gave him away.

'Does she know how you feel?'

Manfri was alarmed at being caught out. 'No, no, Gillie is a fine woman and a good friend, that's all.'

Gillie caught up with us, she nodded approval at the pan and showed us the large sheet of canvas she had found. 'They had some blankets, but I didn't think we could manage to carry any more than this.'

We shared out the load and walked away from the town heading back into open country. The constant wind had dried the ground and our footsteps on the unmade surface kicked up a cloud of dust that followed us.

Gillie said. 'Did you learn anything from your questioning Manfri?'

'No, nothing. But then that was a busy little place they must be used to strangers passing through, we will get lucky, even if it takes a while.'

For two more days we trudged on, asking if anyone had seen a large black and white horse hauling a flatbed wagon, only to meet blank stares and shaken heads.

We ate only bread and cheese that first day, the second day we stopped at an inn around lunchtime for bowls of soup. The nights were spent, the three of us huddled together wrapped in blankets and the canvas. We found sheltered places away from the road and Manfri would cut bracken and pile it up into a mattress, it was moderately comfortable, and it insulated us from the cold ground.

The days had turned cold, and the nights were bitter, the eager enthusiasm we had at the start had hardened to a kernel of grim determination.

When we woke on that third morning our routine was well established. A few mouthfuls of dry bread and hard cheese, then the canvas was folded, and we picked up and settled our loads. We shared quiet smiles and took to the road.

I didn't complain, neither did Gillie or Manfri, but my shoulders and back screamed from the hours carrying my bag and my feet were an agony of blisters. I suspected theirs were too.

Around mid-day we stopped at a roadside cottage, Manfri went to ask the usual questions, the woman who answered the door looked from one to the other of us with suspicion. She didn't seem to be listening to him.

'Yes, yes young man, my eyes aren't so good,

can the ladies come closer so I can see them.'

Gillie and I moved a little nearer.

'You have walked a long way,' we nodded. 'I can tell, blisters all over your feet.'

'Can you tell us Madam, have you seen our horse and wagon? A large black and white horse and a flatbed wagon.

'Two days ago, great big brute of an animal, and the noise that wagon made.'

'Which way did it go?'

'Up the track to Barney's farm. I wondered what he were doing, where would he find the cash to afford a get-up like that.'

'Where is this Barney's farm?'

'Up that track over there, of course. He's not there now, taken it off down the road he has. Be back soon I dare say.'

'Thank you, madam, we're very grateful.'

She started to shut the door then opened it. 'Salt water, my dears, soak them feet in salt water, and mind how you go, Barney and those brothers of his they're a bit rough.'

The door shut, we could hear her footsteps as she walked away, she was muttering to herself.

We drew together, wide eyed with excitement. 'Come on, let's try and get there before they get back.' Manfri was already striding away, Gillie and I shared a grin and followed him. We reached the turning to the farm and turned onto the rough track, it wound its way up a gentle slope then dipped down and there was the farmhouse with a barn and pigsties nearby. The whole area appeared shabby and dilapidated.

As we approached Manfri said, 'I'll go and knock at the door, to see if there is anyone in there, anyone who is prepared to answer the door that is. You two wait round the side of the house, in case.'

From our viewpoint, peering round the corner, we watched Manfri knock the door. There was no answer, so he shrugged, signalled for us to stay put and walked right along the front of the house then all the way round, trying the windows.

'I think we should find somewhere out of the way, where we can see when they come back.'

We decided the best place would be a cluster of pine trees further along the track, up at the top of the next rise. We would have cover there and shelter from the wind.

Once we reached the trees, we settled as comfortably as we could and waited, grateful for the thick layer of needles, softer than the bare earth and better insulation.

I wrapped my skirt round my knees and pulled my shawl tighter then tried to ease a shoe away from the blisters on my feet. Manfri noticed, he reached out to touch my arm.

'Leave your shoes alone or you won't be able to put them back on.' then he went back to watching the house.

The light was almost gone when, faint on the

wind, we heard the slow, steady hoof beats of a large horse. We pulled further back into the trees, sat very still, and watched Moonlight and the wagon appear over the brow of the hill.

The three brothers took the wagon into the barn, they weren't inside for long, they soon emerged and walked erratically into the house.

'They're drunk. Well, that's helpful.'

We waited. In the bitter cold that settled down with the night, we heard snatches of singing, then shouts, then at last the lights went out and the house went silent.

We waited a little longer before unwinding stiff limbs and getting to our feet.

'We'll take it slow and careful down the track, the last thing we need now is a broken ankle and we don't want to wake them up.'

It seemed to last for ever, that walk down the track and we thanked our guardian angels for the occasional patches of weak moonlight, but eventually we reached the yard between the house and the barn.

The wagon had been left by the wall to the right of the barn door. Manfri eased the door halfway open and the light through the doorway showed Moonlight tethered in a corner. He turned his head and snickered a greeting.

Manfri made a fuss of Moonlight then untied the rope and whispering soft reassurances led him outside. Gillie and I found the harness and heaved the wagon into place and between us we fitted the harness. We were ready to go.

'We can either take it slow so that the wheels squeak slowly or we can put on some speed and raise the risk of waking the sleeping beauties. What do you think?'

We each voted for slow so with Manfri walking at Moonlight's head, Gillie, and I beside the wagon, taking it cautiously we set off.

When we considered we had gone far enough, we climbed up onto the seat Manfri spoke to Moonlight and the great horse picked up speed. I looked back at the house, looking for a light to flare in a window but there was nothing but darkness there.

Chapter 18

We kept moving all that night and deep into the next morning. The country we passed through was high, bleak, and empty. Just as Gillie and I were starting to mutter about being tired and hungry and could we please stop before we lost the will to live, the road dipped into a wooded valley. We passed small farms and fields of sheep. A small village was tucked along the banks of a river.

'Ah, an inn, would you like a drink and if possible, some lunch, ladies?'

We didn't bother to answer.

The only food the landlord could offer was a loaf of bread with ham and pickles. We took our drinks to a corner by the fire, and he brought the food over to us. The bread was freshly baked, the ham came as thick juicy slices, and the dish of pickles were sharp and tangy.

After our mean fare of the last few days, we fell on the fresh tasty meal, sharing round the ham, sharing happy smiles.

When every scrap was eaten, we sat back,

replete and satisfied.

'Can you imagine those men coming down in the morning and finding Moonlight gone?'

'I wish we could have seen their faces. We were lucky that they came home so drunk mind you, it wouldn't have been so easy if they were sober, and we would probably have had to run for it.'

It was the first time we had discussed the events of the previous night, we had each been locked in our own bubble of anxiety, now the realisation that we had travelled far enough to be safe from pursuit dispelled all of that.

The warmth of the fire along with a full belly and the feeling of relief made us sleepy. 'Can we stop here and get some sleep Manfri?'

'I would love to Gillie, but I think we need to move on, I will just ask if anyone here has seen Camlo before we go.'

'Let's have a few more minutes by the fire first.'

I felt so warm and comfortable that I closed my eyes. I heard the outside door open, and a blast of cold air blew in, I opened my eyes again to see who had come in and found myself looking into the face of Camlo. I couldn't breathe. The iron band that clamped round my chest squeezed my heart into my throat and someone was beating it with a sledgehammer.

He stood with his back to the door, for whole seconds he stood motionless. We had planned how to tell him that I was still alive, now it was too late; his face showed the shock. Then, before

I could react and call out to him, anger replaced the shock.

He turned and opened the door. He was through it and had slammed it behind him while I was trying to speak.

I was on my feet and moving towards the door when Gillie called out. 'Wait Jess, let us...'

I didn't hear the rest; I was running by the time I left the doorway behind me. Camlo was striding down the hill towards the river, I lifted my long skirts and ran as fast as I could, I reached him as he started to cross the bridge.

'Camlo, wait, talk to me.'

He had stopped with his head down, now he turned to face me, and his expression froze me where I was, one foot on the bridge, hand raised to reach out to him.

'Talk to you? Why on earth would I want to talk to you? You ran out on me at the worst possible time. The next thing I hear of you, is that you are dead.'

He stopped, struggling for control. My heart was breaking for him.

'Couldn't you at least have let me know you were still alive?'

'I couldn't, they took me to a safe house, I couldn't.'

It sounded weak, a feeble excuse.

Camlo looked me up and down, the contempt on his face shrivelled my spirit and I stood helpless as he walked away from me.

Gillie and Manfri rushed up to join me. They had stayed long enough to pay for our lunch so only caught a glimpse of Camlo before he disappeared. Both stood in silence, staring at the empty lane.

'Jess.' She took my arm and shook it gently. 'Come away my dear, we'll talk this over and decide what to do. Alright?'

With an arm round my shoulders, she eased me away from the bridge and towards the wagon. 'Go and get her a whisky, get us all one.'

She took me to the wagon and sat me down on the back then she found a handkerchief and passed it to me. 'Here Jess, wipe your eyes.'

From somewhere amongst all the pain I was feeling I found a scrap of determination and a small flame of courage. I took the handkerchief and wiped my eyes. I raised my chin and straightened my back.

Manfri arrived with three tumblers of whiskey. I swallowed mine down, took a breath.

'He must be living nearby. Someone must know where. I don't care if he hates me now, I'm staying here until he listens to me, talks to me, then whatever he decides I will accept.'

I handed the empty glass back to Manfri.

He said, 'Let's see if we can get a room for you and Gillie for tonight, I'll sleep in the wagon. Then in the morning we can talk it over.'

He started walking back to the inn. I turned to Gillie. 'If you both want to speak with him first, because he will talk to you, ask him if he wants to go home. If he does, fine, you take him, and I'll follow. If he wants to stay and you decide to go home anyway, I'm ok with that but I'm staying.'

When Manfri got back Gillie told him what I had said, I barely heard, it was as though most of my senses had closed down and all that was left was this determination to fight for the man I loved and had damaged.

They wanted to see him and speak with him. Manfri needed to know that his son, if nothing else, was settled, earning a living and healthy. I thought that he would try to persuade Camlo to go back with them and that was why I had said I would make my own way.

'How will you pay your way if we leave you here? I can leave you some money but not enough to last indefinitely and your wait may be a long one. You do understand that Camlo may never forgive you, Jess.'

I wouldn't think about that. 'I will try to find a job. I'm strong and fit and I would do anything.'

Manfri nodded, satisfied. 'I think the first thing to do is get a room, then we will ask if anyone can tell us where to find him, first stop the inn, come on.'

All three of us went back to the inn; there was only one small room to let. We had hoped it would be large enough for all of us but when we opened the door it was tiny, a narrow single bed took the whole length of one wall. A small cupboard sat below a widow in the end wall.

Manfri asked if the landlord knew of anywhere else in the village with rooms to let.

'No sir, the farm and the big house, they have places for their workers but that's all.'

'I think if you plan to stay, Jess, this will suit you, Gillie and I will bed down in the wagon.' He turned to the landlord. 'The young man who came into the bar and left right away, just before we paid for lunch, he's my son, Camlo, do you know where he is living or working?'

'Yes sir, like I said, places for workers. Young Camlo he's been taken on as a shepherd, there's a hut at the top of the long acre field two miles out on the north road. He's living there.'

We thanked the landlord and Manfri paid for a week in the room for me. I walked out to the wagon with them.

'Will you be alright in the wagon? I feel bad that I have the room.'

'We'll be fine. I think we will move on a little, find somewhere sheltered for tonight, closer to the hut. Then we'll see Camlo in the morning, early. I am going to ask him to come home.'

I swallowed hard. 'I hope you can persuade him. He belongs there. Look, if it's possible ...'

'I will tell him what happened to you, but any decision must be his. I won't fight your corner, Jess.'

'I wouldn't ask for more. You have been so kind, thank you. Will you let me know?'

'Did you mean what you said about making your own way home, if Camlo comes with us?'

I nodded vigorously. 'Of course.'

'Then if we don't come back to you tomorrow, we will be on our way home.'

Manfri dug down into his jacket pocket and brought out a wad of notes, he peeled off some and held them out to me.

'In that case you will need this, good luck, Jess.'

The moment felt awkward, charged with emotion and yet strangely formal. I held out a hand and Manfri shook it. I offered it to Gillie, but she ignored it, she put her arms round me and hugged me tight.

Without another word they climbed onto the wagon. Instead of moving off immediately, they waited. Manfri was coughing, a hacking cough that curled him over and took his breath. When at last he had recovered he smiled and raised a hand, with a flick of the reins Moonlight pulled them away.

Back in the room I tried to form a plan, should I ask around for a job? But then if Camlo started for home the next day I would be leaving too. I wanted to walk along the road, look at where he was living, just a look, but that would be a mistake. In the end I lay on the bed and gazed into space. I wasn't feeling the pain; I had locked that away. Besides, it was only self-indulgence anyway. I was the one responsible for ruining our lives.

When the last of the light had gone and the chill in the room finally found me, I kicked off my shoes and wriggled under the blanket. I finally slept as the first faint hint of light showed in the sky.

When it was fully light and the sounds from downstairs were more consistent, I got up, washed in the cold water that had been left on the cupboard and went down to the bar.

I sat in a corner and waited. Lunchtime came and went with no wagon in sight. I felt like a breath of air, so I went for a walk around the village. Then I sat outside the inn, on the wooden bench by the wall, sheltered from the wind and warmed by the sun.

Out of the quiet of the afternoon I became aware of a familiar sound, cartwheels on rough ground, the rattle of harness and the heavy drum from the hoofs of a large horse. The wagon was coming, fast.

My heart started beating hard, something was wrong. I was on my feet waiting as the wagon appeared from the trees.

Camlo was driving, he stopped Moonlight close to me.

'Manfri and Gillie are ill, I think either flu or pneumonia, I have to get them home and I need you to come along and help, get your stuff.'

I dashed inside and up to my room, I grabbed my bag and checked I had everything then back downstairs to find the landlord. I told him that

I wouldn't need the room anymore and thanked him for his hospitality.

Back outside I flung my bag into the back of the wagon and climbed in. As soon as I was on board Camlo snapped the reins and whistled and Moonlight was off.

Camlo had laid them side by side on a bed of bracken and covered them with blankets. One look at the pair of them was enough to fill me with cold, solid fear. They were feverish and barely aware. I settled down between them. All I could do was watch and comfort them, they needed antibiotics, we had to get them home.

Camlo looked back over his shoulder. 'How long did it take you to get here?'

'A week, but three of those days we were on foot. Moonlight and the wagon were stolen, we had to find them and get them back so say five days.'

It was too long.

'Not good enough. We will have to keep moving and only stop when Moonlight can't go on, understood?'

'Of course. Would it help if I walked beside the wagon? Lessen the weight?'

'No, it will be faster to keep pushing Moonlight until he can't go on. Then feed and water him and get him moving again, do you agree?"

I looked around me, it was a beautiful autumn afternoon, the wind had dropped and the sinking sun through the trees lit bright patches of colour contrasted by long shadows, but two special people lay almost comatose in this jolting wagon.

I hadn't replied, now an angry voice snapped at me. 'You don't agree? Do you think that would be too cruel to Moonlight? Have you got a better idea?'

'No, I agree, we need maximum speed. I suggest we take turns driving.'

'Right.'

We pushed on, way into the night, thankful for the rents in the clouds that allowed us to find the road. I wasn't driving so I sat with Manfri and Gillie, wiping the sweat from their burning foreheads, soothing and comforting as much as possible, until Moonlight slowed to a halt. The poor animal stood with his head dropped low and his sides heaving with exhaustion.

Without looking at me Camlo said. 'Help me tend to Moonlight.'

I climbed down and helped release Moonlight from his harness, we let him find a patch of grass and while he ate, we rubbed him down with an old towel. All the while Camlo spoke gently to the great horse, stroking and rubbing.

When the horse stopped grazing Camlo held Moonlight's head and explained into his ear that he was sorry, but we had to move on, then we put him back into the traces and buckled it all back together again.

'You take a turn now.' He handed me the reins,

turned his back, went round to the back, and climbed up into the wagon. He chucked the old towel into a corner. 'Go on then.'

'Come on then Moonlight, be kind.'

I flicked the reins and sighed with relief as Moonlight started to move. At first, I struggled to see the road and strained to see every dip and bend, then I realised that Moonlight was picking his own way perfectly well. I sat back and relaxed, only contributing occasional encouragement.

I could hear the sounds from the wagon, one or the other one of them coughing or snatches of muttering. I heard Camlo talking, more to himself than to them.

When Moonlight stopped again there was a misty grey light in the east. The bitter cold of the early hours had chilled my fingers on the reins. I rubbed them together, trying to get the circulation going.

I looked behind me into the bed of the wagon; it had been quiet back there for a while. I could see that Camlo hadn't slept, he was brushing the hair from Manfri's forehead. Manfri was muttering, restless but Gillie appeared to be sleeping peacefully.

Without lifting his head to look at me, Camlo said, 'I think Gillie might be through the worst of it, but Dad is about the same. We must do something different Jess, we're not moving fast enough,' He looked at Moonlight. 'And we can't keep pushing that poor old horse like this.'

I climbed down and started undoing the harness, Camlo came and joined me. Nothing was said for a while; I was trying to gather my thoughts.

'Do you think Gillie will be able to wait a few more days?'

'Probably, the fever has gone, and she has been sleeping for an hour or so.'

'Is there any way you could take Manfri on Moonlight, just the two of you? You could make much better time and you could send someone back for us.' I could tell he had been thinking along the same lines, for a moment he looked at me, searching my face.

'If we could sit him in front of me and bind us together, I think that might work, we could be home in a day, maybe less.'

He looked round at the wagon. 'If I pull the wagon off the road, you should be safe enough, until someone comes back for you.'

We urged Moonlight into the trees, well back from the road, then took all the harness off, fed and watered him and left him to graze. By the time we had done that the day had arrived, and we could take stock of our surroundings, we had, by sheer luck, stopped in a sheltered spot, our shelter was a spinney of trees in a dip in the road.

We all needed to rest for a while, we sat on the bench and discussed the best way of securing the two of them together. Camlo decided that with his belt and Manfri's and one of the long reins he could manage to hold his father in place.

They would be riding bareback, but Camlo was confident that wouldn't be a problem, 'It's how I learnt to ride.'

We had been talking not as friends but as colleagues, now the shutters came down again, so I wandered off and found a stream where I filled the saucepan I found in the wagon. The one Manfri had bought in the village.

I sat on the wagon bench and took from my bag the loaf of bread I had bought the previous morning. I tore off a hunk and offered it to Camlo. He accepted with a nod, ate the bread, and drank some water. I ate a little and carefully wrapped the remainder. I would need something for Gillie.

Camlo went to Moonlight and brought him over to the wagon. He would soon be gone and there was a chance I wouldn't see him again. I didn't fool myself; he had needed my help to get this far, but now he didn't need me at all. There was no warmth, there would be no reconciliation.

I watched him, the rhythm of his movements, the way his hair, now longer and tousled, fell over his forehead, the dark stubble framing his lips. I would try to take these memories and hold them close, like living snapshots, I would add them to the rest of my treasured memories and keep them safe.

When he and Moonlight were ready Camlo went to the back of the wagon. He wrapped Manfri in a blanket then lifted him and carried him to the horse. I went over to help and between us we got him into position on Moonlights wide back. Then I helped hold him in place while Camlo climbed up behind.

He looked down at me, I couldn't read his expression.

'Look after Gillie.'

I nodded. 'I will, send someone to bring us home.'

He turned Moonlight's head and in a matter of seconds they were out of sight. I stayed staring at the space where he had been for as long as I could still hear the steady beat of the horse's hoofs fading into the distance, when they were gone, I went to tend Gillie.

Chapter 19

She was sleeping; the illness had wiped the colour from her face, apart from her eyelids which were tinged with blue and looked as fragile as a dragonfly wing. The best thing I could do for her in that moment was to leave her in peace, so her body had the time to begin the recovery.

I wondered how the two of them had become so ill so suddenly but then we had been through some harsh conditions on this journey, they had both been coughing over the last day or so.

As for me, I made the interior of the wagon as comfortable as possible. Moonlight had pulled it under the cover of a couple of yew trees, they should provide some shelter. I walked to the road and looked back at the wagon, a traveller passing by might not notice the encampment, but no-one would miss the gouges the wagon wheels had made in the soft earth by the roadside. The last thing we needed was someone else taking a fancy for our wagon.

I used my feet to push earth back into place

and smooth the ruts, I found handfuls of leaves and debris and scattered them over the raw earth. Then I stood back, I was quite pleased, I just hoped I would be awake when someone came for us. It wouldn't do to miss them.

We still had our shawls and two blankets, one covered Gillie and the other had been discarded on the floor. Either we had one each or we shared so, with my shawl wrapped securely round me, I lay down close to her and arranged both blankets over of us. Even though it was full daylight I was so exhausted that in no time at all I fell asleep.

I must have slept for hours because the light was fading when I opened my eyes. My bones ached and I was stiff. I struggled to sit up, then looked at Gillie. She was awake,

'How long have you been awake Gillie?'

'A little while, I don't know.'

I felt her forehead, she felt cool.

'Where is Manfri?'

'Camlo has gone ahead with him; he is going to send someone back for us.'

Gillie turned her head away and closed her eyes but not before I saw the tears.

'How long do you think?'

She meant before someone came. 'I don't know, maybe a couple of days.'

'Are we safe here Jess?'

Again, I didn't have an answer. I broke the bread in half and passed one piece to Gillie.

'Let's eat this while we can still chew it.'

Gillie made a start on hers. I went and re-filled the saucepan while there was still enough light enough to see. We dipped the hard bread in the water to soften it a little then when the bread was gone, we drank some of the water.

We each stepped into the trees to relieve ourselves then with nothing left to do we lay back down, side by side, and covered ourselves again with the blankets.

There had been no traffic on the road that day, at least during the hours I spent awake. The next day there must have been a market in the nearest town. Starting in the early hours a steady stream of people passed by some on foot carrying bundles or baskets, others walking beside well laden donkeys and a few on horseback.

I had been sitting in the wagon watching the people passing by since first light. Because we were tucked into the trees in deep shadow, and it was a dull day only a few noticed our little camp. No-one showed any interest in us.

The day seemed endless, we didn't talk much, we drank water to fill our stomachs and fend off the hunger. Towards the end of the day the people from the morning passed back in the opposite direction, then, when they had all gone, the only sounds were the wind in the trees and the movements of small animals, hunting and being hunted in the dark.

I wondered who would come for us, and how much longer we would have to wait.

It was a long, cold night. I slept little and every time the clouds parted and gave enough light to see Gillie, her eyes were open. At some time, we had moved together, and the shared body heat helped us, at last, to sleep.

The day we woke up to was brighter than for many days, bitterly cold but with brittle glittering light. We kept close, hanging on to the body heat as long as possible.

We talked. For some reason Gillie started to tell me about her childhood, about the moving from place to place, meeting old friends, finding work, and staying until the job was done, then moving on. As she talked, I got a strong image of how that life had been.

After she had finished, we were silent for a while, then Gillie said, 'Tell me about your childhood, Jess.'

I closed my eyes and thought about that. 'Childhood? Oh yes, that. The first thing I remember is being in a car and being very frightened, I believe that is because I had been in the back of my parents' car when they were killed in a crash. Anyway, I was being taken to my first foster parents.'

'You were in foster care, I didn't know.'

'No, I don't talk about it.'

I had started, now I wanted to tell Gillie.

'Some of them were alright, I would be with them for a while but then they would want to move or have a holiday and the foster child is just an inconvenience, so they moved me on. One couple said they wanted to teach me to be independent and self-reliant, so I had to do everything, my own washing, ironing, put myself to bed.'

'How old were you then?'

'Eight, I think. When I was fifteen, the couple I was with then, the husband – well, everyone said what a kind man he was – he liked to cuddle, liked me to sit on his lap. I asked to move on. That was my last move, I liked the couple I went to then. I was there until I was eighteen.'

'What happened then?'

I had been gazing into space while I answered Gillie. Now I took deep breath and closed my eyes. 'When a foster child reaches eighteen the money stops, so those people I had been with for three years, called me into the lounge and told me they were sorry, but I would have to move out.'

I turned away to hide my face and rubbed angrily at the tears. Neither of us said anything for a long time.

'I think I'll get us some more water, Gillie.'

I slipped off the back of the wagon, walked to the stream and filled the saucepan. I was on my way back when I heard a horse coming along the road, a large heavy horse, this could be it. Had someone come for us?

I hurried back and reached the edge of the trees just as Tobar slid down from the back of –

not Moonlight, another horse – and ran over to the wagon.

I held back to give mother and son a moment together then went and stood beside the wagon.

After giving Gillie a huge hug Tobar pulled back and looked into her face.

'How are you feeling now, mum?'

'A lot better now son, starving hungry, we ran out of bread ages ago.'

'I nearly forgot. I brought you some sandwiches.'

Tobar reached into the bag he had slung round his body and brought out a sandwich box. 'Here tuck into these while I harness Shadow, then we'll get going.'

Gillie reached a hand to me. 'Come on Jess, share these with me.' I don't think Tobar had realised I was there, the glance he flicked at me was hostile then he looked back at Gillie who was smiling at me.

'Hello Jess.' Guided by his mother he was prepared to be polite even if a little grudgingly.

I climbed back up beside Gillie. 'Hello Tobar, are we ever glad to see you.'

With a reluctant grin Tobar went to bring the horse over and while he guided it into place and started to buckle on the harness we tucked into the sandwiches, lovely fresh bread, and thick juicy ham with a smear of mustard.

When we had finished and had searched the bottom of the box for the last crumbs we sat back and sighed.

'Better?' I said.

'Better.'

We all drank some of the water then I poured the rest away.

Tobar climbed onto the bench and gathered up the driving reins. 'Are you women going to ride up here with me? It will be a rougher ride back there.'

We scrambled out of the back. Gillie said, 'Pull out of the woods first then.'

When Tobar had driven out onto the road Gillie climbed up next to him, I followed her up then as soon as we were settled, we were on our way home.

'How long will this take us?'

'A few hours, we'll be home this evening.'

There wasn't much talking on the way back; we all had a lot on our minds.

The first to break the silence, Gillie said, 'How is Manfri?'

'Camlo took him straight to outpatients, they say it's flu, not pneumonia so not so worrying.'

I could feel the relief radiating from Gillie. Tobar took her hand and gave it a squeeze. He knows, I thought.

As for me, there was no relief. I knew there was nothing left, Camlo had turned his back on me and that was that.

To hammer the point home, Tobar leaned forward a little to look past Gillie.

'I'm sorry Jess, Camlo asked me to tell you that he doesn't want to see you again, he wants you to collect your stuff and leave right away.'

The shocked intake of breath came from Gillie. I turned my face to study the roadside and swallowed hard.

'It's alright, that is what I was going to do anyway, I didn't need telling.'

My voice sounded strange to my ears, thin and remote. I couldn't turn and look at Gillie, I had felt her stiffen and, in my mind, I thanked her, she was still my friend.

The closer we got to home the more I wished we would never arrive, but the wheels kept turning and eventually we rolled out into the camp. Eight in the evening and it was mostly in darkness. The canteen was brightly lit though and as Tobar eased us to a stop the door opened, and Lela walked out followed by Oshina and Miri.

Tobar was helping Gillie down, the girls came over to where I was climbing down from the wagon, stiff and aching after the hours on the road.

'Jess, thank God you're back safe. We have missed you so much.'

I stood still and stared at them more surprised and more touched than I would have believed possible, even more surprised at the tears that were brimming in my eyes.

'I have to leave, get my things, and go. Camlo sent me the message.'

They all stepped up and put their arms round me, Lela said, 'Come on, let's go to your place.'

'Oh, my bag.' I retrieved my bag from the back of the wagon and the four of us went to the place that had been my home. On the way I wiped away the tears. At the door, while I rooted for my key, Lela said, 'when did you last eat?'

'Gillie and I shared the sandwiches Tobar brought.'

Miri said, 'I'll get something. I won't be long.'

She disappeared into the gloom, I unlocked the door, switched on the light and we walked in. Everything was exactly as I had left it.

Oshina asked the question I had dreaded. 'Why did you go, Jess?'

'To find Camlo, to explain everything and ask him to take me back.'

'No, not this time, before, when Camlo came back with Rose, you just left.'

So, I told them, about how I had mistaken their body language, about what Jenny had said and then everything that happened after.

Miri arrived back with burger and chips. While I ate Lela told her my story. When I had finished, I looked at them.

'I am going to miss you all so much, I never had any friends before, not proper friends I could trust.'

Miri, put a hand on my arm. 'Must you go?'

I nodded, 'Camlo wants me to go, I can at least do that for him. Can I keep in touch?'

'Please, we want to know what you do, where you go.'

'We could meet up, outside the camp of course.'

'You'll stay near then?'

I hadn't given it a thought, now I knew. 'Yes, I will stay nearby.'

I changed into jeans and a sweater then presented the pile of soiled and shabby clothes to Lela. 'Sorry, they have had rather a hard time of it. Look let's exchange numbers and please let me know how Manfri gets on.

When we had done that and the only things, we had left to say were too complicated to put into words I collected up all my stuff, shoving it anyhow into any bag I could find. I handed the key to Lela.

'Give this back to – someone for me. I had better go now.'

I put my stuff into the boot of my car and walked round to the driver's door. We hugged our goodbyes, I climbed in behind the wheel, the engine started first time so, waving goodbye, I drove away down the track.

Chapter 20

I drove without thought, hardly able to breathe I felt so crushed, this was it, I had left.

I ended up in Chichester. I found myself a hotel, took a long hot shower and washed all the travel dust from my hair then I fell into bed. I slept until mid-morning then I lay in bed and decided what I would do with the immediate future, further ahead could take care of itself.

I had said that I would stay near and yes, I would do that, though not too near, that would be too much like stalking. That brought a smile to my face, no that wouldn't do at all. Should I draw an imaginary circle and start looking for somewhere to rent inside that space?

I had fired up my laptop and started looking at a map of the area when a thought drifted into my mind, I could probably afford to buy a place.

I sat back and gave that some thought. The contents of Phillip's accounts had been transferred into my new account and Simon had said that there would be more when his shares and other investments had been processed. I had put all that out of my mind, now I began to wonder.

I logged into my online banking and checked the balance. Then I sat rather still for a while. Oh well, I could buy a house all right.

I was hungry, the share of Gillie's sandwiches and burger and chips were the only things I had eaten in over two days. I checked my watch; the hotel restaurant would still be serving lunch, so I dressed quickly and went looking for food.

I ordered prawns in tempura batter with sweet chilli dip and pasta with spicy sausage in a tomato sauce then I had lemon sponge and custard.

While I ate, I wondered at how the body still demands feeding even while the whole of your insides is squeezed into a tight ball of misery. I finished with a coffee then I arranged to stay at the hotel for at least another week, collected my coat and went out to look for a house.

I trawled the estate agents for the rest of the afternoon and didn't find anything that appealed until, as I was about to give up and go back to the hotel, I was shown details of a pretty, modern house with a good-sized garden. It was located on a country lane a few miles south of Midhurst. I arranged for a viewing the next morning.

Back at the hotel I phoned Lela to ask about Manfri. She told me that Camlo had spent all night at the hospital with him. In the morning he popped home to see Gillie, to shower and change and then went back.

He told them that Manfri was making good progress and would soon be home. Manfri's weakened condition, which they put down to depression, was the reason he was so ill.

I asked her to pass on to Manfri my delight that he was getting better, not to Camlo.

The next morning, I drove towards Midhurst to look at the house. Although my heart wasn't in the search, I did like the house, it was a manageable size with three bedrooms. There was a pleasing flow to the rooms, and it sat back from the road, secluded and private. I made an offer which was accepted. I moved in two weeks before Christmas.

I saw the girls many times during this time, we shopped for the house and spent evenings in the local pub talking over a bottle of wine. They kept me up to date with life in the camp. Manfri was home and recovering, he had been worried that when he was better Camlo would leave again but he had promised to stay.

In fact, Camlo had taken on some of the responsibility of running the camp, as well as working at the hotel, until Manfri was strong enough to resume leadership. When he had first disappeared, the day-to-day management had been transferred to Jason. Lela had acted as his part-time assistant and continued now with Camlo.

'In fact, I have ideas I would like to try, with

Camlo's agreement of course, for a start I want to run murder mystery weekends, that sort of thing could bring in more business. What do you think Jess?'

'I like the murder mystery idea a lot. One thing has occurred to me, there are a couple of wagons parked out behind the canteen, ones that were once lived in but are now unused, how about doing them up then putting them out on the field and renting them out. Offer them as 'An Authentic Gypsy Experience.' We had laughed at that, but I could see the idea appealed to her.

We had discussed whether they should let the people in the camp know that we kept in touch. Miri had said why not, there was no reason not to, but we agreed they wouldn't tell that I was only a half hour or so away. I didn't want Camlo to know.

Christmas day was long and lonely, Lela, Miri and Oshina were spending the day with their families. I avoided the TV, cooked myself a chicken bake and opened a bottle of wine, then I went to bed and settled down with a book.

I was reading a lot. I had always enjoyed a good book, now I used reading as a way to block out the real world. I would read into the early hours, until I was so exhausted that I could sleep.

The girls came to visit a couple of days after Christmas, Lela had spoken to Camlo about running murder mystery weekends and got the go ahead. She had spent a while researching what other people did and wanted to start right in. She wanted us all to help her with the planning.

We spent hours working on a plot, the method of murder, when and where the 'body' would be deposited.

Oshina said she thought the body should be in the resident's lounge, to be discovered after dinner on the first evening. The guests could 'investigate' the next day and gather together before dinner to compare theories. Anyone naming the correct suspect would be given a bottle of champagne.

Lela said. 'I want to delay the murder until lunchtime on the Saturday. I will tell them that the murderer and the victim can be anyone in the hotel, guests, or staff, which will give them all plenty of time to watch each other and work out their favourite suspects.'

Miri said, 'There would have to be clues for them to find and the staff would have to be primed with answers to the most likely questions. Then you'll need someone to play the part of the murderer, blend with the clients, look guilty at the right moments and of course you will need a body.'

Lela grinned round at us. 'I was thinking three people, the body, the murderer and the police officer who interviews the clients and then arrives teatime on Sunday for the denouement.'

We looked round at each other, Miri said, 'It's a set up. You planned this you cheeky moo.'

'But you will do it won't you? It will be such fun, the four of us working together. I would be much more confident if you were all there with me.'

'I would love to Lela but what if Camlo came along? Having me there might be too close to the camp.'

'I can tell him before-hand and anyway we're good friends and I would like to have you there.'

The weekend was set for the end of January. It was publicised in the local papers, we put up posters round the area and plastered it all over the hotel's web site and social media.

Oshina was to play the murderer. Miri the body and I would be the police inspector. Lela as assistant manager would ensure that everything went smoothly and deal with any hitches.

We were all looking forward to it, regarding it as a mix of fancy dress party and amateur theatre. When we had all the plans set and were sitting round my table feeling pleased with ourselves Miri nudged my elbow and nodded towards Lela. She was sitting elbows on the table, gazing into space.

'What are you planning, Lela?'

'Let's do a period one next time, with everyone in fancy dress, maybe roman, what do you think.'

Miri threw a pencil at her. 'Let's get this one over with first shall we.'

It was the Friday of the chosen weekend, and we were as ready as we could be. Ten people, four couples and two singles, had booked and arrived. Two of the couples were friends, they had arrived together. There were two young couples, an elderly man, and a middle-aged woman. All the staff were primed, we were ready. Friday's dinner and the Saturday morning breakfast would be uninterrupted, to lead the customers in and to build some suspense. Saturday lunch would be when it all kicked off.

Both Miri and Oshina were booked in as clients, ready to play their parts. I wouldn't be needed until after the 'murder' but because we didn't see the point of me being half an hour's drive away, I had a make-shift bed made up in my old office.

We gathered in there when the clients had all gone to their beds. Lela was pleased, so far it was going well, the group had talked together, politely, during dinner, but you could see them sizing up the opposition.

'Tomorrows the day, it should be exciting, right let's get some sleep.'

Breakfast came and went. The clients passed the morning, first, by looking round the hotel, familiarising themselves with the layout, then some of them congregated in the lounge and socialised. Miri sat in the lounge with a book, pretending to read but keeping a close watch on the others.

At a moment when only Miri and one other person were in the lounge, she sent Oshina a text.

Oshina joined her and the pair of them staged an argument, beginning with an angry dialogue in hushed tones and escalating into a brief shouted exchange.

Lela and I were keeping a watch on the rest of the clients to see if any of them had also heard, between us we observed three people pause and pay close attention. We wondered if the information would spread rapidly and that soon everyone would know about the row or if the ones who knew would keep that nugget to themselves.

Lunch time. The dining room was ready, the table laid, the clients were taking their seats. When everyone apart from Miri had arrived, the waiter would count to a hundred then run into the room and shout out, 'There's been a murder.' That was the plan.

It didn't happen like that because that was where everything went terribly wrong. There was a murmur of conversation, the room was waiting for the last four diners to arrive: one of the couples, Miri and Oshina. I was watching from the kitchen, behind the window in the service door.

The missing couple walked in. They smiled apologetically at the others before walking to their places. As they took their seats a scream broke into the quiet of the room. Everyone instantly knew that this was no theatrical scream, there was true grief and shock in the intensity, the way when all breath was gone there was a pause for more air and then the scream became a wail, then sobs.

Lela and I reached the stairs together and pounded up them towards where the scream had come from. We looked at each other, I saw the panic on her face, I could hardly breathe.

On the top landing we found Miri on her knees, she was clutching Oshina in her arms and rocking backwards and forwards. There was blood everywhere.

'Where is the blood coming from, has she got a pulse?' I realised that I was shouting.

'I don't know Jess, I don't know.'

I had my phone out. I grabbed a wrist and tried to feel if there was a pulse there. 'Police and an ambulance, there has been a stabbing.'

The voice at the other end of the line was so calm, I answered her questions feeling like I was in a bubble of silence. From a long way away I could hear Miri's anguished wailing and Lela shouting at the clients who were clustering round, pushing, and shoving, eager to see: 'Go away please, all of you, this is real, go, get out, can't you understand English? Fuck off.'

I heard myself giving details, describing the scene. I thought I was in control until I saw a face peering round the corner of the stairs. Still holding tight to my phone, I stood up and ran towards the stairs, I aimed a belter of a kick at the curious face. The face disappeared and my foot connected with the edge of the wall.

I went back and knelt beside Oshina again, the voice on the phone was telling me that an ambulance was on the way, and could I find a pulse, was the person breathing?

'I don't know, I don't think so, please hurry.'

Miri was still holding Oshina, she was sitting on the floor and had pulled Oshina close. I went and sat with my arms round both of them. Lela came and joined us, all of us holding tight to each other.

Someone else had taken charge downstairs, a strong competent voice giving orders. I heard sirens, vehicles driving up at speed, stopping outside then running feet. The paramedics arrived first.

'Move away, give us space.' I saw the look they exchanged. 'You shouldn't have moved her.'

They were fast and professional, for endless minutes they worked to save her, in the end Oshina was placed on a stretcher and taken away. We tried to go with them but a policeman arrived and put out an arm to bar the way.

'Sorry ladies. Let them do their job. I'm afraid you can't go anywhere until you have talked to us.' He kept us there until we heard the ambulance drive away. 'Come on downstairs now.'

We followed the policeman down the stairs, at the bottom he looked us over.

'I think maybe you had better clean up a bit

first.'

He waited for us while we went into the staff toilets and washed off as much of the blood as we could, moving like zombies. The tears still falling, our shocked silence broken by sobs and occasional keening cries. One of the others brought us those white suits they wear at crime scenes.

'Here put these on.'

He was waiting for us when we had changed. We were ushered into the clients lounge. We were holding ourselves together, our grief was private, not to be shared with strangers. Extra chairs had been found and everyone who had been in the place had been gathered there. The clients, untouched by grief were trying to hide that they considered all this drama an unexpected bonus. Someone had called the camp and Camlo had arrived. He sat apart from everyone else, he looked tired and grey, his face rigid with anxiety.

One by one we were taken into the office where the police were taking statements. While I waited, I made a mental list of clients and staff. The vision of that still body being carried off with the sheet pulled all the way up over her face was still there in the back of my mind. I swallowed hard and blinked back the tears.

When we had all made our statements, we were free to go. The clients went back to their rooms. We stood, uncertain, in our white overalls.

Camlo walked over to us, he spoke to the girls. 'Come on I'll take you home.'

He waited a little apart while we said our goodbyes. Silently we gripped hands, embraced, and then Lela and Miri followed Camlo. At the door Lela turned, she managed a bit of a smile. 'I'll call you tomorrow.' I raised a hand to them and then they were all gone. I collected my coat and went back to my house.

Chapter 21

I made myself breakfast the next morning, then struggled to get any past the lump in my throat. I managed a few mouthfuls then gave up. I took my coffee into the lounge and stood by the window watching the raindrops splashing in the bird bath.

My phone rang. I grabbed it from the table. 'Hello.'

'Jess, its Lela, I just wanted to hear your voice,' Her voice sounded strange, lifeless.

'How are you, and everyone?'

'Her family are in a bad way.' There was a long pause. 'We all are. We can't arrange the funeral yet, not until after the post-mortem. I'll let you know when, you will come, won't you?'

'Yes, I'll be there, just let me know. Keep in touch Lela, please.'

'I won't let you go. Alright?'

'Alright. Speak soon.'

'Yes, speak soon.'

I clicked my phone off and slowly placed it back on the table then I sat and let my thoughts wander. After a while I went and found a notebook and a pencil. I made a coffee and settled back on the sofa.

Struggling to find a place to start I settled on simply writing Oshina at the top of the first page. That freed my mind, and I started jotting random thoughts.

*

Was Oshina the intended victim or just in the wrong place at the wrong time?

If she was the intended victim, why? There must be a reason, a motive. If there is a reason someone must know.

I sat back and considered what I had written. Then I continued.

The police will be considering the same questions, keep your nose out. But it wouldn't hurt to keep my eyes open, as long as I don't confuse the issue.

This will be for Oshina.

*

I drew a line under that list, turned over to a clean page then put the notepad and pencil into a handy drawer, ready for any thoughts or memories. I would jot them all down as soon as they came to me and try to make sense of them.

My coffee had gone cold, so I took it back into the kitchen and poured it down the sink. Suddenly restless I walked back through the lounge picking up my phone, bag and keys on the way and my coat from the hall cupboard. Outside

I threw my coat and bag into the back of the car climbed in behind the wheel and turned on the engine.

Initially I just drove, after a while I realised, I was on the outskirts of Brighton, so I drove on into the town. On my way along the seafront a watery sun found its way through the clouds and glittered on the waves and the wet road. I found a place in a crowded car park and walked out into the town. Shopping. That was what I would do.

An hour later I struggled back to the car loaded down with bags which I loaded into the boot then I went looking for food. After an excellent lasagne at Donatello, I worked it off with a long walk by the sea. For a long time, I sat on a sheltered bench just gazing out to sea. Then, feeling cleansed and chilled to the bone, I went back to the car and started back home.

As I turned from the lane into my drive, I saw a familiar car parked in front of my garage. My heart rocketed into my throat, then, as though I needed to advertise my arrival, as I pulled up beside him, I stalled the motor and the car jerked forward.

I could see Camlo behind the wheel. As I sat trying to compose myself, his door opened, and he climbed out. He leaned against his car and looked towards me. Oh god, if only I could read his expression. I had to move at some time, so I let go of the steering wheel, clenched my hands in an effort to stop them shaking, then went to join Camlo.

He greeted me with, 'Well, you don't get any easier to find.'

'I wasn't expecting you to look for me.' I walked past him and unlocked the door, opened it, and walked indoors. Camlo followed me in.

'I'm making coffee, would you like one?'

'Yes please.'

He peered round, identified the lounge, and walked right in. I went into the kitchen and clattered about making the coffee trying to sound nonchalant while I steadied myself. By the time I carried the drinks into the lounge I was in control. I switched on the light to banish the shadows, then I sat opposite Camlo. There were a few awkward seconds when our eyes almost met and then we both quickly looked away.

'How is everyone, have they said when they plan to do the post-mortem? Lela sounded awful this morning.'

There was a despairing shake of his head. 'No, no idea yet. If only the family could plan the funeral that would give them something to focus on. The camp is an incredibly sad place. Lela is blaming herself. She thinks that running a murder themed event was somehow the trigger for whoever attacked Oshina.'

'Oh Christ.'

'I feel like I have to do something Jess, talk to someone, that's why I came to see you.' He looked me straight in the eye. 'Do you think it was a random attack?'

'I'm not a great believer in random attacks.'

'So, you think Oshina was specifically targeted?'

'Yes.' I went to the drawer and took out the notepad; I walked back and handed it to him. he spent a couple of minutes looking through it.

I said, 'I don't think either of us can go round questioning people, the police need to do that. Because they are trained for it and because when it is all over, they will be gone and any resentment they cause will go with them.'

'I have been trying to think, turning it over in my mind, hour after hour. She was just such a nice person. I knew her all her life and I don't think I ever heard of her being unkind, it wasn't who she was.'

I had nothing to add to that, we both sat in silent thought.

'Something she knew?'

Camlo shrugged then laid back in the chair with his eyes closed. I sat and thought back through the time I had spent in the camp, right back to the evening when I had pushed my bike up the track in the dusk of a wet day and Camlo had stepped out from the trees and challenged me.

'What?' He had opened his eyes and was watching me; he must have seen something in my face.

'Nothing, I was remembering the night I came

to the camp, and you took me prisoner.'

A fleeting smile lit his face and just as quickly was gone. I looked away and took a sip of coffee to hide my emotions.

When I glanced back, I was surprised to see that Camlo sitting forward in his chair, I could almost see the air crackling with tension.

'That's right. I thought you were Sinfi Miller. It was only a couple of weeks before then that she sneaked into camp and pinned a page of abuse and threats on the office door.'

'Why? '

'Her family belonged to the tribe, there was Sinfi, she was only a little girl then, her mother and her father. He was always a problem, argumentative with a quick temper, especially after a few drinks. Because we knew him well, we all knew not to let him drink too much, he had never attacked any of us.

The problems started when he went out into the world. One night about ten years ago he got into an argument in a pub which escalated into a fight. During the struggle he pulled out a knife and killed the man

'He didn't get away without injury and when he was seen coming back into camp staggering and trailing blood, Manfri was informed. A group of us went to see him, we found him washing the blood out of his clothes.

When we demanded an explanation, he admitted that he had knifed a man but claimed that he had been attacked. He tried to persuade us to shelter him. We said that if he had been attacked there would be witnesses and he had to go to the police. In the end we had to take him prisoner, when we arrived at the police station, they were already looking for him.

'He was put on trial and sent to prison. The wife and Sinfi decided to leave the camp and went to live near the prison. It was Oshina who saw him that night and told us. Because she was ill and couldn't sleep, she was kneeling on her bed looking out at the stars.' Camlo's voice, full of distress, had faded almost to a whisper.

'Why look for revenge so many years later?'

'He died in prison, he got into a fight with several other inmates. One of them cut him with a knife he had made from a tin can. How ironical is that. He got blood poisoning, and it killed him. That was when the threats were made.'

'But she didn't do anything then, why now?'

'I don't know. I'll go to the police station tomorrow and tell them all of this, see if they think it is worth looking into.'

He looked towards the window, it had grown dark while we were talking and the wind had got up, it would be a wild night. It was painful to see the sorrow and exhaustion on his face, without thinking I reached and touched the back of the hand that was clenched on the arm of the chair.

The hand jerked away, and he looked at me his face rigid with anger. 'Don't touch me.'

I jumped back. 'I'm so sorry.'

'Bit late for that isn't it? You walked out on me. There was no explanation. Then I hear, on the bloody TV news if you please, that you are dead. Your leaving broke my heart then if that wasn't enough, thinking you had died destroyed me. Months later up you pop, all in one piece, lovely as ever. You didn't even have the decency to let me know you were still alive.'

'Now hang on a minute. I waited and waited, all that time, longer than you said you would be gone, then one day there you are, rolling back into camp with that gorgeous woman by your side. If you remember rightly, she gave you a huge hug before she jumped down off the wagon and went to greet everyone. I had thought you would look round to find me, no, you looked down at the ground as though you wanted to avoid seeing me. On top of all that, the final straw, that bloody Jenny stood behind me and said, "look he's brought Rose back with him, I knew he would go back for her one day. He always loved her."

'Of course, I ran away, and you think you know about a broken heart. What is more, I couldn't let you know I was alive because after the fire, I was taken from the hospital straight into a safe house so they could quiz me about the Chinese men who tried to burn me alive.' By this time, we were both on our feet, facing up to each other as though we were in a boxing ring. 'Why would

I let you know I was alive anyway when I knew you were happy with someone else.' The room rang with the sudden silence after our shouting.

'She was married to my best friend, he wanted to go back to the old life, and he took her with him. When I found them, he was dying, the old life killed him. Rose didn't want to stay there, that's all it was. 'His voice was subdued now.

'Gillie told me all that, after we met in Plymouth. That was when I decided to come and find you, to let you know why I ran away.'

'She tried to talk to me, I wouldn't listen. What Chinese men?'

I sat back down, Camlo, rather hesitantly, did the same. I told him everything, right up to me leaving Plymouth. When I run out of things to say I sat and waited for some sort of reaction.

Camlo rested his elbows on his knees, his face in his hands. I heard a huge sigh, then his head lifted, and he looked into my face. His eyes held mine for a second then moved away.

'Christ, what a mess, what a waste.' He stood up and walked towards the door then he stopped with a hand on the door handle. 'You don't have to avoid the camp. You have friends there who would be pleased to see you and I'm glad to know the full story. I'll keep you up to date with any progress.'

He closed the door behind him, I heard him open and close the front door then his car started and moved away.

It was a whole week later and the day of the funeral. The post-mortem had concluded what everyone knew that a person or persons as yet unknown had attacked and killed a young woman named Oshina West, it went on to identify the time and place of the death and that the body had been released for burial.

The service was to be at the village church with drinks and food afterwards in the camp hall. Apart from the Romani, four people Oshina had worked with would be at the service. I would be there to give what support I could to my friends.

I visited the camp, paid my respects to Oshina's family then went for a meal in the canteen with Lela and Miri. Afterwards I paid Manfri a visit. We sat together in his office, and he made me a cup of tea. I thought he was looking well, when I said that to him, he smiled over the top of his teacup.

'It has been good for Camlo, taking responsibility for the camp, and it has stopped him from talking about going away again.'

I smiled back at him.

'He told me he had a long talk with you, cleared the air.'

'More of a long shout actually.'

'Ahh.' After a thoughtful pause he said, 'I understand you have bought a house Jess.'

I nodded. 'I didn't want to be too far away, but because of … well, not too close either.'

'Nonetheless.' He opened a drawer and passed me a key. 'Keep this, use it as and when you want to, it's the key to your room.'

When I left, he walked me to the door. I said, 'Have you spoken to Gillie yet?'

'We speak all the time.'

'Don't be obtuse.'

I kissed his cheek and left. As I walked to my car, I gripped the key tightly then once I was inside, I put it safely into my bag, to keep it safe. That had been three days ago.

Now I was ready to go to the funeral, I picked up my bag and closed the door behind me.

The funeral was awful, I had only been to one before, that one had been for a politician, an acquaintance of Phillip's and had felt impersonal. At that funeral, the small cluster of family at the front of the church had held each other and shed tears but most of the people there had gone to see and be seen.

This was different, Oshina had been loved. The church was crowded with the Romani and full of shared grief. When I joined the silent crowd on their way out of the church, I was going to go home but Lela found me and insisted I went back to the camp with her and Ruslo.

'There is so much food, you can manage just a little of it and a couple of drinks.'

'I have to drive home. I can't get drunk.'

'Who said anything about getting drunk? Anyway, I know Manfri gave you back your key.'

So, I went back to the camp. The hall thronged with people, all eating and drinking, releasing the tension and grief they had been living with. Camlo was there, passing from group to group, talking to people but a little withdrawn.

I sat in a corner and drank it all in, being with these people again. By the end of the evening, I definitely couldn't drive home, not silly drunk but certainly well over the limit. I slipped quietly away and went to my room.

I sat on the bed, the room surrounding me with its comfortable familiarity. Then I went and had a shower. I was wrapped in a towel, combing through my wet hair with my fingers when there was a knock on the door.

Holding on tight to the towel, expecting it would be Lela or Miri, I answered the door. It was Camlo and he was drunk. He walked right in and perched on the edge of the table.

'Ah yes, Jess, I came to let you know I went to the police, I told them what we talked about -- I haven't told you this have I?' I shook my head.

'Interested, yes, definitely interested, they said they would investigate. Thought you would like to know.

'Well thank you Camlo.' I still stood with one hand on the door handle.

He started to leave but when he reached me, he pulled me into his arms and his mouth found mine, fierce and desperate, a long kiss that ended with him pushing me roughly away and striding unsteadily off into the darkness.

Chapter 22

I locked the door, dropped the towel onto the floor and crept between the covers.

'Oh Camlo.' I curled up into a tight ball and let the tears flood into my pillow.

I didn't sleep well, waking frequently then dozing off again. As the morning light started showing through the window I went to the window and watched the early risers starting their day, greeting each other as they set off to work.

The room still felt like home, but it had been empty for ages, it needed a little loving, so I searched out the cleaning materials I had left there, all that time before. I cleaned and polished right through. After giving the window a final rub, I stepped back and admired the result. I would come here and use the room on a regular basis, Manfri wouldn't have given the key to me if I wasn't welcome.

I took a mooch around the camp to re-familiarise myself. Wrapped in my coat and scarf I wandered the familiar paths, pleased to find that it was much the same. I poked my head into the canteen and received a cheery wave from Mary. The aroma of coffee wafted towards me, warm and inviting. I walked on.

I had noticed more cars taking people off to work and there were a couple of others parked where another small area of woodland had been newly cleared. The place was looking more prosperous. On my way back to my car I turned a corner and almost bumped into a familiar figure, she was standing on the path, looking lost and staring into space.

'Hi Lela, I didn't expect to see you today, I thought you would be at work.'

'I'm going in for the afternoon and Camlo's doing this morning. Things are a bit quiet in the hotel now.

'Have you got time to come for a coffee?'

'I'd love one, let's go to the canteen.'

We settled in the furthest corner of the lounge area. I had a good look at Lela. She looked a little pale with huge sad eyes.

'You don't look any better than me you know Jess.'

'No, I don't expect that I do. Are you sleeping?'

'A bit better now thanks. I think we all did her proud yesterday. I didn't see you leave. Did you see how drunk Camlo was? I have never known him get that bad, I don't know how he got off to work this morning.'

'He seemed OK, he went off at the usual time.

I happened to be looking out of the window.' I tried not to notice the expression on Lela's face, concentrating on my coffee. In the end I gave in and put my cup down carefully before I looked her full in the face.

'He came to see me on his way home last night; he told me that he had been to the police.'

'I see, and…?'

'Stop prying you awful woman. Alright, he kissed me, and it wasn't sweet, and it wasn't gentle, then he pushed me away and he left.' My voice had wobbled, and my treacherous eyes had filled with tears. I brushed them away.

'That's good. Drunk or not you have to believe it was a start, Jess.'

I shook my head. I wasn't going to read anything into the actions of a drunken man.

Lela changed the subject. 'A few of us think someone from the camp gave the murderer details of that night, about who would be working. I can't get my head round that.'

So that was what was bothering her. 'That's not good, it would be a tragedy if people started suspecting each other. Have the police given any hint to what they think happened? Do they believe Oshina was targeted?'

Lela shrugged. 'They're not giving anything away. Camlo gave them the address that Sinfi and her mother moved to. I suppose the first we will hear of it will be if they arrest anyone.'

We finished our coffee and Lela looked at her

watch. 'It's time I got off to work. Come often and use your room, we will have to plan a few nights out.' She stood up to leave so I got up and we walked out of the door together, said our goodbyes and went our separate ways. I went back to my room and picked up the bag with my change of clothes. I smiled at the room before walking out through the door and locking it carefully behind me.

As I drove back to the house my mind wandered through the last couple of weeks. I was curious about the people who had booked in for that weekend. Logic said that the murderer was one of them. No-one had reported seeing anyone unfamiliar in or around the hotel.

There had been four couples and two singles, I considered the singles first, an elderly guy, skinny and stooped, no not him, he could never overcome Oshina. The other single was a rather large woman, she had been sitting at the dining table well before the lunch was due to be served.

Not either of them so what about the couples? Well of course there were the newlyweds, totally absorbed in each other. The other young couple, smart with expensive clothes, had appeared to be well into the spirit of the weekend. Notebooks in hand they had explored and discussed possible hiding places and escape routes, made sketches, written notes and were constantly watching the other guests, waiting for something to happen. This had made them quite conspicuous; the other, less obsessed clients had been quietly amused by them.

The last two couples had been in the lounge, their rather loud conversations easily heard, before walking into the dining room.

Which had really narrowed it down to the newly married couple. The ones who were the last to walk into the dining room. I searched my memory for descriptions of them and found that I had registered their behaviour rather than anything else.

I found a field entrance and pulled off the road then took my phone out of my bag and rang the hotel. I was surprised when Lela answered – I had expected Donna to be manning the phone.

'Jess? Is everything alright?'

'Yes, I was wondering, can you give me the address that young couple gave? The newly wed ones.'

'The ones at that weekend?'

'Yes.'

She went silent while she checked the register.

'It's a Morton address, 23, Cornfields, Morton. Do you want the post code as well?'

'Might as well if you have it.'

I wrote it all down on the back of an envelope. Thanked Lela and told her I would contact her soon. I stared at the address, was I going to follow up such a random idea? Bloody right I was. I had no idea how to find Morton, so I put the post code into the sat nav and let it lead me there.

Morton turned out to be a small town of new build houses, flats, and shops that had sprung up round a core of ancient cottages. I drove through avenues of tree shaded detached properties then streets of semi-detached houses.

The place I had been looking for was one of those, a small semi, the last at the end of a row of increasingly shabby houses, where the road led back into farming land. Fields of grazing sheep, broken by patches of woodland. There was a decent sized wood right next to the house.

I drove on by for a mile or so then turned back and drove past in the other direction. In the town centre I put the car in a car park and went to explore. I huddled down into my coat, it started to rain, light and persistent and I was cold. I found a high street with a collection of shops, an Italian restaurant and two cafes. I went into one of the cafes and sat at a table by the window. I ordered a brie, bacon and sweet chilli panini and a coffee.

The waitress brought my lunch to my table. I ate while watching the people passing by. I didn't believe I had much chance of recognising anyone in the crowds and I didn't, but the food was good, and the café was dry. I lingered as long as I dared then walked round the shops. I found a warm hat that covered my ears and an extra sweater to put on under my coat.

By the time I had completed a tour of all the shops, lingering to examine the goods, I stepped out into a gloomy dusk. The rain had stopped, and the temperature was dropping. With my hat pulled down low, avoiding the puddles and the patches of light from the streetlamps, I made my way back to the house.

At first the roads were busy with people making their way home, by the time I reached the house only the occasional car passed by. Good, if Sinfi, her mother and maybe even the young man: the one who had played the husband, were living there they should surely be home by now on such a bleak winter night.

There was a car parked outside that hadn't been there earlier and I could see lights in the downstairs windows. It wasn't dark enough to get close to the windows to see inside so I walked on and when out of sight of the house I turned off the road, into the wood. Among the trees it was much darker. Slowly, as quietly as I could, I worked my way back through the trees, ignoring the showers of drops every time I brushed against a branch, until I had an unobstructed view of the house.

I felt quite pleased with myself, with luck I would find out if this Sinfi was the female half of the couple at the hotel. The last thing I expected was the whisper that came from just behind me.

'What the hell do you think you are playing at?'

'Camlo?'

'You were expecting someone else?'

'Don't be so bloody smart you sarcastic…'

A pause, then in a subdued tone, 'you're right, sorry, I don't know why I keep doing that. Let's start again, why are you here?'

'I want to see if Sinfi was the girl at the hotel.'

'That's why I'm here too. Oh well as you're here you may as well stay. We had better wait a while before we try to get closer.'

It felt strange, in the wet dusk, making polite conversation with the man who had rejected me so completely. We talked about the hotel and the camp, almost like we used to. When we ran out of things to say there was a period of silence before Camlo said, 'it's quite dark now. Ready?'

'Ready.'

'Come on then and try not to make any noise.'

'What if someone sees us?'

'Then we pretend we've had a row and you walked out on me. You can shout at me all you like. OK?'

In the dark wintry night, a spark of warmth broke through, and I smiled to myself.

We were almost out of the trees, moving closer to the house when the front door opened and a figure stepped through, brightly lit, then turned and waited. We didn't need to identify the man who stepped out after her because we knew her.

I whispered, 'That's her, the one from the hotel.'

We stood perfectly still and watched them get into the car and drive away.

After they had gone Camlo said, 'She's the image of her mother. That's Sinfi.'

Stepping out of the trees we moved right to the edge of the road and looked at the rear lights growing smaller, then there was a swing away and headlights coming towards us. Not fast but deliberately, they had turned the car and were coming back.

'Push me or hit me.'

I bunched my hands at my sides, took an aggressive step forward and lashed out, catching his face a stinging slap. As the car drove slowly past us, I screamed out at him. 'You bastard.' Then I turned my back on him, walking away.

I kept on walking until the car, picking up speed, had turned a corner and gone.

Camlo caught me up. 'You didn't have to make it so real.'

'When they walked out, they saw us watching them, didn't they?'

'I think they did, yes. Let's hope they didn't recognise us, anyway there's nothing we can do about that now. Where's your car?'

Camlo walked with me back to the car park. He had parked in a side street, so he said goodbye and left. Rather weary and distressed I started the motor and drove home, the heater in the car bringing a welcome warmth.

By the time I had taken a shower and made a mug of hot chocolate I was ready to crawl into bed. However, once I had drunk the chocolate I lay, sleepless, in the dark. My mind kept trawling through not just that day but everything, all the recent sad and tragic days.

I heard a car turn slowly onto the gravel of the drive. It stopped, a door opened and closed, then, after a long pause, long enough for me to begin doubting my ears, there was a soft knock on my front door.

I went to the window and peeped round the edge of the curtain. I recognised the car. Taking my dressing gown from the hook on the back of the door I put it on as I walked downstairs. The knock didn't come again, the bloom of light in the hall would tell him that I was on my way.

I took a deep steadying breath and then I unlocked and opened the door. Camlo stood on the step. He raised a hand from his side in an unspoken appeal. I stepped back and aside, inviting him in. He took off his coat as he walked past me, dropped it on the chair and stood there while I closed the door.

I waited for him to say something because I really needed to know why he was there in my hall. Then I noticed that Camlo had shaved since he said goodbye to me in the Morton car park.

He still hadn't moved and wouldn't meet my eyes. So, scared of ruining everything again, I took a step closer, reached out and touched him gently on an arm. Slowly and gently Camlo gathered me into his arms. I breathed in the scent of him and leaned my head on his shoulder.

I could feel both our hearts beating, strong and fast. Leaning back a little, at last our eyes met. The emotion I saw there would have had me in tears if he hadn't kissed me. At first the touch of his lips, still cool from the cold night outside, was hesitant and gentle. Seeking reassurance, needing a welcome from me. I forgot all my fears and let my body respond instinctively. Feeling my response, Camlo pulled me closer, now our kiss was pure passion.

When we pulled apart, shaken and breathless, I was sure even the air around us was vibrating. I slipped the lock on the door and took Camlo's hand. Without a word I led him up the stairs.

Now I could see the desire in his eyes, powerful enough to drown in. I could barely breathe, my need for him was overwhelming. The hands that slipped inside my dressing gown were eager and demanding. He breathed in my ear, 'Jess.' just the once. We stumbled to the bed, and without thought or plan, at last, we made love.

Afterwards I cried. All my carefully constructed barriers had been broken down. Those months living with the pain of loss, wiped away by the man who held me close, soothed me, shed his own tears, and shared with me the joy of love rediscovered.

We talked for hours, until we each understood – and forgave. Repairing the damage I had done. We had so much to catch up on, so much still to learn. We made more love and talked more and then at last we slept. As I slipped into sleep, an echo of our lovemaking shivered through me and melted my bones again. I hadn't realised it could be like that.

I woke when Camlo climbed out of bed to go to the bathroom. I watched him walk out, shadowy in the dim winter light. On the way back he peered through the curtain before getting back in bed.

'It's a cold day, there's a thick frost out there. What? What are you grinning at?'

'You, here in my bed, walking naked round the room like that. Do you have any idea how gorgeous you are? Or how much I love you?'

Camlo lifted onto an elbow and looked down at me.

'I won't ever let you go again, not now.'

I reached up, wound my fingers into his hair and pulled his lips down to mine. As we kissed the alarm on Camlo's phone went off, with a sigh of frustration he rolled over and turned it off.

'We'll have to wait until later.'

'I smiled, 'sure, we have plenty of time, you get ready for work, and I'll get us some breakfast. Is toast, ok?'

'Toast and coffee would be great, have you got marmalade?'

'Of course.'

Why don't you come with me today and we can plan what to do next, how we can present our latest information to the police, now we know for sure Sinfi is the killer.'

'I'd like that. Look, we know it was her, but we have no real proof to take to the police.'

'It's a start. I'm sure the police will get there, but I'd like to feel we did something to help.' He rolled out of bed, flashed me one of his vivid smiles and headed into the bathroom.

The coffee was made and a pile of toast on the table when Camlo walked into the kitchen. I had almost finished eating so I popped in the last mouthful and picked up my cup.

'Help yourself. If I'm coming with you, I have to get ready, I won't be long.'

In the bedroom I put my cup on the bedside table and went for a shower. When I was dressed and ready, I checked the time, I had time to wash up the breakfast stuff, so I hurried into the kitchen to find that Camlo was putting away the last plate.

'You didn't have to do that but thank you.'

'No problem, here give me your cup. There's no rush but I need to go to the camp first to change.'

We collected our coats and walked out into a cold February morning. A few clouds had moved in from the north, small and harmless looking but scudding along at a brisk pace, followed by a thick bank of cloud. Cursing, Camlo turned on the motor and set the air to blow towards the windscreen then he scraped the ice from all the glass.

Settling himself back in his seat he said, 'I

wouldn't be surprised if it snowed later.'

We made the journey in good time, as we turned onto the track he said, 'I think I have time to check in with my dad, will you come with me, we can tell him about us.' I smiled and nodded, feeling a bit emotional. Camlo stopped outside the office and took my hand as we walked to the door.

When Manfri opened the door, he said. 'Yes, what can I do for you?' The slow smile that spread across his face showed that he understood perfectly well why we were there. 'Funny thing, I called round to see you last night, couldn't get an answer.' He opened the door wide and stood aside to let us pass then closing it behind us stood and waited for one of us to speak.

'We want you to be the first to know, dad, Jess and me, we're back together again.' The smile on Camlo's face and his arm round my shoulders said more than his words.

Manfri's voice was husky. 'I'm delighted son, about time too.' He hugged Camlo and then me.

'You're a fine one to talk.' I said to him giving him an extra squeeze.

'Anyway dad, there's something else, Jess and I did a little snooping. We went to the address. The one the young couple used when they checked in that weekend. We were watching the house when they came out and drove away. We both recognised her. It was Sinfi Miller.'

'Good work. Give me the address, I'll phone the police if you like and let them know. We'll get her yet.' Manfri's expression showed the same relief and satisfaction that we all shared.

Chapter 23

We left and walked to Camlo's rooms. I sat on the bed while he changed into a suit from his jeans and sweater, I watched him, marvelling at the miracle that had so unexpectedly transformed my life.

When he was ready, he stopped in front of me and held out a hand. 'Come on, let's go to work.'

Climbing into his car and looking at his face as we drove down the track gave me a weird sense of Deja Vue, no not Deja Vue, these memories were real. I had made this same short journey with Camlo so many times, so long ago and yet here I was, again.

It was another disturbing feeling, driving up to the hotel. My last visit was when I had collected Lela, Miri and Oshina from the camp and we had arrived, all taking at once and bubbling with excitement, to prepare for a weekend of fun. Before that I had last been here with Camlo on the day Pellow found me.

We went into Camlo's office. Before he had even started on the emails Donna arrived wanting his help with a problem booking. For the next two hours he was totally engrossed, so while he worked, I occupied myself quietly in the corner playing games on my phone, but my eyes kept straying back to him. I couldn't help it.

I ran through in my mind the very few times I had seen Camlo since leaving the camp, incredibly, almost eighteen months before. First there was the search, then I had watched him ride away on Shadow, taking a desperately ill Manfri home. Even that had been several months ago. Then nothing until the dreadful day we lost Oshina, when he had briefly appeared to deal with the police and take the girls home. There had been that drunken kiss. The day he had arrived unexpectedly at my house to talk through his worries, and then there was the previous night, our first night. That memory stirred a thrill of electricity that caught at my breath.

Back in the past, when we found him, he looked every inch the young Gypsy he would have been if they had stayed. Working boots and trousers, a striped shirt with the sleeves rolled up to his elbows, a small red scarf tied round his neck. There had been dark, heavy stubble on his chin and round his mouth and a thick mop of uncut hair that fell almost to his eyes.

Yet, there in front of me, the same young man in a very different role, smart suit, styled hair, running a business. He had moved between those very different worlds with total ease, he felt at home in both of them.

At last, he sat back in his chair and regarded me with an amused smile. 'I can feel you doing that you know.'

'What?'

'Watching me.'

'You're worth watching. Do you mind?'

'No. Except you make it hard to concentrate. You make me want to lay you down and make love to you right here, right now.'

I was actually looking round for somewhere suitable when Camlo took me by the hand and pulled me up to my feet.

'Coffee, that's what we need and something to eat. Come on.'

Donna was the only person in the staff canteen. She seemed unsurprised to see me with Camlo. We chatted briefly while she finished her tea and sandwich.

'I had better get back to the desk. Delighted to see you back Jess, it's about time.' She patted Camlo on the shoulder and made for the door.

After she had gone, Camlo and I exchanged a grin. I said, 'do all the staff show you that much respect?'

'Yes. That's about average.'

At the end of the day, as we walked out to the car he said, 'I want to go back to the camp, to check if they have heard anything from the police, why don't you stay tonight, and I'll drive you home in the morning. I'm not working in the hotel tomorrow so no problem.'

I didn't know if he found that simple suggestion as thrilling as I did. I spent the journey home thinking about another night with Camlo, feeling a thrill of anticipation. I looked at his face and there was a slight smile that I hoped meant he was thinking much the same.

He parked by the office, we left the car there and tried the office door. Locked.

'Right Jess, where do you think we'll find him?'

'I think either at Gillie's place or in the canteen.'

'Let's try Gillie first. We can tell her about us.'

'I think he has already told her and Tobar, plus anyone else he has happened to speak to.'

We stopped at Gillie's place. She wasn't home either, so we headed for the canteen. Sure, enough, they were both there with Tobar. They had just started on their dinners, fish, and chips all round. They spotted us and waved us over. Tobar called out, 'Hey you two, great news. Drag some more chairs up and join us.'

We found two chairs and sat down. I sat beside Gillie, who took my hand and squeezed it. 'So happy for you both.'

She said that with such simple sincerity, I put my arm round her and hugged her. 'Thank you, Gillie, from you that means the world to me.' I glanced over at Camlo, where he sat on the other side of the table. The acceptance from the people he was closest to obviously made him happy.

Camlo turned to Manfri, 'I was wondering, what reaction you had from the police when you told them about Sinfi.'

'Ah yes, it took me a few minutes to explain, but once they got the hang of it, they seemed eager to follow it up. I asked them to keep us in the loop so we might hear something soon.'

They started talking about our little spying trip, I had seen Miri waving like an idiot from the lounge area. Lela, who had her back to me turned round and started as well. I told Gillie I would be back and went to see them.

'Wonderful news, Jess.' That was Miri.

Lela added, 'We heard this morning, we hoped you would call in so we could tell you how pleased we are. So, Camlo stayed the whole night. You must have really worn him out.' Her grin was wide and wicked. I didn't react to her teasing, beyond raising my eyebrows and grinning back. They both laughed joyfully. I stayed a few minutes, just passing the time with good friends then left and went back to the others.

Manfri was putting his phone away, his mood had changed. We all just waited for him to speak.

'That was the police, they went to that address. She wasn't there, none of them were, the house was stripped and empty.'

Camlo and I looked at each other. I said, 'Bloody hell! She saw us, instead of getting useful information we let her see us and he took that as a sign to get out.'

'We don't know that, she would have realised that the police would investigate everyone there that night and pinpoint her as suspicious, she had to disappear.'

I said, 'think of it this way, innocent people wouldn't have run like that. The police have to believe they're after the right people, they will keep looking.'

Manfri nodded, 'As long as we get them in the end.'

We left them to finish their meal. I was feeling hungry, so I started looking for a table. Camlo took my arm, 'I seem to remember we have something to celebrate. Let's go out for a meal.'

'So, we do. Let's just go to the pub, I don't feel like going far.'

At the village pub we found a table close to the fire, placed our order and sat quietly waiting for our food. I looked at the man sitting an arm's length away across the table. It had taken so long for us to finally learn to trust, to understand each other. He caught me looking at him and smiled into my eyes. I wondered if it would always be like this, the lurch inside, the flush of warmth. I could still hardly believe that the two of us were there, together.

'Can we make it work this time round, Cam?'

'Yes. Don't ever have a second's doubt. One thing for sure, it will never be dull, we both have short fuses.'

We shared a grin. I raised my glass, 'To the future.'

The food arrived. We were famished so had both opted for steak and jacket potato. When we had finished, we sat for a while just relaxing, chatting, comfortable together.

The restaurant area was quiet with only two other tables in use. The front of the pub was busy with groups of people sitting round tables and crowding the bar. At one point, as I glanced in that direction, something caught my attention, but my eyes had moved on before I registered what I has seen.

'I think I've just seen Sinfi, in that crowd at the bar.'

Camlo took a good look, appraising the crowd. 'I can't see her anywhere. It's easy to imagine you recognise people in a crowd like that.'

By the time we had finished our meal the crush had thinned, people were going home.

Then someone walked into the bar shaking snow off their coat.

'You said this morning that it looked like snow. Should we make a move do you think?'

'Yes, we'd better. Ready?'

Outside a proper snowstorm was raging, thick fluffy flakes blown by an icy wind. I almost slipped over on the way to the car. Glad to get out of the weather we slammed the doors and sat with the engine running until the car was warm and the screen clear.

'Good job we haven't far to go.' I said.

Camlo eased the car along the narrow country lane, we hadn't gone far when a car blasted past us, going much too fast and throwing up clouds of snow from the rear wheels. After passing, it cut in front of us, causing Camlo to swerve and slide. He controlled it nicely and drove on, cautious in the poor visibility until, no more than half a mile from the camp, we saw the same car side on across the road.

Swearing quietly to himself Camlo brought the car to a slithering stop.

'Has it crashed do you think? I can't see anyone inside.' He was leaning close to the windscreen, as though that would help him see. He undid his seat belt. As he opened the door he said, 'Stay in the warm, I'll just go and take a look. Get your mobile ready in case we need to call an ambulance.'

I watched him walk up to the side window of the car and peer inside, then turn and look around. He looked confused. Not seeing anything outside the car he turned back, leaning closer to the glass, a hand up to shield his eyes.

From out of the trees at the side of the road three dark figures converged on Camlo. He didn't see them until it was too late, nor did I. As soon as I realised the danger he was in, I shouted a warning but instead of alerting Camlo to the danger it only brought his attention to me. I was struggling with my seatbelt but there was no way I could reach him in time.

They were each carrying a club, long and heavy-looking and Camlo was trapped against the car. As I ran towards them, slipping in the snow, they lifted the clubs and started to attack him with them.

Screaming at them to stop, I reached the nearest figure and tried to grab hold of an arm. He was strong; he shoved me away as if I were nothing. The force of the thrust sent me sliding until I lost my balance and crashed to the ground.

Disorientated I got onto my hands and knees. The car that had blocked the road was reversing, turning to face away. The last two figures leapt in and with the engine revving hard, sliding all over the road, it drove away.

Choking on my sobs I reached Camlo. He lay spread-eagled, not moving. Where his head was half buried in the snow a dark stain was spreading into a brutally bright patch of moonlight. Help. I had to get help. Trembling hands found my mobile. I made the call, begging them to please, please hurry.

I didn't dare move him and I was too terrified even to hold him, I thought the best I could do was try to keep some warmth round him, so I took off my coat and laid it gently over him, then I searched the car, found an old blanket in the boot, and added that. I sat beside him and held the out-flung hand.

The ambulance arrived. I had no idea how long it took. It seemed like a lifetime but there it was, with scurrying people who knew what to do. They wanted to know his name and what had happened. The questions were asked while they worked on him.

In no time, with Camlo's head in one of those clamp things and he had been tenderly lifted inside the ambulance. They were ready to go. They turned to me then. 'Come on, you need to come too.'

I was so stiff with the cold I had to be helped into the ambulance. They sat me in a corner out of their way and kept on working on Camlo all the slow journey to hospital. Once we got there Camlo was whisked away. I was prevented from following, I would only get under their feet they said and anyway I needed treatment too.

'Is he alive, please keep him alive, lots of people need him, keep him alive for me.'

They wanted to bring my body temperature up to normal, so I was persuaded into a bed and given an injection that dropped me into a deep sleep.

When I came round Gillie was sitting beside me. She looked so pale and strained that I panicked. I couldn't speak, couldn't say, 'Is he alive?' I sat rigid in the bed and gripped the cover, begging her with my eyes to have good news.

You can trust Gillie to be honest, there is no-one more kind, but she doesn't lie, and she doesn't fudge her answers.

'It is too soon to know yet Jess. They have worked hard on him, but it could go either way. They have put him into an induced coma to try and give him time. We won't know anything until they judge it time to bring him out of it.'

Chapter 24

I started pulling off the cover.

'Wait Jess, I'll take you along soon but first the police are waiting to talk to you. Stay here and I'll let them know you're awake.' That was alright with me, I wanted to see the police.

I waited impatiently while Gillie went to bring them in. A female plain clothes officer came in with a young, uniformed, male constable. She introduced herself as Inspector Naylor and the Constable as Peters. They drew chairs up to the side of the bed and the Constable took out his notepad. Inspector Naylor began the questioning.

'Your name is Jess Hampshire, I believe.'

At first I had thought she looked professional, but a bit soft, her blond hair was immaculately styled, she wore elegant, heeled shoes. Wrong. This woman's gaze was pure steel.

'That's right.'

'And the young man is a Camlo Walker.' I nodded. 'Can you run through the events for me as they happened, please?'

I clenched my hands into fists and recounted the whole thing. As I approached the attack I took a deep breath, my voice had started strong but remembering was tearing my heart out and now my voice was all over the place.

'It's alright. Take a minute to compose yourself, I have a couple of questions I would like to put in here. Can you tell me about your relationship with Mr Walker and how long you have known him?'

'He is my boyfriend and I have known him two years.' I didn't bother to mention all the time we had spent apart.

'His home, I believe is the Gypsy camp in Long Wood.'

I didn't like the tone of her voice. My answer had a sharp edge. 'Romani, he's a Romani and yes, his home is in Long Wood. I spend a lot of my time there; I have rooms there they keep for me.'

Aware that she had made me feel defensive, she moved on. 'So, Mr Walker approached the car. What happened then?'

'These figures, three figures walked out of the woods, they had their faces covered with what looked like black tights, they were carrying clubs, Camlo was standing by the car, he had been looking inside but he turned and looked at me. He didn't see them coming. They started hitting him and he couldn't get away. I ran, I tried to get to him; one of them, the nearest one to me pushed me. I slid and fell over, by the time I got up the car was driving away and Camlo was laying on the road bleeding into the snow.'

Tears were running down my face, but I had more to say. The Inspector glanced at the Constable, they thought I had finished, the constable was closing his notebook. The inspector slipped a card out of a pocket and handed it to me. Her voice was kind now. 'Thank you for your help, Miss Hampshire, feel free to contact me if you think of any further information ...'

'Wait, I haven't finished. It must be obvious to you that there was nothing random about that attack. If you check your records, back about nine or ten years, you will find that one of the Romani men, Miller was his name, murdered a man in a pub.

'Camlo, along with his father and others, handed him in to the police. Then, only a few weeks ago a particularly good friend of mine was murdered at the Hurst Hotel, a Romani girl. She happened to be the person who saw Miller returning to the camp that night, covered in blood and she told the others. Please do those checks. Miller's daughter, Sinfi, threatened revenge and she was at the hotel the night Oshina was murdered.'

I was thinking, 'damn, damn, damn.' I had garbled it out, made a mess of it, she would never take my story seriously now. I turned away and pressed my face into the pillow, they would be gone in a minute, smiling together at the fantasy story I had told them.

'She was at the Hotel that night?'

I looked at her again, surprised. 'Yes, she didn't book in under her own name of course but she put the correct address down, the one she moved to with her mother after her father went to prison. We told the police, the ones investigating the murder, and they went to the house, but it was empty, they'd gone.'

'You believe she is behind the attack on Mr Walker?'

'Yes. I'd bet my life on it.'

'Leave it to me, I'll look into it.'

And that was that. They left, and Gillie came back in. Her eyes searched my face.

'Oh Gillie, I messed it up.'

'You did alright.'

'You heard?'

'I was listening in. Come on, let's get you tidied up, then I'll take you along to see Camlo.'

She handed me some tissues to wipe my face and eyes. My clothes were in the locker, but they were still wet from the snow, so she gave me her coat to put over the hospital gown.

There was a nurse at the desk outside, she looked up.

'I'm going to see Camlo Walker, perhaps you can tell me, do I have to stay here tonight?'

'We did want to keep you under observation tonight, but if you're feeling alright, I'll get the doctor to sign your discharge.' She looked at the soggy bundle of clothes in my hand and passed me a bag for them. 'Bring the gown back next visit.'

As I wanted to be free to leave after visiting Camlo we waited, a little impatiently, until I had been officially released then finally, we went to find Camlo.

As we approached the ICU I reached for Gillie's hand, I was so afraid.

Camlo was in a side room all by himself. As we walked in a nurse was completing some checks.

'You won't get any reaction from him. They say that some patients have a degree of awareness so by all means identify yourselves and chat to him. He is breathing on his own and doesn't need a ventilator. Either myself or another nurse will be coming in every fifteen minutes to monitor him.'

The figure lying silent in the bed with his head neatly bandaged showed no sign of life apart from the steady rhythm of his breathing. His eyes were closed, and he looked peaceful. Manfri sat in a chair beside the bed. He got up and came to welcome us, taking my hand and leading me to the chair.

'Here, you take the chair, Jess. Gillie and I will go and get a coffee. Would you like us to bring some back for you?'

'That would be nice, thank you.'

They left and I sat and looked at Camlo,

thinking how strange to see the face that was usually so expressive, so totally blank. I reached and took his hand.

'I'm here Cam, sweetheart. I'm waiting for you to come back to me. When you can, when it is time. We will take care of everything. You just get well again. I will come every day and tell you all the news. I love you. If you can hear me, remember that.'

That was all I could manage so I leant over and as gently as I could I kissed him.

Manfri and Gillie came back with coffee and the three of us stood round the bed watching Camlo intently.

The nurse walked in, smiled around at us, and began her checks, making notes on the clipboard. When she had finished, she slipped the clipboard back into position at the end of the bed and made for the door.

'Just a minute nurse, do you mind, could you explain how long this is likely to last, before you can tell one way or the other?'

I wished Manfri hadn't asked, I didn't want to know if there was any sort of limit to the time they would wait.

The nurse was kind.

'I'm not a doctor so I can't say. Sorry.'

As the door closed behind the nurse Gillie touched Manfri's arm. 'Tomorrow, in the daytime. That will be the time to speak to a doctor, we will learn nothing tonight. I suggest we finish our coffee, go home, and get some rest.

I hated leaving that room, leaving Camlo motionless, shut away from the world. At the doorway I stopped and looked back at him. Manfri took my arm and moved me on, we walked the long corridors and out into the cold snowy night.

Manfri's car was covered with a thick layer of snow, he unlocked the doors, Gillie, and I climbed in, shivering. As he cleared the snow from the screen I said to Gillie, 'I will make that bitch pay, I know it was her.'

Gillie leaned slightly to see Manfri's face through the screen.

'Oh yes, she has to be stopped, but anything we learn we give to the police. Ok? Camlo needs you safe for when he comes back to us.'

'Like Manfri needs you but he won't say so. I don't know what you are both waiting for. One of you needs to take a chance for god's sake.' Manfri got into the car, and we started for home. I sneaked a look at Gillie and was surprised to see tears running down her face. I took a tissue from my bag and passed it to her.

I had no tears. I was way beyond that. I had a pain inside as though Moonlight the horse had kicked me and a stone cold determination that Sinfi would pay, for everything. I spent the journey home turning over ideas in my mind.

There was a police car parked next to the office, right in front of it was Camlo's car. As we pulled up two officers climbed out, they walked over to meet us.

'We have finished with the car. We thought it would be safest back here.'

He held out the keys to Manfri.

I stepped up. 'Will you keep us informed, please?'

They didn't say they would or that they wouldn't, they bid us goodnight and left.

Manfri said, 'I need a drink, would you like to join me?'

I realised that I was crushingly tired, and I wanted to be alone.

'Thanks, but not tonight. I'm just going to go to my room. Would you run me back to my house tomorrow, I'd like to bring my car down.'

'Can we do it fairly early in the morning, leave here at seven?'

'Perfect, thank you. Goodnight Manfri, goodnight, Gillie, see you in the morning.'

I walked to my rooms, my footsteps echoing in the silence of the sleeping camp. My key sounded loud as it turned in the lock, I closed the door behind me and locked it. I was so overwhelmed with everything that had happened that my mind and emotions had shut down. I dropped my clothes onto the chair and crawled into bed.

In the morning Manfri took me to my house, the temperature had eased, and a light rain had washed away most of the snow leaving only patches still lingering in the hollows and in sheltered places under hedges and between the trees. When he dropped me off, we agreed to meet at the hospital later. He turned the car, then before driving away he leaned over and lowered the widow.

'We have to believe Camlo will come back to us, Jess.'

I swallowed hard, nodded, and waved him goodbye. In the house I collected a bag of clothing and other useful stuff. I checked that the house was secure, locked the door and stood for a moment, looking back, before getting into my car and driving away. I was fond of the house; it had been my refuge when I had needed one.

If I never needed to live here again, I would rent it out and I would make very sure to find tenants who would love the house. I turned my thoughts back to my plans. I wanted my car at the camp not only because I needed to get to the hospital but because Sinfi knew Camlo's car but not mine. I was going to chase that woman down and make her pay.

After dropping off my stuff I drove straight to the hospital. On my way to his room I could feel my heart beating and I felt sick. I took a breath before opening the door. Camlo looked exactly the same, so I went to the nurses' station and asked if it would be possible to speak to a doctor.

I was told the consultant in charge of Camlo's case would come to the room as soon as he could. With nothing else I could do I resumed my bedside vigil.

'Hello Cam sweetheart, it's me again. Come back to us as soon as you can, please, I miss you so much.'

There was no reaction, steady breathing, and warm flesh the only sign of life.

I pulled the chair up closer to the side of the bed and slipped a hand round his fingers, so still and unresponsive, willing his body to heal itself. After a while Manfri and Gillie arrived. We greeted each other quietly.

Manfri said, 'have you managed to speak to anyone yet?'

'No, I asked to see a doctor and was told that the consultant will come here to the room when he has the time.'

'How long ago was that?'

'Half an hour or so.'

They gathered chairs and made themselves comfortable. We waited.

When the door opened and a thoughtful looking man in a suit came in, we all jumped, the room had been so silent until then.

He introduced himself, I smiled and shook his hand, but I forgot his name immediately. I watched him intently, willing him to say Camlo would be alright.

'I know this isn't what you want to hear, don't worry it isn't bad news, but it is too early to know yet how well Mr Walker will recover. We have to give it time, there is no quick fix. We are keeping a close watch and when the time is right, we will bring him back. Then we will find out how successful we have been. In the meantime, we are taking particularly good care of him.'

He turned to go.

'How long?'

'Before we bring him out of coma? A week. Maybe longer.'

The door closed behind him. I sat back down. There had been no comfort in his words. Manfri and Gillie were frozen in time staring at the closed door.

'Will you both come and sit with us. If Camlo has any awareness I don't want him distressed. We will believe he will be whole when he comes back, no doubts. Ok?'

Without replying they pulled their chairs closer to the bed and sat again. I looked at the impassive face on the white pillow. I reached for his hand again.

We talked on for a few more minutes, conversation that dispersed the urge to whisper and tiptoe. A nurse, not the same one as the previous day came and checked Camlo, smiled and left. Manfri and Gillie prepared to leave soon after. On his way to the door Manfri paused, he walked over to the bed and looked down at his son.

'Take the time you need my boy. We will keep you informed.'

I stepped out of the door with them. Gillie said,

'Let's all eat together in the canteen this evening, shall we say seven?'

'I would like that. I'll just stay here a while, see you at seven.' I stayed a little longer, sitting quietly, then I kissed Camlo, said goodbye and left.

Driving back to the camp I re-ran the scenario of that evening in Moreton, visualised the walk past the house, remembered Sinfi and her boyfriend leaving the house and driving away in the car. There was something about the car. Something had made my spine tingle but then I had met Camlo and forgotten to chase that feeling down.

The police had gone to the house and found it abandoned, well, places to stay are easy to find. I concentrated my memory on the car that had been standing outside the house when I walked past and that she and her boyfriend had driven away in.

It came to me when I had almost given up, in fact my mind had wandered off subject, thinking about the rain that day. When I walked past it that night, the car had been dry. I discounted my original thought that someone had driven home from work in it, in that case it would have been wet. It had to have been in a garage and there wasn't a garage with that house. She must have rented one nearby. Maybe, just maybe when she moved out, she had kept on the garage, as somewhere to hide the car away.

I checked the time, lunchtime. I wasn't going back to the camp now, so I stopped at the next pub I came across. I locked the car and scurried into the warm bar where I ordered a bowl of their homemade mushroom soup and a coffee. I went to sit at a small table close to the fire. While I waited for the food, I found the card Inspector Naylor had given me. A quick look around confirmed that there was no-one close enough to overhear, a group at the bar were perched on stools, chatting to the barman and at a table the other side of the fire two elderly men were playing chess. I dialled the number from the card. She answered after a couple of rings.

'Yes?'

I identified myself and explained why I had called, about the dry car on a night after rain and my thoughts about the car being kept in a garage. She thanked me for the information, said she would definitely look into it. She must have sensed my hesitation because she finished by warning me that it was a matter for the police.

The soup was good, hot, and it came with fresh crusty bread. It reminded me of our days on the road, in the past. When I had finished, I ordered a coffee and spent the time it took to drink it with my phone, studying a map of the area of Morton around Sinfi's house. I found two possible sites, both within a short walk from where she had lived, that could be garage blocks and feeling that I had a reasonable idea where to find them I put away my phone and left.

The remaining drive to Morton was spent trying to decide if I should leave my car in the same car park as before, because I knew how to find it and it should be safe there, or should I try and find somewhere to park closer. I chose closer as I was fairly sure she wouldn't recognise my car. I parked in the next road over from where Sinfi had lived and walked towards my first target. That one turned out to be a block of flats. Well, that explained why there was no garden space. I retraced my steps and went to the other option.

I had got that one right, at least I had found some garages. Situated off a residential road where a turning between the houses led to two rows of garages facing each other across a tarmac turning space. At the far end a jumble of municipal re-cycling bins were ranged in front of a high brick wall. Bitterly cold winter sunshine lit the space, it was silent and deserted. A torn plastic bag stirred among the bins. I don't know what I had expected, an open garage door perhaps or a sign saying, 'This way to Sinfi's car,' with a big arrow?

I had set out to test a theory, to prove a possibility and I had done that. Time now to go home.

I was wondering how much space there would be behind the largest bin, the one for unwanted clothing, and how much of a view there would be from there. If there was no result from the police, I would have to find out for myself if Sinfi did indeed rent a garage here. I went to have a look. I rooted about, looking for something to sit on in case I had a long wait. I found a sturdy box that would do for when my legs got tired.

I was peering out from one side and then the other, to discover how much I could see from that hiding place, when I heard a car approaching. Not wanting to be seen loitering around the bins I stepped back into the shadows. When I saw the car that pulled into the garages my heart lurched. Stupidly, having come to find Sinfi, I hadn't expected her so soon. Yet there she was, climbing out from behind the wheel and walking over to unlock the third garage along.

Chapter 25

I froze, it would be alright, I could stay still and silent until she had put her car away and left. Then I would phone Inspector Naylor, tell her where Sinfi garaged her car and go home. Then another car door opened and slammed shut and I recognised a voice.

'Get a move on Sin, get the car put away. Don will be here in a minute. I'll just put our fish and chip wrappers in the bin. Right?'

The general waste bin was next to the clothing bin. I didn't dare move; I stopped breathing and stayed very still, hoping she wouldn't notice me. I watched her walk up, lift the lid, drop in her bundle of greasy paper, and drop the lid back down. It was as she turned that she saw me.

'You! What the hell are you doing here?'

'Well hello Jenny, I could say the same.'

'Who are you talking to Jen?'

'It's that bitch that latched on to Camlo.'

I stepped back and out of the other side of the bin, I didn't want to be trapped behind it, making a run for it seemed the best plan. Sinfi had moved like lightning, she had snatched up, from a pile on the floor of the garage, two wooden stakes. She ran to block off the exit from the garages.

'Jen, come and get one of these.'

Jenny dashed over and picked up a stake. Now they had one each and they were closing in, I searched desperately for something among the random rubbish dumped around the bins, something that I could use to protect myself, to fight back with.

They weren't in any hurry, enjoying the hunt, confident that once they had me backed into a corner, I would be an easy victim. One slow step at a time they closed in on me forcing me back. I had to check every step to make sure I didn't trip. I had to find a way of fighting back.

'Jenny, you wanted Camlo for yourself, don't you feel anything for him? I know you were there, at the ambush. That was you, hanging back, not getting involved, wasn't it? While Sinfi and her boyfriend tried to kill Camlo. Do you know that he is in hospital in a coma, they don't know yet if he will ever wake up.'

She stopped. The wooden stake lowered a little.

'Don't listen Jen, she's lying.'

'Am I? Come to the hospital with me and see him then, see for yourself. What did she tell you, that they only knocked him about a bit as a warning?'

She still wasn't moving, she looked from me

to Sinfi, she was wavering, undecided. Come on, I thought, put it down.

Sinfi turned away from her; she would take me on by herself. She grinned at me.

'Too bad you still have me to deal with.'

Another vehicle drove in and stopped, blocking the entrance. I thought, Oh, bloody hell. It was Jenny's faithful follower, Don, what was more he had brought the camp minibus. Not sure what was expected from him he climbed down and stood waiting for Jenny to tell him what to do.

Sinfi yelled out, 'Come on Don, here take this, help us get her.'

Don looked at the offered stake, then at Jenny who still stood undecided.

'I don't know, I don't want to hurt anyone.'

'I am very glad to hear that.'

Inspector Naylor, flanked by Constable Peters and two others had appeared behind Don. I had heard the sound of yet another motor and I had hoped. Flooded with relief I leaned against the nearest garage door while the officers took charge, one of them removed the stake from Jenny's hand, two others walked towards Sinfi.

'Don't come any closer, bastard coppers. Don't think you'll get me that easy.'

Despite her bravado and lashing out with the stake she still had in her hand she was overwhelmed by numbers. Still screaming out abuse, she was taken out through the entrance to the police car, then they came back for Jenny. As Jenny was being taken away, Don turned to the officers. 'What's happening, don't they want a lift now?'

'No, not now. You go back home. We will come and talk to you later. Alright? Go home and stay there.'

Don got back into the minibus, he reversed out and went on his way. Which left me. Inspector Naylor walked up and stood, staring into my face.

'What do we do with you, what bit of leave it up to us do you not understand?'

'I was only taking a look, to see if I could find the garage, then I was going to let you know, that was all.'

'Go home Miss Hampshire, when we want a statement, we will come and find you. You're not planning to go anywhere, are you?'

I shook my head. 'Do you have enough now to get a prosecution?'

Her expression softened. 'Go home, Jess, trust me to get the job done.'

I smiled at her as I walked past. She had everything under control. On the street I took a quick look at the two police cars parked at the roadside. I went in the other direction, to my car and then back home.

I arrived back at the camp at a little past four; all the way I had been wondering what to do about Jenny. She had been working to cause trouble for me from the time I arrived at the camp, and I disliked her intensely, I had never stopped to consider if she had a family.

Manfri should know, right away, what had happened, so I walked to the office and knocked on the door. Manfri called, 'come in.' I walked in and smiled at the domestic scene inside. He and Tobar were sitting at the desk with cups of tea and a packet of biscuits in front of them.

'Come in Jess. We're having a tea break, would you like –?' He stopped, noticing my lack of response.

'What is it? Something has happened.'

I took off my coat, pulled another chair up to the desk and slumped onto it. 'It has been quite an afternoon; I don't know where to start.'

'Camlo, is he alright?' Manfri leaned forward anxiously.

'Yes, sorry Manfri, it all happened after I left the hospital.'

I told them everything, right through to both the girls getting arrested. It was beginning to sink in now, that the woman who had murdered Oshina and put Camlo on the knife-edge between life and death had finally been caught. It was all a bit much, my mind kept focussing in on irrelevant details.

'Inspector Naylor sent Don away, has he arrived back with the minibus?'

Manfri said, 'I saw the bus come back in a while back, I haven't seen Don though. Who would believe one of ours would do that?'

I shook my head, despairing that I had been so stupid.

'Lela brought it up, that someone in the camp had been passing information. It slipped my mind …' I lost myself in the things that could have been different.

'Don't Jess, don't go there.'

'Anyway, I realised I don't even know if she has a family, if so, they should be told.'

Tobar and Manfri exchanged glances. Tobar said. 'Only her mother, she doesn't understand a lot of what goes on these days, you're right though, look, I'll go, she knows me. I'll break it to her gently, make sure she's alright.'

He stood to leave. 'I'll come back and tell you how it goes, then I must go and tell Gillie. I won't be long.'

After Tobar left, Manfri clattered around with kettle and cups and put a mug of tea in front of me. 'Well done this afternoon, this really is something to celebrate you know.'

'I know.'

When Tobar came back, Manfri made another tea for him. Well, how did that go?'

'She didn't understand, poor thing. Don was there, he had tried to tell her. He told me he would stay and look after her. He seemed shaken, he came outside when I was leaving and asked me if the police would put him in prison. I told him not to worry. I didn't know what to say to him.'

'They will want to speak to him, to find out what he knows but I think he is safe. Inspector Naylor arrived just as he was refusing to take one of the stakes. He said he didn't want to hurt anyone.'

There were relieved sighs from Manfri and Tobar, our small community didn't need to lose any more members. We all drank our tea in thoughtful silence.

I put my cup down. 'I'm off, see you in the canteen at seven.' I pulled on my coat and raised a hand in farewell as I left. Back in my room I found my music file on my tablet and put it on as background while I took a shower. Then, dressed, and warm I used the time left to relax and reflect on everything that had happened in such a short time. When it was time to meet the others at the canteen. I took down my coat from the hook and buttoned it before leaving.

Warm air flooded out of the canteen when I opened the door, bringing the welcome aroma of cooking food. I breathed it in, closed the door behind me and walked towards the table where Tobar and Gillie were waiting. On the way I passed close to where Lela and Miri were already eating. They were sitting with Ruslo and Kem.

Lela leapt up; she came over and flung her arms round me. 'Jess, we came to look for you this afternoon, but you weren't home. Oh my god, how could anyone do that to Camlo. Is there any news?'

'Not yet, it's too early to know anything yet but … the police arrested Sinfi this afternoon.'

Her eyes grew huge with surprise. 'Christ, that's wonderful, where, how?'

'Look, you're busy tonight, when do you next have time off work?'

'I'm not working tomorrow.'

'Come round in the morning and I'll tell you all about it. Then I am going back to the hospital. I'm going to stay there until they bring Camlo out of his coma. One other thing though, do you remember saying to me that someone from the camp was collaborating with her?'

'Yes, I was sure she had a spy.'

'I forgot. I forgot what you said.' My voice wobbled, 'It was Jenny, all along it was her.'

Lela gripped my arm. 'Her? I never would have believed it. Look you're eating with the family tonight. We will come to yours in the morning and you can tell us all about it. Now go and be with them, have a drink or three. Ok?'

Lela sat back down, and I went to join the others. As I sat, Tobar poured me a glass of wine. Manfri arrived and we ordered the hot meal of the day, a thick rich beef casserole with dumplings. When it arrived, it was so good no-one spoke until we pushed our empty plates away.

Manfri held the empty wine bottle up to the light. 'Does anyone want more wine?'

We all declined the offer, choosing coffee instead, but somehow the coffees arrived with a glass of brandy for each of us.

Totally unrepentant Manfri lifted his glass.

'I want to raise a toast, to all of us, to courage and to optimism.'

I saw it in Manfri's face, his determination to cling to hope, how close he was to despair. We all raised our glasses and drank. When we were finished, we left as a group. Outside, we said our goodnights and separated to walk back to our own homes. I was so tired that I went straight to bed and slept peacefully until later than I had intended. I was only just out of the shower when Lela and Miri arrived. I let them in and finished dressing.

We sat at my table, and I told them the details of what had happened. They lived every word with me, horrified when I described how Camlo was attacked, then when I described him closed away from life in that hospital bed, and I had to stop to steady my voice, we all shed tears. I stood and fetched a box of tissues from the bedside table, taking a handful I put the box on the table for the girls and made us all another coffee.

'So, now tell us how you got Sinfi arrested, it was you wasn't it?'

I described how I had wondered about Sinfi's car and gone looking for garages then what had happened right down to Tobar going to tell Sinfi's mother. By the time I had finished we were all smiling.

Lela said, 'you are talking to Camlo, in case he can hear. Tell him we all love him and to stop mucking about and come back to us. Do you know when they plan to wake him up?"

'Apparently they don't prolong the coma beyond a couple of weeks, so nothing to worry about there.' Somehow, I had kept my voice level and confident.

I stood at the door, and we hugged as they left, there had been nothing more said, it wasn't necessary. I knew that I carried their love and best wishes with me.

I collected enough clothes to last me a while, I would worry about laundry when I needed to, I made sure I had my phone, tablet and chargers and dumped them into a bag.

Manfri was nowhere to be found, or Gillie, when I went to tell them I was leaving. Assuming they had left already for the hospital I got behind the wheel of my car, started the motor, and headed off in the direction of the hospital.

Once I had found a parking space, I locked the car and walked towards the main entrance, taking a deep breath so I could pass through the smog of cigarette smoke from the patients clustered outside the doors, shivering in their dressing gowns and slippers.

The route to Camlo's room was now familiar, past the reception desk, turn right, take the lift up one floor then right and on to the end of the passage. At the door to his room, I said a silent prayer, in case there was a helpful god floating around somewhere and opened the door. As I had expected, Manfri and Gillie were there, chairs close together beside the bed. Manfri was reading to Camlo from the sports pages.

I smiled at them, tucked my bag in the bedside locker, hung my coat and pulled up the last chair. Once he had finished with the final item of football gossip Manfri folded the paper and put it down. 'There, that's about all that's worth reading, son, I expect you heard the door just now. Jess is here now.'

'Hello, Camlo sweetheart.' I turned to Manfri, 'Have you given him the good news?' Manfri shook his head. 'Well yesterday afternoon the police arrested Sinfi, isn't that great, and Jenny, she has been helping Sinfi, so they arrested her too.'

We chatted on, telling Camlo everything that had happened in the camp, even what we had eaten at dinner the previous evening. Gillie gave him an update on the hotel, assuring Camlo that Jason was making a good job of running the place.

When they left each of them bent to kiss his cheek and said they would be back the next day. At the door Manfri paused, 'you still intend to stay?'

'Unless they pick me up and chuck me out, yes.'

'Good, see you tomorrow.' He took my hand and gave it a gentle squeeze then as they turned to walk away, Manfri put an arm round Gillie. I caught her eye, and we shared a smile. I closed the door after them.

I went back to my chair. 'Do you know Camlo I do believe that those two are finally getting together.'

I opened up my bag of stuff from home and brought out a paperback thriller.

'We haven't got round to discussing what sort of book you read but I have one here that I enjoyed. I shall read it to you and if you hate it you will have to wake up and tell me.'

I settled down and began, I read aloud to Camlo for hours, until I couldn't continue. The nurse doing the regular checks had smiled and asked how many books I had brought.

In the early evening I went down a floor to the café and bought myself two packs of cheese and pickle sandwiches and a tea. I drank the tea, ate one pack of sandwiches then took the rest back to the room with me.

I found the earphones in my bag and listened to some music for a while then got as comfortable as possible and tried to sleep. At some time in the night the nurse asked me if I was going home. When I told her that no, I was staying, she went away, returning with a blanket and a pillow.

I managed to get a little sleep. In the morning

I freshened up in the loo down the passage and breakfasted in the café, taking a second coffee back with me.

During the morning the doctor came in with the nurse, she did the checks, passed him the clipboard, and left while he studied the charts.

'Well?'

'He's nice and stable.'

The door closed behind him, and I settled back to a day that was just a repeat of the one before.

That evening, bored with sandwiches, I had cottage pie with carrots and followed with sponge pudding and custard. Back in the room I brought out my emergency supply, a bottle of wine. I poured a healthy slug into a coffee cup and carefully put the rest of the bottle back in the locker.

'Now don't you go telling on me, Camlo Walker.'

I sat back beside him and sipped at the wine, passing the time by stroking the wrist that lay by the edge of the bed, running my fingers down to the tips of his fingers.

I slept better that night, right through to morning. I woke with a dream still echoing in my mind. I had been walking through a field; I could still smell the thick honeyed scent of lush grass warmed by sunlight. Sunlight that dazzled so I couldn't see to move. And the grass was growing, fast. Twining round my legs and holding me to the earth. I opened my mouth to shout for help, but no sound came.

Then, out of the blinding light came Moonlight and on his back Camlo, riding the horse bareback. At a word Moonlight stopped beside me and Camlo reached an arm down and pulled me up in front of him. Moonlight turned and – I woke up, heavy eyed and for a moment confused.

I didn't feel like eating but after my morning freshen-up I went down for coffee, again taking a second one back up to the room.

That day the doctor didn't visit until after Manfri and Gillie had been and gone. I had given up waiting for him, deciding in my own mind that he wouldn't come but when he finally arrived, shortly after the nurse's late afternoon visit, he bustled in radiating energy. This was so unlike his usual casual stroll that my heart rate leapt to panic mode, what could be wrong that could cause this change.

'What? Please tell me what has gone wrong?'

He turned and beamed at me.

'Nothing Miss Hampshire, nothing at all. We think Mr Walker is now well enough to begin bringing him out of his coma.'

Chapter 26

The doctor disconnected the drip from Camlo's arm and pushed the stand back to the wall. He waited a few minutes and checked Camlo's vital signs again. 'There, now we wait. Good day Miss Hampshire.'

'But what, how long, is that all?'

'Yes, that is all. We can't tell how long it will take, that is up to him, so all we do now is keep checking him and wait.' The door closed behind the doctor. I pulled my chair up closer to the side of the bed and with my heartbeat choking me, watched intently for that first flutter of Camlo's eyes or tiny movement of muscle.

Nothing. Long, painfully slow minutes slipped away becoming one hour, then two. The tense eager anticipation slumped into bitter disappointment. I told myself to be reasonable, the doctor had said, no, more implied, that it could take a long time. 'We can't tell.' he had said. So, I would be patient. I was good at being patient and for that man I could wait.

I still watched, closely, for every minute that

passed, but now I was calm. I didn't need food or drink. I stayed at Camlo's side and waited. In the dark of the night, I fought back and defeated the small voice that tried to tell me that the man who came back would not be the man I loved. Yes, he would, because I believed so very strongly in him.

In the end I failed. Time after time my head dropped onto my chest, and I snapped it back up again, but when I fell asleep, I didn't even know.

It must have been a tiny movement in the hand that I held that brought me back, instantly alert. I waited. Had I imagined that? Was it just another dream?

There was a dim light in the room. The other side of the blinds another dawn was beginning. A deeper breath, then the head on the pillow turned towards me and the eyes opened. Dark and shadowed, I couldn't tell if there was any recognition in them. I couldn't breathe properly.

'Camlo? Hello sweetheart.' The worst seconds of waiting in my whole life ticked by.

'Jess. Hello my love.'

There was joy and relief and tears and a few minutes of magical reunion before I rang the bell to bring someone to see the wonder that had happened. Medical people clustered round Camlo, talking together in the shorthand language people develop when they work in close groups. Someone brought him a cup of tea. He was answering their questions, but his eyes constantly searched for me.

When they had finished, they drifted away one by one until only the usual doctor remained. The lights were on now. I could see that the bruise spreading down from under the bandage was already fading. What made my heart sing was the relief on the doctor's face.

'Thank you; I don't know how to tell you how grateful I am.' We both looked at Camlo, he appeared a little thinner. He had dropped off to sleep as soon as the crowd left.

'It looks as though he will make a full recovery, he is an incredibly lucky young man. We'll let him sleep now. I'll come back later to remove the bandage. If he continues as stable as he is now, he can come home tomorrow. Why don't you try to sleep too?'

'I think I will.'

We both slept, when I woke up Camlo was already awake and the nurse was there, she had just finished taking Camlo's blood pressure. He smiled his old vivid smile. 'Help me persuade Nurse Campbell to let me get out of bed and make my way to the bathroom, I need a wash and now I'm free of that tube thing I am not going to use a bedpan.'

Nurse Campbell gave in and took Camlo to the bathroom, he returned clean and shaved. Instead of getting back into the bed he settled himself in a chair. 'Any chance I can have something to eat now nurse?'

'I'll get the kitchen to send up something suitable, don't try to eat anything too heavy for a while, keep your meals small and keep off the alcohol.'

A little later a plate of scrambled eggs with bread and butter arrived. When Camlo had finished he looked a little better although he was still weak and pale.

Manfri and Gillie arrived, the meeting between father and son was quietly emotional, they hugged, then stood a moment and smiled at each other. Manfri cleared his throat and they both sat down, positioning their chairs close together.

'Has Jess told you what happened, you missed quite a drama.'

'No. Not yet, what sort of drama and how bad was it, Jess?'

'I like the way you assume I was involved.'

Camlo grinned, his eyebrows raised in challenge. So, I told him the story and watched his reactions. He turned his head away and gazed through the open blinds at the bright day outside. I wasn't sure if he was looking at the sky or hiding his emotions. I sat on the bed and took his hand, his strong fingers gripped mine tight, but his eyes stayed fixed on the view.

Manfri signalled to Gillie. 'We fancy a coffee; we'll bring you both back some.'

After they had closed the door behind them Camlo stood and walked to the window. I slipped off the bed, went over and wrapped my arms around him, Camlo pulled me close, and we stayed like that until we heard footsteps approaching the door.

Instead of the expected Manfri and Gillie it was the doctor who walked through the door. He placed the tray he was carrying on the bedside cabinet.

'It's time now to replace that dressing and see how that wound is healing.'

I moved to the other side of the bed to allow the doctor plenty of space, staying standing so that I had a good view. I watched as the bandage was removed and then the dressing pad. The hair had been shaved along the side if Camlo's head. Once the dried blood had been swabbed away the cut didn't look as bad as I had expected.

'The cut didn't cause the internal swelling Miss Hampshire. That was down to the blows. The wound is doing well, a small dressing and a plaster is all it needs.'

Gillie walked back in followed by Manfri carrying our coffee as the doctor was preparing to leave.

'Oh, now that looks better son.'

Once the doctor had left, we had a quiet family afternoon. When Camlo's eyelids started to droop I signalled that it was time for our visitors to leave. Camlo noticed of course.

'You go too Jess, no don't argue with me, how many nights have you slept in that chair?'

I shrugged.

'How many?'

'Three.'

'Go and get a decent sleep then you can come back for me tomorrow. I will be alright you know.'

Gillie was already gathering my stuff together; she tossed my coat onto the bed. 'Here put this on, it's cold outside. There's no point in arguing with him you know he's just like his father.'

I gave in, the thought of a comfortable night's sleep was tantalising, so I put on my coat, picked up my bag and kissed Camlo goodbye. At the door I looked back and although he raised a hand, I could see how close he was to sleep. I closed the door on him and went out into a freezing evening to find my car and go home.

After a good hot meal and many conversations with people asking after Camlo I went back to my rooms and slept so deeply that I woke confused because I was in a bed and not screwed up in a chair. Too excited at the prospect of bringing Camlo home to even think about eating breakfast I spent a while tidying the room and changing the bed.

After a last look around I went to my car and started off to the hospital. By the time I had parked I was desperate to reach him. Once inside I wanted to run all the way, but I kept it down to a fast walk. When I reached his room, I found the door open. There was no-one inside apart from a woman stripping the bed. The world froze. I saw her lips moving but heard nothing above the voices screaming in my head. She stood there with her arms full of sheets waiting for an answer.

'What? Sorry, what did you say?' My lips struggled to form the words. I didn't want to hear her saying how sorry she was that Mr Walker had died.

'I said, if you're looking for Mr Walker, he is waiting for you in the patients lounge. He said I was to be sure to let you know, it's through the door opposite then two rooms down on the left.'

'Thanks.' I said as I spun away from the doorway. I slammed through into the corridor, gathering speed so that I reached the lounge at a run. The door was open. I grabbed at the doorframe to help me stop. Standing in the doorway, I looked into the room.

Camlo was by the window, looking out into the car park. Hearing me arrive he turned. 'Jess, I've been waiting for you.' He said and the joy in his smile scorched into my soul.

I can't remember how it happened that I was in his arms, I may have run, I would have crawled that short distance over burning coals but there I was, holding him close, feeling his heartbeat.

'I'm here Cam, I've come to take you home.'

Books By This Author

Consequences

When Beth chose a new life in the country, she didn't expect to find herself hunted by a killer. Surrounded by danger, her courage is tested to the limit. So she reaches out for help from new friends. But what part will the mysterious man from the valley play? The tall man with the brown hair and the green eyes.

With her life under threat, Beth encounters true friends and hatred, betrayal and love. Most of all she learns to accept as real the impossible, the unbelievable.

Dusty Windows

The action takes Beth, Jack, and her family to Italy for a wedding. The anticipated happy event becomes a journey into tragedy when they are entangled in a local war between the Mafia and a rival criminal empire.

The return to England doesn't bring safety, a killer bent on revenge has come to hunt them down.

A Step From The Shadows

A violent attack during a robbery puts Billy's life in Jeopardy and throws a shadow of fear over Valehurst. Similar robberies are happening all over the area. Beth and Jack, together with their close band of friends determine to discover the identities of the thugs and see that they face justice. However, there is also mortal danger from another source. Someone from the past has come for revenge.

Books By This Author

Consequences

When Beth chose a new life in the country, she didn't expect to find herself hunted by a killer. Surrounded by danger, her courage is tested to the limit, so she reaches out for help from new friends.

But what part will the mysterious man from the valley play, the tall man with the brown hair and the green eyes.

With her life under threat, Beth encounters true friends and hatred, betrayal and love. Most of all she learns to accept as real the impossible, the unbelievable.

Dusty Windows

The action takes Beth, Jack, and her family to Italy for a wedding. The anticipated happy event becomes a journey into tragedy when they are entangled in a local war between the Mafia and a rival criminal empire.

The return to England doesn't bring safety, a

killer bent on revenge has come to hunt them down

A Step From The Shadows.

A violent attack during a robbery puts Billy's life in jeopardy and throws a shadow of fear over Valehurst. Similar robberies are happening all over the area. Beth and Jack, together with their close band of friends, determine to discover the identities of the thugs and see that they face justice.

However, there is also mortal danger from another source. Someone from the past has come for revenge.

Printed in Great Britain
by Amazon

28839174R00188